DEATH COMES
DARKLY

DEATH COMES DARKLY

by

David S. Pederson

A Division of Bold Strokes Books

2016

DEATH COMES DARKLY

ISBN 13: 978-1-62639-625-8

This Trade Paperback Original Is Published By
Bold Strokes Books, Inc.
P.O. Box 249
Valley Falls, NY 12185

First Edition: April 2016

Credits
Editor: Jerry L. Wheeler
Production Design: Stacia Seaman
Cover Design by Jeanine Henning

To Alan Karbel, the key to my lock, and to my family and friends
for their never-ending support and love.

Special thanks to my mom, Vondell Pederson,
and Jacques Coulliette and Glenn Koos,
for reading my early drafts and providing valuable feedback.

Chapter One

In times like this, a man's got to do what a man's got to do. I hurried out of the bathroom of my small apartment, wiping my wet hands on my shirt since the clean towels were still in the wicker basket on my bed. Like I said, a man's got to do what a man's got to do. I padded over to the telephone, ringing incessantly from the entryway.

"Hello?" I answered, somewhat irritated. A ringing telephone can be full of promise, but it can also be annoying when one is indisposed.

A woman's voice came through the handset, rather tinny. "Hello, Heath?"

"Oh, hi, Mom," I said, trying to hide my irritation.

"I didn't think you were home, dear, it just rang and rang, probably fifteen times or more."

"Or more. I was in the bathroom." I glanced at myself in the mirror above the phone table and smoothed out my hair as I talked.

"I hope you didn't wipe your hands on your shirt again."

Sigh. "I'm thirty-two, Mom, I can take care of myself."

"You should be married, dear. A wife can take care of you better than you can."

A still heavier sigh on my part. "How's Dad?" I asked, hopefully changing the subject.

"Oh, he's fine—doing the crossword in the paper. We wanted to know if you're going to be coming by the house this weekend."

"No, Mom, I can't this weekend. I'm going down to Lake Geneva."

"Lake Geneva! What on earth for? No one goes down there this time of year. It will be deserted."

"It's sort of related to my last case, Mom."

"You mean your only case so far." Her voice sounded rude, but I know she didn't intend it that way; it's just how she comes across sometimes.

"My first case. There will be others."

"I don't like you doing this police work, Heath. It's too risky. You managed to stay out of the war because of your feet, and because you were a policeman, but the war's over now. Do something safer. Your cousin Chuck was killed in the war. It could have been you."

"Chuck was in Pearl Harbor, Mom. He was killed during the attack."

"I'm just saying war and police work are both dangerous. Why take chances? Chuck thought being in Pearl Harbor was like going to heaven. Well, he was right in a way, I suppose, but I don't want anything to happen to you."

I rolled my eyes. "I'll be fine. I'm a police detective now, Mom. I'm not chasing down bank robbers anymore, not that I did much of that, either."

"Well, I still don't like it and neither does your father. Who are you going to Lake Geneva with?"

"I'm going down by myself, and a friend is joining me the next day."

"You spend too much time with friends, Heath, and by yourself." I could hear the tsk, tsk, tsk in her voice. "You need to date more, settle down. Mrs. Addison's daughter, Estelle, is home from Boston this weekend, and we thought the two of you might like to have dinner with us at the house. I'm making your favorite, fried chicken."

"That was my favorite when I was ten, Mom. Maybe the following weekend. I'll let you know."

"But Mrs. Addison's daughter will be gone back to Boston by then, and she's such a lovely girl. She's a Methodist, you know."

"I'm sorry, Mom, but I have plans."

She made that clucking sound with her teeth that she always does when she's annoyed or frustrated. It drives me crazy. "Well, that's too bad. She'll be disappointed, but we'd like to see you, too. You don't come around much anymore."

More sighs. "I know, I know. Like I said, maybe the following weekend. I've been really busy."

More clucking sounds from her teeth. "I just don't see why you want to go to Lake Geneva when it's not even summer yet. You could come over here and have a nice home-cooked meal and visit with your parents and talk with Estelle."

"I know you don't understand, Mom. I'm sorry, it's work related. I'll come over soon, I promise."

Her turn to sigh, but at least she stopped the clucking noise. "Verbina tells me you had lunch with her last week."

My aunt Verbina, my mother's sister, married well. Several times. She understands me in ways Mom never will, and I enjoy spending time with her, but of course I couldn't tell Mom that.

"It was just lunch, Mom. She happened to be downtown, I had to eat."

"Well, I'm glad to hear you're eating, even if it is diner food downtown."

"It wasn't diner food, Mom. We ate at the Pfister, where she and I always have tea."

"What, diner food's not good enough for you? Don't go putting on airs like Verbina does, son."

"I won't, Mom. I'm not. I eat at diners all the time."

"What about the evenings? Are you eating okay at home? Your vegetables?"

"I'm a good cook. You and Dad have been here for dinner, remember?"

"It's not the same when you're by yourself, Heath. It's better to have someone to cook for, or to cook for you."

"I'm sure Mrs. Addison's daughter is a wonderful cook."

"Don't get sassy, Heath. Estelle is a lovely girl."

"And she's a Methodist," I added with sarcasm that was always lost on my mother.

"Yes, she is. Your father and I are just concerned about you, that's all."

"I know, Mom, but I'm fine, really. I have to go. I'll talk to you soon."

"Don't you want to say hello to your dad?"

"Let him finish his puzzle, tell him I said hi."

"All right, son. Be careful."

"I will, Mom, bye."

I hung up the heavy black receiver, looked at myself again in the mirror, and rolled my eyes once more. "You confirmed bachelor, you. My mother is either going to drive me to drink or vice versa or both." I shook my head, watching my reflection, and then I opened the hall closet door, taking down my well-worn leather-bound scrapbook from the top shelf.

Back in the living room, I made myself comfortable in the old wingback chair by the window and settled the scrapbook on my lap, turning the pages again, many of them already yellowing and faded. Nothing lasts forever, I guess. The highlights of my life so far were all glued, taped, or pinned there, with captions printed below in black ink: my school play programs, glee club announcements, my ribbon for drama club, the senior prom. My high school graduation announcement—class of 1933—had its own page. The more recent articles were about me making the police department, my promotion to the detective division, and my first big case this past March. I had solved the murder of Mr. Murdoch, a wealthy local businessman, that had at first appeared to be suicide.

The article was accompanied by a photo of the victim, Spencer Murdoch, and an almost ten-year-old department photo of me when I was a vibrant twenty-two. Next to the *Journal* article, I had pasted a similar one from the morning *Sentinel* and a smaller one from the *Chicago Tribune*, neither of which, I noted sadly, had included the picture the *Journal* had run.

That was three weeks ago and I still couldn't help feeling a bit proud of myself, but also spooked. Some fellow who was acquainted with the late Mr. Murdoch, a complete stranger to me, reads one of those articles and suddenly invites me to a weekend at his home in Lake Geneva. I set my scrapbook down carefully on the small desk next to my chair and picked up the mysterious letter again. I must have read it five or six times since it arrived four days ago. Of course I let Keyes read it. Alan Keyes is a close personal friend of mine. At least that's how I'll introduce him to my folks if they ever meet. They just wouldn't understand my personal life. Most folks wouldn't, I'm afraid.

I looked once more at the envelope, addressed to *Detective Heath Barrington, Milwaukee Police Department, Milwaukee, Wisconsin*, in a rather shaky hand. The return address was: *D. Darkly, Dark Point, Lake Geneva, Wisconsin*. I took out the engraved stationery, a calligraphic *D* at the top, and unfolded it carefully, reading it again even though I knew it by heart:

April 3rd, 1947
Dear Mr. Barrington:
You obviously don't know me, and I hope you won't find this too forward, but I read in the Milwaukee newspaper a couple of weeks ago with great interest that you single-handedly solved the murder of Mr. Spencer Murdoch. I was raised in Chicago but spent many years in Milwaukee, on Newberry Blvd., and in the past I have had dealings with Mr. Murdoch. I must confess I cannot say we were friends, or even on friendly terms, but still his violent murder and the subsequent solving of it by you made the papers and, of course, interested me.

I know all too well that public servants such as yourself get little reward for your work, and I should like to remedy that in some small way by offering you an invitation to spend the weekend of April 19th at my summer home on Geneva Lake. I know this is rather short notice, and that it may seem unusual to you as we have never met, but I am in the position financially to do such things, and I must say I am curious to meet you. From the account given in the newspaper, you sound like a very bright, inquisitive young man, and I am always eager to meet new acquaintances.

You would, of course, be welcome to bring your wife or a companion. My summer house has eight bedrooms, and though I am inviting other guests, you and your wife would be quite comfortable. If you choose to bring a companion, you would each have your own room.

I can offer you hiking trails, a billiard table, music room with a piano, of course, croquet on the lawn, books by the dozen in the library, and an excellent console radio for you to enjoy. The folks on the coast are really talking up this television phenomenon, but I've seen one and really don't think it will last. The picture is small and grainy, and who would want to cram around and stare at a little box? At least with radio you can do other things while you listen. But I digress. The weekend will be casual—no need for black tie—just casual clothes for daytime, simple suits for dinner.

Please RSVP to the address below as soon as possible so that I may make arrangements.

There is an early afternoon train from Milwaukee to Lake Geneva on Friday, April 18th. I would have my butler meet you at the station and bring you to the house. If it is not possible to make the Friday train, there is an earlier train on Saturday, departing Milwaukee at 8:00 a.m. and arriving here at 10:30. Just let me know your preference when you RSVP.

If you have questions, please don't hesitate to contact me by telephone at Lake Lawn 5-3445, Lake Geneva; feel free to reverse the charges.

I await your response.
Sincerely,
Dexter D. Darkly

When I first read the letter, I had no idea who Dexter D. Darkly was. But it didn't take me too long to find out at least some basic information. A stop at the main library on Wells Street told me a few things. He was listed in the most current volume of *Who's Who*, a wealthy industrialist, family money.

He was born in 1875 in Chicago and raised there, and moved to Milwaukee in 1926 for business purposes, and he did indeed own a house on Newberry Blvd. No police record or gangster ties that I could find, either in Wisconsin or Illinois.

I've always been a curious sort, so after finding everything to at least appear on the up-and-up, I accepted the invitation and let him know I would arrive on the Friday train, with my friend Alan Keyes joining me on Saturday. I had hoped I could talk Keyes into coming with me Friday, but he was on duty that day.

I put the letter back into its envelope, set it down on my desk, and then walked back out to the hall and picked up the telephone receiver, putting on a sweater from the hall closet. I was fortunate not to have a party line—policemen automatically get their own phone lines. I dialed and waited as it rang once, twice, and then I heard a click.

"Hello?" That deep voice that could melt an iceberg. Too bad the *Titanic* hadn't had him on board.

"Hey, Alan, it's Heath!"

"Hello!" he repeated, this time more upbeat, and I could tell he was glad to hear from me.

"Is this a good time?" I asked.

"Always. Just sitting here reading the paper, listening to the radio."

"Ah, the advantages of radio. You can do two things at once," I said.

"Huh?"

I smiled to myself. "Just remembering Mr. Darkly's comment in his letter about radio versus television."

"Oh," Alan said. "He's wrong about that, you know. One day everyone will have a television, mark my words."

I smiled to myself. "Maybe, but I've heard they're very

expensive. They'll be out of date by the time you save up enough to buy one. Interesting concept, though."

"I agree. So what are you up to tonight?"

I leaned against the wall next to the mirror and arched my back. "Just talked to my mom. She wants me to come to dinner this weekend and meet the daughter of some friend of hers."

"Interesting. And what did you tell her?" Alan asked.

"That I was going to Lake Geneva with a friend. Police business, more or less."

"A safe excuse, but I bet that didn't go over very well."

"She made that clucking sound with her teeth, so I know she was annoyed, but like I told her, I'm not a kid anymore."

"But you'll always be her little boy," he replied wisely.

"I guess in some ways you can never grow up."

"I guess so. Hey, at least you still have your folks."

"Yeah, you're right, Alan, I know. As much as they drive me nuts. Though sometimes I wonder…"

"You wonder what they'd do if they knew about you?"

"Yup. I can't help thinking about it sometimes. I mean every time she brings up my settling down, meeting some nice girl, I wonder what would happen if she knew, how she'd react."

"That's natural, but better she doesn't find out, Heath. Don't court trouble. Honesty always comes at a price."

I stared at my reflection again. I liked myself, I accepted myself. Why couldn't they? But I knew he was right. "Good point, Alan, though they must wonder."

"If they do, they make up excuses for it—you just haven't met the right girl yet, you're too busy with work, you're too picky."

"Well, I am picky," I replied, laughing.

"My second cousin Tony was like us, you know. His dad

found out, threw him out of the house. He turned up two weeks later hanging from the rafters of an old barn we used to play in as kids."

"Holy cow, Alan. I had no idea."

"He was a year older than me, scared the heck out of me. I swore I'd change then and there, and I did for a while. Thought I did, anyway. Dated a girl named Dorothy. She was a sweet kid, but I knew deep down I was lying to her, and to myself."

"I'm glad you came to your senses, Alan."

"Me too, I guess. But we can't be too careful, especially with our work and your family. You can't afford to be too honest, and neither can I."

"I'll always try to be honest with you, Alan. I know we've only known each other a very short time, but I feel I can be completely myself around you."

"Good to know, Heath. And likewise."

We both paused for a few seconds, both of us pondering, I suppose, then Alan said, "So, all set for your big Lake Geneva adventure?"

I laughed. "Yeah, just finished packing earlier."

"I'm surprised," Alan replied, sounding amused. "I would have thought you'd done that days ago!"

I laughed again; already he knew me too well. "Yeah, well, you know, I don't want my clothes to get too wrinkled."

"Very true, though I'm sure this Darkly chap would be happy to have his butler press things for you."

"I don't want to take advantage."

"You mean considering you don't even know this guy?" His voice had turned to annoyance.

"I know it's strange, Alan."

"Strange to say the least! Who is Dexter Darkly anyway? I've never heard of him."

I sighed. "A wealthy philanthropist from Chicago who also lived here in Milwaukee. I told you that."

"Yeah, I know. Family money, in his seventies, and he invites you to spend the weekend with him out of the blue." I could hear the annoyance growing louder in Alan's voice.

I sighed again, this time more heavily. I seemed to be doing that a lot lately. "Not out of the blue. He read about the Murdoch case in the paper and was impressed. We've been over this before. You read the letter."

"But it still strikes me as odd."

"He's a fan of mine, I guess."

Now it was Alan's turn to laugh, rather sarcastically. "I hate to burst your bubble, Heath, but policemen, even detectives, don't usually have fans. Movie stars have fans. Cary Grant has fans."

"You included!" I countered.

"Hey, he's a great actor!"

"And rather dashing, I might add," I said, picturing Grant in *Notorious*, which I'd seen last year.

"Well, yes, yes, he is. And so is a certain police detective I know, but back to the point. How do you know this Darkly fellow doesn't hold some grudge against you? How do you know he's not luring you to this house in Lake Geneva to do you in?"

I shook my head. "Alan, you've really got to stop listening to the guys on the force who think everybody has some sinister angle they're just waiting to spring on someone. I checked on him at the library, and I ran a criminal check with the guys downtown. He's just some eccentric rich guy who wants to meet me and reward me for my public service. Remember he said in his letter he wasn't very fond of Murdoch? Why would he want to lure me to his house to kill me because I solved Murdoch's murder?"

"If he wasn't fond of him, why would he want to reward the man who brought his killer to justice?"

"Alan, you're overanalyzing this, really. Besides, you're coming along. You'll be there Saturday morning, and you'll get to see for yourself. Unless you've changed your mind and want to stay here instead."

"Ha! Not a chance! You gone for the weekend at some rich man's summer house on a lake and me here? Not likely, Heath. Maybe you have a thing for rich older men you haven't told me about."

"Not likely, unless he's Cary Grant," I replied with a chuckle.

"Now that's not likely," Keyes said, laughing himself, this time more warmly. "So what all did you pack for this excursion?"

"I wasn't sure what to pack, but I think for the train my brown tweed suit with the green silk tie will look smashing, so I'll wear that tomorrow. Then I packed my dark navy suit with that ivory tie you admired. I'll wear that for dinner Friday night, and then my black wool double breasted with the red and white tie for Saturday's dinner."

"Nice. After all, you are the best-dressed detective on the force, as I recall."

"Very funny, but true!" I turned and glanced at myself in the mirror again, picking a minute speck of lint off my gray cardigan.

"Also the best looking, I might add."

"Says you, and thank you," I replied, blushing just a bit and stealing one more look.

"Cufflinks?"

"Of course. I wouldn't be dressed for dinner without them. I'm taking my gold pair and the black opals that match my ring."

"I like those. They're the ones you wore to dinner last week."

"Yes. I fit everything in the suitcase and my train case."

"Your *matching* train case, as I recall you mentioning."

"That's right, brown leather suitcase and matching train, monogrammed. If one is going to travel, one might as well do it in style."

"One might as well. I hope you won't mind when I show up with my beat-up old suitcase that belonged to my dad," Alan said.

"As long as you show up, I'm sure I won't even care what your clothes are packed in. Besides, you could be dressed like a hobo and still look smashing."

"Glad to hear you think so, though I believe I can manage to dress a bit better than that. Not up to your par, of course."

"Oh go on, Alan. You dress fine, in and out of uniform, but especially out, if you know what I mean."

"Why, Detective, that's awfully suggestive."

"I have lots of suggestions for you, Officer. Just wait."

"I can't hardly wait. So, I'll see you Saturday?"

"Absolutely. I'll try to call you tomorrow night and let you know what it's like. That is, if old man Darkly hasn't done me in by then!"

"Ha, very funny. Night, Heath. Safe travels tomorrow."

"Good night, Alan. See you soon."

CHAPTER TWO

I awoke the next morning too early, but I couldn't sleep. I usually can't when I'm anxious or excited or nervous. It was the same on Christmas Eve when I was a kid. I guess in some ways you never do really grow up. I showered, had breakfast and read the *Sentinel*, and then took the #115 trolley car over to the station at the end of Wisconsin Avenue, arriving at eleven a.m., a full two hours before the train was scheduled to leave.

I passed the time perusing *LIFE* magazine at the newsstand, reading a bit in my book about the life of Oscar Wilde, and observing the general public, always a fascinating study. I watched an expensively dressed fat little man in a black bowler hat follow a pretty little thing in a green and white striped dress. She circled the newsstand with him close behind, all the time pretending to be interested in the periodicals, until finally she turned and walked briskly across to the ladies' room. Defeated, the fat little man circled one more time, then set out in search of a new target.

I smiled to myself, knowing some pretty little thing would probably let herself be caught, since clearly the fat little man in the bowler hat was rather well off. A little after noon, I got a pastrami sandwich on rye, hold the mustard, and some black coffee from the lunch counter. The pastrami was dry and the coffee weak, but it was enough to tide me over until dinner, anyway. I hoped Mr. Darkly was right about the skills of his cook.

At long last it was time to board, and I found myself a seat toward the back of the second car, put my hat in the overhead rack, and relaxed a bit, taking out my book on Oscar Wilde once more to pass the time. There weren't too many fellow passengers, so I was glad to have a seat to myself as the leg room left something to be desired.

I read, watched the little towns of Racine and Kenosha fly by out the window, dozed for a bit, and read some more. After I'd finished several chapters, the train at last pulled into the small Lake Geneva station. I stowed my book inside my case, put on my hat, and adjusted my tie before stepping down onto the platform, the porter following me with my larger case. I tipped him a quarter and looked about, squinting into the bright light of day. A small, older man in a dark suit and a tweed cap was standing just off the platform, and as we made eye contact, he came forward.

"Mr. Barrington?" he asked in a low, gravelly voice.

"Yes, that's right." I nodded, sizing him up.

"Bishop, sir. Mr. Darkly's butler. I have a cab waiting to take us to the dock. Allow me."

The meter must have been running on that cab, because Bishop wasted no time on pleasantries. He lugged my bag down the platform and through the station to the parking lot, where a younger man in a taxicab uniform took it from him and lifted it into the trunk.

Bishop held open the back door of the cab for me and closed it after I'd settled in. He climbed in up front next to the driver, and we were off. It was a short ride to the dock, not more than ten minutes, tops. The driver stopped the cab, retrieved my bag from the trunk, and then stood by until Bishop paid him off. Before the cabbie was even back in his taxi, Bishop was lugging my case toward the water.

"Just this way, sir," he said over his shoulder, huffing a bit. I marveled at how quickly he could move, considering he had to be well past sixty.

I followed him once more as he led the way past the beautiful Riveria ballroom on the water's edge. I'd attended a dance there once a few years ago. Swanky place. All the big names played there—Artie Shaw, Glenn Miller, Les Brown— all of them, right here in little Lake Geneva. It was built in 1932, during the Depression, and it turned out to be quite an attraction, with shops and changing rooms for the nearby beach on the first floor and the ballroom up above. Alongside the Riveria, long wooden docks jutted out into the water, where an old-fashioned lake steamer from the '20s seemed to be waiting just for us as no one else was about. The name *Mercury* was printed on the side of the steamer in gold letters, a somewhat grandiose name considering I highly doubted this old tug could move anywhere near that fast.

"Pretty deserted around here."

"It's the off season yet, sir." Bishop stopped at the foot of the dock and set my suitcase down. I put my train case next to it. "Mr. Darkly arranged for the steamer to bring me over and wait while I retrieved you from the station."

"I'm honored," I replied, not sure what else to say. The sun was brilliant, the sky cloudless, and I squinted again in the brightness. I looked about the empty pier and parking lot, glad to have worn my wide-brimmed hat. I wondered why we stopped where we did, but I figured Bishop must know what he was doing.

He motioned to a group of brawny men working on the shore. "In five or six weeks, Memorial Day weekend, this place will be spilling over with people, sir. They're working on getting all the private docks back in the water now. Once the docks are in and the boats back in the water, the place is filled with people right up until Labor Day."

"I guess it's good to come off season, then." As I finished my sentence, I noticed a handsome young lad bounding down the dock toward us. Good things come to those who wait, as Mom always says. Of course, my aunt Verbina always says good things come to those who go out and get them.

"Let me get those for you, sir," he said to me with a smile about as wide as Wisconsin Avenue back in Milwaukee, lifting my heavy case as if it were a feather and tucking the smaller one under his arm.

"This is Adam," Bishop said. "He's the deckhand for the *Mercury*, the lake steamer we're using today."

"How do you do, Adam?" I asked. I extended my hand but then realized his arms were full, so I let it drop back to my side.

"Just fine, sir. Thank you," he replied, still grinning, his teeth amazingly white. "Lake's calm today, so it should be smooth sailing. All ready?"

"Absolutely!" I answered, grinning myself. Adam's enthusiasm was contagious, at least to me. Bishop seemed nonplussed.

Mesmerized, I watched as Adam turned on his heel and bounded back up the dock effortlessly and onto the steamer, his white sailor pants hugging his hindquarters like the water to the shore. By the time we caught up with him, he had stowed my luggage and was standing by to help us aboard. I gladly took his large, calloused hand and let him pull me on the deck.

"Captain Boone already has the steam up, sir. We're ready to make way once you two are seated and I let go the mooring ropes. The trip to the Darkly dock will take about twenty-five minutes. It was one of the first to be put back in the water, per Mr. Darkly's request." It was all I could do to focus on his words and not let my mind and eyes travel farther down. I hoped Bishop hadn't noticed my distraction; I generally pride myself on my discretion.

"Why do they take them all out?" I asked.

Adam's clear green eyes shimmered in the sunlight. "The lake freezes over completely in winter, sir. It's spring fed."

"Ah, I see. I wasn't aware of that." I smiled back at him. "Hard to believe such a large body of water freezes over."

Adam nodded in agreement, a lock of his wavy brown hair dancing across his broad forehead. "And yet it does, sir. It's actually kind of pretty."

"I've never been here in the winter. I suppose that's true for most folks," I replied, still concentrating on his eyes and that lovely hair, but letting my mind wander.

He turned back and looked at me. "For the most part, just the townsfolk winter over, sir. Most of the homes on the lake are summer homes, used Memorial Day to Labor Day."

I marveled to myself at anyone having that much money as to own a massive summer home like those dotting the lakeshore. "Amazing. Well, I'll let you get to work," I responded, realizing we needed to get under way, and knowing Alan would not appreciate me drooling on my green silk tie.

"Yes, sir. Make yourself comfortable and let me know if you need anything." He grinned that grin again, and I wondered if he meant that.

As Adam started preparations to make way, I went inside the small cabin, Bishop trailing me. We were indeed the only passengers, so I made myself comfortable by a window along the port side. The water below was still and looked a rather muddy greenish blue. Bishop settled one row behind me. I looked back at him. "Really, Bishop, come up here and sit with me. No need to stand on formality, and I'd like to talk with you."

"As you wish, sir," the old man said, moving up to the wooden bench seat beside me.

We watched out the window as the steamer got under way, the shore slowly growing smaller behind us, the engine making a churning, thumping, rhythmic sound. I turned to Bishop, hoping to pass the time and perhaps get some answers to my questions. "Adam seems a nice chap."

Bishop nodded. "Indeed. So many young men never came back from the war, you know, or if they did, they were never the same. Adam's one of the lucky ones, I guess."

"Very lucky. Let's hope we never have another war, Bishop."

"I can't even imagine, sir. I lost my cousin in the first war. His mother took it hard."

"I'm so sorry."

"Thank you. War is a nasty business, and the price far too high." He glanced past me out the window. "Lovely day, today, sir—let's not talk of war."

"I agree, it is a lovely day."

"Yes, sir, it is," Bishop said again. "It's almost sixty degrees today and sunny, very little wind. Weekend's not supposed to be as nice, though, I'm afraid."

"Oh?"

"Rain predicted tomorrow and colder; probably only in the forties tonight, maybe even the thirties, according to the radio, anyway. Possibly frost tomorrow night."

"That's quite a difference from today."

"Indeed, sir. It's that time of year. Warm and sunny one day, cold the next. We've even gotten snow this late in the year, though that's not typical."

"Have you worked for Mr. Darkly long, Bishop?"

He shook his head. "Actually, sir, my wife and I were just hired by Mr. Darkly last fall as he was preparing to close the house for the winter. For reasons he didn't go into, he had dismissed his previous staff and needed a couple to be the caretakers in the off season and his butler and cook during the summer months."

"Curious. Where does he live during the winter?"

"Apparently he had an apartment in Chicago, sir. On Lake Drive."

"Had?" I said, surprised.

"He told us he gave it up last fall. He had quite a few of his belongings, boxes and such, shipped out here."

"Curiouser. Why would he give up his year-round place?"

"I don't really know, Mr. Barrington. I suppose he travels so much during the winter, he didn't feel a need to maintain a winter residence any longer. He spent this past season in Monaco," Bishop said matter-of-factly.

"Sounds lovely. I've never been there, and Monaco was neutral during the war, so no ravages and burned-out buildings to contend with."

"That's true, sir. Though Europe is making hasty repairs, it will take many years to recover. I know London was especially hard hit. Let's hope they never have another war."

"Amen to that. Sorry, I didn't mean to get us back on the war subject," I said, quite sincerely.

Bishop looked at me, his eyes penetrating. "It's all right, sir. Only natural, I suppose. It changed so much, changed us all. Were you over there?"

I shook my head slowly. I get asked that a lot. "No. Unfortunately, or fortunately, I have flat feet, and I'm a cop, so I was exempt."

He nodded. "Police put their lives on the line every day, too. I have to respect that."

"Thank you, Bishop. So I understand Mr. Darkly had a home in Milwaukee, too."

"Yes, sir. He mentioned that when we interviewed for the position. He was born in Chicago and his family's main house was there, but apparently he relocated to Milwaukee later in life, probably for business reasons. Nora, that's my wife, has a sister who lives there, though she doesn't see her much anymore."

"I see. Why did he move back to Chicago?"

Bishop shrugged. "I don't know, sir, though I imagine being by himself, he didn't want to maintain a big house in Milwaukee and a big summer house out here. An apartment in Chicago seems quite cosmopolitan, though now he's given that up, too, so he's down to just this place. Most of the homes here are owned by folks in Illinois. It really took off after the Chicago fire."

I stared at the old man next to me, his face lined and worn, but his gray eyes still so bright. "I bet. People with money and means had the opportunity to escape up here while the rebuilding was going on."

"Money perhaps can buy happiness, sir."

"Or rent it, anyway," I replied. "I remember my grandmother talking about the Great Chicago Fire. I can certainly understand why this beautiful little area would hold an attraction after that."

"Indeed, Mr. Barrington."

"So, Mr. Darkly travels all winter and summers here? Quite the life. What's Mr. Darkly like, Bishop?"

He scratched his gray, dimpled chin. "Difficult to say, Mr. Barrington. We only met him briefly when he gave us our instructions for closing up the house, and then when he arrived for the season a few days ago. He keeps to himself."

"Keeps to himself?"

"Yes, sir. With us, anyway. He's rather traditional. Servants and employers don't mix, and perhaps that's for the better, though times are changing."

"Indeed they are, Bishop. Is there all that much to closing up a house for the winter?" I asked, envisioning closing some shutters and maybe turning off the water.

"Oh, more than you would imagine, sir. All artwork and furniture has to be wrapped or draped in sheets, bedding stripped, laundered, and stored, all the light fixtures cleaned, the upper floors closed off, windows shuttered, draperies taken down and cleaned, the good china washed, rugs aired and beaten, silver polished and put away, the dock taken out of the water and stored. Mr. Darkly is very particular. It took Nora and I close to two weeks to finish everything."

"And then what did you do?"

Bishop looked a bit sheepish. "To be honest, sir, very little. It seemed almost criminal accepting pay for basically just living in his house all winter. Most of the homes here are weekend or summer houses, as Adam mentioned. The people usually bring their servants with them from the city, and the homes sit vacant all winter. Mr. Darkly had heard talk of vandalism and break-ins at some of the properties last year, however, so he felt having us winter over was worth it."

"A wise precaution, I'd say, speaking from a policeman's perspective. Where were you working previously?"

"My wife and I are semi-retired. The family we had been working for moved out West, and we decided not to follow. They were generous to us and gave us a year's salary. Truth be told, I think they were relieved we didn't want to go. I think they felt we were getting too old to keep up with them full-time, and maybe so, though don't go telling Nora that." His laugh was surprisingly light.

I smiled at him.

"But we like to work," Bishop continued, "so when we read the advertisement for this position, it seemed ideal. Still, as I said, it was a long winter at the house by ourselves. One can only read so many books or play so many games of canasta."

I nodded understandingly. "I would imagine so."

"Yes, so we were very pleasantly surprised to get the telegram from Mr. Darkly asking us to have the house open for the season several weeks earlier than originally anticipated. Generally, houses here open for the season Memorial Day weekend and close in October, though Labor Day weekend officially marks the end of season."

"Is Mr. Darkly easy to work for?"

"Well, as I said, sir, we only met him briefly last fall and then again just a few days ago when he arrived. He seemed satisfied with our preparations and the menus Nora had planned. He didn't say much, really, though he discussed a few things with us. Mr. Darkly seems rather private, as I said before."

"He's older, I understand?"

"In his mid to late seventies, I suspect. Not too much older than me. He seems rather frail, though he's quite tan. He wintered in Monaco, as I mentioned."

I nodded again. "That does sound exotic. The pleasures of the idle rich," I replied, thinking about my seventy-two-dollar-a-week salary with two weeks' paid vacation. "His letter said there would be other guests this weekend?"

"That's right, sir. Most of them came in yesterday, though Mr. Doubleday arrived first thing this morning, just after breakfast, rather unexpected."

"I didn't think there was a morning train on Friday."

"Mr. Doubleday's in from Chicago, sir."

"Ah. He's a friend of Mr. Darkly?"

"Donovan Doubleday is a relative by marriage, apparently. As I said, we didn't really expect him this weekend. It caused a bit of an uproar."

"He wasn't invited?"

Bishop shook his gray little head. "No, sir. It seems he got wind of the weekend from Mrs. Atwater, his niece."

"Strange. So he just showed up?"

"This morning, sir. Though Mrs. Atwater says she invited him. The whole thing was very awkward."

"No doubt. Who's Mrs. Atwater?"

"Mrs. Atwater and her husband, a doctor, arrived yesterday. She never mentioned Mr. Doubleday, probably because she knew it would upset Mr. Darkly."

"Very curious," I said. "So many curious things. Good thing I'm not a cat."

Bishop shot me an odd look. "A cat, sir?"

I smiled. "Oh you know, curiosity killed the cat. I'm a very curious sort of fellow."

He nodded but looked a bit confused. "Indeed, sir. Oh, and Mr. Acres arrived yesterday also, along with Mrs. Darkly—Mr. Darkly's ex-wife, I understand."

"Really? That seems unusual."

Bishop raised his white brows a bit. "Nora and I thought so, too, sir. But it's not our place to say anything. The whole weekend seems unusual, if I may say so, sir. Curious, as you would say."

"Of course, Bishop, I am the picture of discretion. You can tell me anything."

He smiled at me. "I appreciate that, sir, as I, by nature and trade, am very discreet myself."

"Good to understand one another. So, five other guests besides myself."

"That's right, sir. And we understand your companion is arriving tomorrow morning?"

"Alan Keyes, yes. He's a fellow police officer. I thought he could do with a weekend away."

"Indeed, sir. Very considerate of you. As I said, I have the utmost respect for policemen, servicemen, and firemen. Mr. Darkly has reserved the room behind yours for Mr. Keyes."

"Sounds like you, your wife, and Mr. Darkly have everything under control, then."

We rode in silence for a while, watching the homes along the shore glide by. The largest, the Wrigley estate, stood silently like a temple, awaiting the gods and goddesses of chewing gum to arrive shortly. Eventually Bishop pointed out the Darkly dock, a flagpole standing at the end of it, flying the forty-eight.

"The flagpole," Bishop explained, "is actually a signaling device. If Mr. Darkly is in residence and is welcoming guests, he flies the blue flag with a large white D in the center of it. If the steamer is needed, a yellow flag with a red circle is flown. If he's in residence but not accepting visitors, he flies the US flag."

"So why isn't he flying the blue flag now?"

"The blue flag, I understand, is for when other people who live on the lake are out boating. If they see the blue flag, they know it's okay to stop at the dock and go up to the house to visit."

"Ah, I see. And just where is the house?"

"There, sir, at the top of the hill." He pointed to a speck of white, just visible through the trees, which had already leafed out considerably.

"Prepare to dock," a voice said over a tinny speaker. Soon after, I felt the steamer scrape against the bumpers tied to the side of the pier, and we came to a stop, the rhythmic thumping of the engine throttling down to idle. Rather entranced, I watched through the window as Adam leapt off the steamer deck, secured the mooring ropes to the dock, and made way the gangplank.

I retrieved my hat and train case and walked down, Bishop trailing behind dutifully once more. Once we were off, Adam bounded back on board to retrieve my larger case, which he quickly sat at my feet not too gently, but I didn't mind. I obliged him with a fifty-cent piece, probably too extravagant, but he did have a nice face. Nice everything, and it all came together so well, too. He thanked me with a tip of his cap and a flash of that killer smile, and then released the mooring ropes and boarded the old tug once more.

As the steamer moved off, Bishop turned to me. "Well, sir, here we are, then."

"Yes, here we are. What's with the mailbox?" I asked, gesturing toward a mailbox at the end of the pier.

"Homes this far out on the lake get their mail by boat, sir, during the summer months. There isn't much of a road."

"Fascinating."

"Yes, sir. The rest of the year, any year-long residents pick up mail at the main post office in town, using the old road, or Edgar will eventually drive it around in his truck."

"I mailed my RSVP back. I'm assuming since you're here, you knew I was coming."

"Oh yes, sir. Edgar had been instructed to watch for it, and he drove it around special. He does that for telegrams, too."

"I see." Lake Geneva was clearly an interesting place to live.

Bishop nodded and pointed. "The house is just there at the top of the hill. Shall we?"

"Let's go," I said, and I picked up my small bag, Bishop taking the larger. "What's that there?" I asked, pointing in the general direction of a rather dilapidated shingled building close to shore, just off the dock. It looked like a garage, but the large doors opened onto the water. The shingles had weathered to a soft gray color, more than a few missing. Some, I noted, were floating in the greenish brown water below.

"That's the oldboat house, sir. Mr. Darkly tells me they used to keep a boat or two here for fishing and whatnot, but he sold them off a few years ago. Too much maintenance."

"Too bad. I'd think a little boating would be fun."

"Indeed, sir," Bishop replied, but I got the feeling he was glad the boats were gone, as he probably would have had to do the maintenance. "Nothing in there now except the flag locker and some supplies, maybe a rat or two and some squirrels."

Next to the boathouse, a small dirt path went up a rise to the base of a large hill. From there a set of weathered wooden stairs climbed up, somewhat steeply at points, zigzagging back and forth to the top of the hill where the house stood.

We started up, but somewhere near the middle of the climb, I became aware that Bishop was falling farther and farther behind me. It wasn't exactly easy going for me, and I'm only thirty-two years old. Poor Bishop had to be in his sixties at least and was struggling with my large case, which, I guiltily remembered, contained six pairs of shoes and a multitude of clothes.

At the next landing, I stopped to get my breath and wait for Bishop to catch up. When he did, puffing like the lake steamer, I said, "Why don't we rest here a bit? The lake looks lovely from here."

"Excellent idea, sir," he managed to get out, his voice even more gravelly and deep.

We waited silently together, staring out at the lake below, until I felt we were both ready to go on. "Let me take the large bag, Bishop. You can handle the small one. It's only fair, you've carried it more than halfway now."

"Oh, thank you, sir." He hesitated and then glanced up toward the house, which was becoming more visible. "But I'd better not. Mr. Darkly wouldn't like it if he saw his guest carrying his own bags."

"But that's ridiculous. I want to carry it. I can use the exercise. I'll be happy to explain that to Mr. Darkly if he says anything."

The old man shook his head. "Thank you, Mr. Barrington. You are too kind, but I'd better carry it for you. When my wife and I interviewed for the position, Mr. Darkly was adamant that we be fit enough for the physical aspects of the job, and he specifically detailed carrying luggage up to the house from the landing."

"You mean you've had to carry everyone's luggage up here?"

"Yes, sir. Except the steamer deckhand, Adam, helped me with Dr. and Mrs. Atwater's bags. That was okay since there were two of them, and they tipped him to assist. He carried nearly all of their bags single-handedly. Quite a strapping young fellow."

"Yes, I noticed." *Who wouldn't?* I thought. I remembered that Keyes was arriving tomorrow and wondered somewhat jealously if Adam would be on the *Mercury* steamer then, too. "Does Adam work on the steamer tomorrow, also?"

"I don't know, sir. But I imagine so. His father is the captain."

I made a note to myself to be on hand down at the dock

when the *Mercury* arrived tomorrow morning, just to make sure Keyes didn't forget me. To be honest, I wanted to get another look at Adam myself.

"All ready, sir?"

"Yes, but if you insist on carrying the large bag, let's at least take it slow. There's no need to rush, all right? We'll rest at every landing."

"Yes, sir. *Thank you, sir.*"

We started off again, resting at each landing until we reached the top. From there, it was a short walk down another dirt and stone path to the house. It was enveloped by the trees, casting it in perpetual shadow, somewhat melancholy and gloomy. I don't know why, but I had the feeling we were being watched from someone in the house. Or was it the house itself that appeared to be staring at me? From above, I glanced a white gull making lazy swoops in the sky. Maybe it was watching me, too. I laughed at myself for being so silly. I think Alan and his detective movies were rubbing off on me.

I turned instead to Bishop and asked, "Rather a big place, isn't it, Bishop?" The house was sheathed in white clapboards and the windows trimmed with dark green shutters, which matched the green-shingled roof. A corner tower was on the right, and a large, deep porch wrapped around the left side of the house until it ran into a wing that jutted out even farther to the left. A large bay window on the second floor rested on the porch roof, sagging slightly, and the attic floor rose majestically above that, soaring to a peak.

Bishop nodded. "Yes, sir. Nineteen rooms in all, including the servants' rooms."

"That's quite a lot."

"Yes, sir, it is. Still, it's smaller than some of the places out here. There's also an ice house out back along with the old summer kitchen. A new kitchen's been added on to the house in the last few years, so that old one just sits empty. Probably full of mice by now. Mr. Darkly only gave me and Nora two weeks to get the place ready for this weekend. That may seem like a fair amount of time, but it goes by in a hurry when you consider all that has to be done."

"I can imagine. Pretty much the reverse of closing it down."

"That's right, only even more so. Everything gets rather stale and dusty over the winter, you know. Beds have to be aired out and made up, mattresses beaten, furniture and artwork uncovered, windows washed, draperies taken down and cleaned and pressed, rugs beaten, floors scrubbed, place aired and dusted from top to bottom, everything spick-and-span, all the yard work, supplies laid up. Everything has to be bought in town, you know, and brought over on the steamer. Then," he paused, looking back over his shoulder, "carried up all those stairs, sir."

"Goodness. I thought Mr. Darkly said in his letter there was a road. You mentioned it, too, the one that Edgar fellow uses to deliver mail and telegrams."

"Yes, sir, there is, sir, but it's not in the best of shape, and Mr. Darkly doesn't keep an automobile here. There used to be a stable, but Mr. Darkly gave up his horses some years ago."

"Well, that's certainly a lot of work for two people." *Especially two older people*, I thought to myself.

Bishop nodded again. "A house like this usually has at least four on staff—housekeeper, cook, maid, and butler. But Mr. Darkly runs things a bit tighter. Most folks do since the war, domestic help is hard to find these days. Nora and I don't mind all that much, though. It's nice to be busy. He told us this will be his biggest party for the season, and it's just a weekend. Mr. Darkly said most of the time he stays out here by himself."

"Seems a lonely place to be," I said, glancing about the

grounds and the big old house once more. The gull, I noticed, was still circling above.

"It is, sir. As I've told you, it was a long winter with just me and Nora out here. Once the lake froze over, we were pretty much marooned. And it was cold, too. The house really wasn't built for year-round use, so it doesn't have much insulation, you know."

"How did you manage?"

"Most of the rooms were closed off, locked and forgotten about. And we shut the water off to the main part of the house. We pretty much lived in the kitchen and rooms just above it. The cook stove and the fireplaces kept it toasty enough most days."

"I can see where that would get to be a *very* long winter, though."

"Yes, sir, very much so. The neighboring houses are all vacant for the off season, and as I said, there was too much ice for the steamer until a month ago or so, so it was pretty much just the two of us from November to February, until the *Mercury* started running again in March. Truth be told, I'm glad to see the house filled up with people. Seems that's how it should be."

"I can't even imagine spending four months out here by myself, with just one other person," I said. *Unless that other person was Alan Keyes,* I added silently to myself. *And maybe Adam.*

The large front porch creaked noticeably under our weight. Bishop sat my bag down, and I waited while he opened the ornate carved wooden door. A scrolled letter *D* that matched the *D* on the invitation was etched in the frosted oval door glass.

"Sir," he said, motioning me into the entrance hall. I stepped inside and had a look around, my eyes adjusting to the dim interior as a musty smell hit my nostrils. The hall was roughly ten or twelve feet wide and ran the depth of the house, with a grand staircase rising up and back at the rear. The stairs were open underneath, and I could see another entrance door under the landing, which led out to the backyard, I assumed. Looking up, I could see a stained glass window on the staircase landing, lighting the stairs up and down. What I assumed were family portraits lined the walls, glaring down at us from heavy, dark gilt frames. The people in them wore somber expressions, as if they were bored at having nothing to do but hang in the hallway year after year.

Bishop picked up my case again and stepped inside, closing the door behind him with a heavy sigh. "Welcome to Dark Point, Mr. Barrington."

"Thank you. Where is everyone?" I asked quietly, noting the silence.

"Resting after lunch, I imagine, sir. Nora will be in the kitchen doing the washing up and preparing for dinner. Everyone else will be in their rooms or perhaps out on the grounds having a look about. Someone might be in the library—back there, just to the right of the stairs," he said, pointing down the hall. "The drawing room is to our right, also known as the music room. There's a piano there, if you play."

I shook my head. "Never learned, always wanted to."

"Never too late, they say, sir. The dining room is to our left. Lunch is at one, dinner at eight. Mr. Darkly is very punctual about dinner times, and he expects everyone to dress, of course."

"Of course, and where is Mr. Darkly?" I asked, having expected him to greet me personally.

"I imagine he's in his study, sir, just to the left of the stairs there."

"The door that's at an angle?"

"That's right, sir. He keeps to himself a fair amount and doesn't seem to mingle much except at meal time. You'll meet him at dinner if not before."

"Shouldn't I go say hello? Let him know I've arrived and thank him for inviting me?"

Bishop shook his head. "I shouldn't be surprised if Mr. Darkly already knows you're here, Mr. Barrington. He'll meet you on his schedule, I'm sure. We've been instructed not to intrude."

"I see," I said, raising my eyebrows.

Bishop continued his verbal tour of the house. "Just before the door to the study is the hall to the kitchen, on the left. You'll find the necessary room down there, too, sir. Last door on the right."

"Good to have the lay of the land, thank you."

"You're welcome, sir. Feel free to nose about. Mr. Darkly said guests are free to go wherever they like, with the exception of his bedroom and sitting room, of course. Shall we go up to your room now, sir?"

"Oh, yes, of course. By all means."

"You're up in the attic. Two more flights of stairs," he said rather resignedly, picking up my large case.

"Bishop really, I don't mind." I reached for my bag.

"No, sir, I insist. It's my job, really."

I sighed. "Very well, then. Lead on."

The stairs creaked under our weight as we climbed slowly. We paused at the second floor, and I had a look around while Bishop caught his breath again. I saw still more portraits on the walls, along with pictures of sailboats, horses, and people in fancy dress. Each of the doors off the hall had a transom above it.

"Four bedrooms on this floor, you said?"

"That's right, sir. There are two servant rooms over the

kitchen, too. Plus the old nursery is straight ahead of you, over the entryway. Mr. Darkly uses that as a sitting room now. There's a door to it from his room as well as the hall."

"Who has the other rooms?"

"The doctor and his wife have the room behind Mr. Darkly's, and Mrs. Darkly has the room just here above the study, sir. You, Mr. Doubleday, Mr. Acres, and your friend all are up in the attic."

"But you've accounted for just three bedrooms on this floor."

I followed his gaze to a closed door across the hall. "Yes, sir. That one is unoccupied, another room off-limits to guests, sir. Shall we continue up?" I was curious about the empty room but got the impression Bishop didn't want to discuss it, at least not where others might overhear. I dropped the subject.

"Up to the attic we go! Lead on, Bishop."

We climbed the final flight of stairs to the top, and Bishop set my case down, breathing rather heavily.

"Mr. Darkly's given you the nicest room up here, sir—the tower room. You can see the lake from here."

"Very considerate of him."

"Yes, sir. I hope you'll find everything satisfactory. Mr. Darkly himself was up here this morning, making sure the rooms were in order. Surprised me, I must admit."

"Surprised?"

"Mr. Darkly has a bit of trouble with the stairs, Mr. Barrington. He told us he rarely comes up here, so I was surprised to see him this morning, checking out the rooms. He must think very highly of you."

"I'm honored, though I'm sure he found everything to be top notch."

"Thank you, Mr. Barrington. I didn't mention to Nora that

I saw him. I think she'd be offended to think Mr. Darkly was checking up on us."

"I won't say a word about it, Bishop."

"Thank you again, sir. I think Mr. Darkly would be embarrassed, too. I don't think he knows I saw him. But it doesn't bother me, being checked up on, I mean. If he'd found anything out of order, we'd have heard about it."

"I can imagine."

"Indeed, sir. Anyway, your room is the second door on the left."

"Thank you, Bishop. I can take it from here, honestly." I picked up my bag and started down the hall. No portraits or family photographs up here, just an old framed map of the lake, and a perspective view of the town dated 1912, the year the *Titanic* sank. I made a mental note to come back and study it later, as I've always been interested in history and old maps.

"Wouldn't you like me to unpack for you, sir, show you your room?" He called out after me in his deep gravelly voice.

"No, thank you. I can manage," I replied, looking over my shoulder and giving him a smile. "I'm sure Mr. Darkly won't mind if I go the rest of the way myself."

"As you wish, sir. May I have Nora fix you a sandwich?"

I stopped and looked back at the little man, very much the gentleman's gentleman. He was still standing at the top of the stairs, breathing rather heavily, his hands folded in front of him. "Very kind of you, Bishop, but I ate at the station in Milwaukee before boarding. I should be fine until dinner. I just want to get settled and change my clothes, relax a bit, maybe do a walk."

"All right, sir. But if you need anything, there's a call button in your room. There's also a telephone in Mr. Darkly's study. Should you need it, just ask."

"Only one telephone in this big house?"

"Yes, sir. Mr. Darkly feels telephones are intrusions. Necessary evils, he calls them. He told us that when he's here, he wants to get away from intrusions and interruptions."

I shrugged. "Seems logical, I suppose."

"Mr. Darkly has also asked me to remind each guest that if you must telephone to please reverse the charges, sir."

I smiled. "I'll remember that, thank you, Bishop."

"Anytime, sir."

I turned and meandered down the remainder of the hall toward the front of the house and my room, which I ascertained must sit above the drawing room/music room two floors below.

CHAPTER THREE

The door to my room was not locked, and I noticed it swung open noiselessly. The room was surprisingly large even with the sloped ceilings, and nicely furnished with a brass double bed against the wall, covered with a thick quilt of red and white diamonds. Next to it, a small round table with a lamp and a clock on it, as well as a drinking glass. A small table and chairs was next to a fireplace in the corner, their paint flaking off in spots. The wallpaper was a small rose floral print, faded and old but in good condition. The woodwork was all painted white, and there was a brass overhead light in the center of the ceiling.

Beside the door to the hall, two more doors stood like sentries, and I discovered two generously sized cedar-lined closets. The wall at the front of the house had a window with a lovely view of the lake, which could also be seen from the private bath in the tower. Red chintz draperies hung on the windows. They appeared freshly pressed and cleaned but still faded from the sun. Everything in this house seemed old and worn out, I thought to myself.

I had just opened my large bag on the bed and had begun to lay out my clothes when someone knocked sharply on the door. "Come in," I called out, expecting Bishop with a hot Earl

Grey tea or something. But instead of the little old man, in walked a rather handsome, nattily dressed fellow in his early thirties, maybe late twenties. He was a tall wisp of a man, clean shaven, with hair the color of the night sky, touched lightly with premature gray streaks like wisps of clouds, and parted neatly down the middle. His eyes were deep brown, one ever so slightly smaller than the other, set on either side of a long, thin nose. The overall effect was a touch asymmetrical, but still quite attractive and sweet looking. I got the feeling he was surveying me just as I was surveying him.

"Harwood Acres, Philadelphia. How do you do?" he said, somewhat affected, as he strode gracefully across the floor. First impressions immediately led me to believe we had something in common. That put me on my guard, yet also aroused my curiosity.

"Heath Barrington, from Milwaukee. A pleasure." I held out my hand, and he grasped it firmly enough, then turned it over to look at my ring. "Gorgeous, Mr. Barrington. Black opal?"

"Ah yes, that's right. Thank you."

He dropped my right hand and took hold of my left. "And no ring on the left. Not married?"

"No, single. You?" Alarms went off in my head, as they always do when someone mentions not being married. I needed to be careful.

"No, I'm not the marrying type," he replied, arching his brow. "You're that policeman fellow they were talking about."

"Yes, that's right. Who was talking about me?"

He shrugged. "Everyone was talking, but not just about you. I must say you don't look like a policeman." He looked me up and down again, and I felt a bit uncomfortable, as if he could see right through my suit.

"Ah, thanks, I think. Actually I'm a detective now."

"Hmm, same difference, I'd say. I bet the ladies are all over you. Handsome young men are in short supply these days after the war."

"Um, thank you again," I said, somewhat embarrassed. "I don't date much." *Careful. Don't reveal too much.*

He gazed into my eyes. "Uh-huh. I don't either, if you know what I mean. My room is just across the hall. I have to share a bath with Mr. Doubleday. Not that I mind sharing a bath, but have you *seen* Mr. Doubleday?" he asked.

"Ah, no. I haven't met anyone yet except you and Bishop."

Mr. Acres smiled devilishly, showing amazingly white teeth framed by very full red lips, rather unusual for a man. "Well, you're in for a treat, Mr. Barrington. I arrived just after dinner last night, but I got the lowdown at lunch today. Everyone was being oh so polite but beneath the surface, tension was steaming more than the soup." His face was lit up, and I could tell he relished telling me all about it.

"Tension?" I asked, my curiosity aroused and my defenses put on the back burner temporarily.

He rolled his brown eyes to the ceiling and whistled. "You know it, mister. Apparently, Mr. Doubleday showed up uninvited, at least by Mr. Darkly. Can you imagine?" He paused for dramatic effect, I think, as he continued before I could respond. "Everyone was on edge and with good reason, it seems. Anyway, after lunch I came up here just for some peace and quiet. That and I was looking for my pocketknife—I seem to have misplaced it, though I could swear I left it on my dresser when I went downstairs earlier. If you see it, let me know, won't you?"

"Sure. What's it look like?"

"It's got a pearl handle, and it has my initials on it."

"H.A. for Harwood Acres. Ha?" I asked, smiling.

He rolled his eyes again. "Ha. Yes, I know. That's me, always good for a laugh. Anyway, if you see it give me a shout. Or whistle or something. I'll come running."

"I definitely will."

"I hope so. Anyway, I came up to look for it and when I couldn't find it I just rather moped about. I watched you and Bishop come up the hill, the poor old man. I thought you two would never make it."

No wonder I felt like I was being watched, I thought. Him and that gull.

"I must say it's nice to have a friendly face in the group," he continued. "And such a nice-looking one, too. You must be what, twenty-nine? That's my age, you know."

"I'm thirty-two." Defenses up once more.

He grinned again. "Wonderful age to be. So what has brought you here from little ol' Milwaukee?"

"Mr. Darkly heard about my latest case and was kind enough to invite me."

He arched his brow, making his one eye appear even smaller. "Do tell. I should like to hear all about it. You're here alone, yes?"

"Yes, though someone is joining me tomorrow."

"Oh, I see," he said rather dejectedly. "I'm alone. Someone to chum about with would be nice. I rather expect it's going to be a long weekend."

"I'm looking forward to a nice peaceful weekend," I replied quite sincerely. "The house seems very quiet."

"It is. Nice, if you like that sort of thing, which I don't. I imagine Mr. Darkly has that comfy big room with the private bath reserved for your friend."

"Yes, I believe that's what Bishop told me."

"I wanted either that room or yours. I got the one with the

shared bath, and I have to share it with Donovan Doubleday, no less. If he hadn't shown up, I would have had the bath all to myself. Well, at least Darkly didn't put me in the little room over the old nursery."

I looked at him, feeling a bit guilty for some reason. "Perhaps we could switch off rooms since yours isn't to your liking. I wouldn't mind. I can sleep just about anywhere. You could stay in my room tomorrow night, and I could stay in yours."

"What a kind invitation, but no, I'll stay put. I wouldn't dream of putting you out, and besides, you've got so many clothes you'd have to move." He scanned the contents of my bag. "My goodness, you've got wonderful taste. And look at all those shoes. Are you staying past the weekend?"

"Uh, no," I answered, rather embarrassed. "I just wasn't sure what to pack. I've never stayed at a lake house before. At least, not one like this."

"Well, stick with me, bud, and you won't go wrong. For this afternoon, just a nice pair of trousers and a long-sleeved shirt will do. That dark suit for tonight, of course—love the double breasted. For breakfast tomorrow it's very casual. Slacks, short-sleeved shirt, you'll be fine. They set everything out buffet style, so it's serve yourself."

"I'm used to that."

"Of course you are. I mean, most folks are, aren't they? I don't come from money myself, but I do like the finer things in life."

"Most folks do."

"Touché. I see you packed some sweaters. Good thinking. You'll need them in the mornings and evenings. It can get quite chilly, and it's supposed to be bone-chilling cold tomorrow, quite unseasonable. I wouldn't mind borrowing that cream V-neck if you don't end up wearing it."

"Sure, Mr. Acres, you'd be most welcome."

He wrinkled his long, thin nose. "Oh, don't let's be so formal. Call me Woody, won't you?"

"Woody? I thought your name was Harwood."

He rolled his eyes again and sighed. "It is. Harwood Acres. God, it sounds like a horse farm in Kentucky. So I go by Woody. You can't really call me just Har. It sounds like half a laugh, and my initials are enough of that. Plain old Wood sounds silly, so I came up with Woody when I was in school."

"Okay, Woody, nice to meet you." I smiled. "Call me Heath."

"Charmed, I'm sure."

"So, have you known Mr. Darkly long, Woody?"

Woody's smile disappeared, and he furrowed his brow. "Oh, God. I really don't know Mr. Darkly at all. Nor do I care to. He's certainly changed, though, from what I remember of him."

"In what way?"

"It's been over eight years since I last saw him, and of course, people change. But I remember him as quite fat, pale, thinning hair, not quite so, so, so old looking," he finished. "I was a friend of Nigel's, his son. Nigel and I were at university together."

"I had read that Mr. Darkly had a son and a daughter," I said. I suddenly realized that everything I knew about Mr. Darkly, which wasn't much, was what I'd read at the library or heard from Bishop.

Woody turned toward the windows by the fireplace. "Nigel took after his mother. I hear she was a lovely woman—Nigel showed me a photograph of her once—she died when he was five. I don't think he remembered too much about her."

"Losing his mother at such a young age must have been hard on him," I said softly.

"It's always hard to lose someone you love, Mr. Barrington. Heath. He died eight years ago, here." His voice was much quieter.

"Here?" I said, glancing about my room.

"Well, not exactly here, but out on the lake. Drowning."

"Oh my, I'm so sorry."

Woody wrapped his arms around himself, close. "So am I. Nigel was a wonderful man, so full of life, yet so under his father's thumb."

"You and Nigel were close?"

He turned back to face me, a queer expression on his sweet face. "Unless I miss my guess, Mr. Barrington, I'm sure you'll understand when I say Nigel and I couldn't have been any closer."

"I see." My initial instincts had been correct, and apparently his were, too. He was breaking through my defenses, seeing through me, and I needed to proceed with caution. A friend of mine back in Milwaukee who worked in a bank got too comfortable with one of the tellers who was also homosexual. Turned out the teller liked to tell, and my friend found himself unemployed. He could have been arrested, or worse.

"I thought you would. I have a sixth sense about that in people. I'm almost never wrong," he said matter-of-factly. He casually fingered my cream cashmere sweater. "I bet we're the same size."

"Probably. I wear a forty-two long suit. You're about my height and weight, maybe a bit thinner."

He laughed. "I've always been thin. It drives my auntie crazy as she puts on weight just looking at food."

I nodded. "So what brought you back here now, after all this time?"

"I received an unexpected letter from Mr. Darkly, complete with a train ticket. Like I said, it's been eight years. I'm surprised he even knew where to find me, though I imagine he has his ways. He invited me here, so he said, to make amends, to let bygones be bygones, though I'm not sure I believe that. I don't know why I came, really. Curiosity? A chance to speak my mind? A chance to speak the truth at last? To feel Nigel's presence?" He shrugged. "I don't know, honestly, but here I am."

"You miss Nigel?"

"All the time, when I think of him, and I think of him all the time." Woody's voice was soft, misty.

"He must have been very special."

Woody put my sweater down and started walking about the room as he softly spoke. "It's been eight years, Mr. Barrington. I've moved on with my life. What choice did I have? But not a day goes by that I don't hear a song we used to listen to, or smell an aftershave he wore, or think of a line he used to say, not a single day. His favorite color was green, like his eyes. I always envied him his eyes. Mine are just a dull, ordinary brown, but his were lit from within."

"I noticed your eyes are brown, but I'd hardly say they're dull or ordinary, Woody. They suit you, they're dark and mysterious yet full of life." I bit my tongue after saying that—stupid!

I watched nervously as he pulled his full lips pulled back even farther in a huge smile. "Why, that's just so incredibly sweet, Heath! Oh, I do look forward to getting to know you better. To be honest, I'm sorry your friend is joining us tomorrow."

"You'll get along just fine, I'm sure."

"Yes, I'm sure." He was less than sincere about it, I could tell.

"So uh, you've, uh, not met any other friends since then? Since Nigel died?"

He stopped in his tracks and smiled at me again, not quite so broadly. "Delicately put, sir. Delicately put. Of course I have. And I've got my eye on that dashing deckhand from the steamer."

"Adam?"

"Yes, Adam. I figured you'd notice him, too. He's hard to miss, and he's dreamy."

"You mean, is he...?" I stammered a bit, glancing at the door to make sure it was shut, and hoping no one was listening on the other side.

Woody smiled provocatively. "Is he what? One of us? Sadly no, at least I don't think so, do you?"

"I don't know what you mean by that."

Woody laughed. "I think you do! Honestly, Heath, I know we've just met, but you can trust me."

"That and a nickel will get me a cup of coffee, Woody."

"Ouch, that hurts."

"Besides, walls have ears."

"Not here they don't. Believe me, when Nigel and I were younger, we made all kinds of noise in almost every room and no one could ever hear a thing. And no one's listening at the keyhole, either." Woody strode over to the door, yanking it open to prove no one was there, and then shut it again.

"Look, Woody, in my profession, in my life—"

He waved his hand dismissively. "I know, I know. One can't be too careful, of course I understand."

"I would imagine you do."

Suddenly Woody turned away, and I could sense his mood had changed again. "We used to have fun, Nigel and I," he said wistfully as he started pacing again. "But that's in the past, isn't it?"

"I suppose we all need to live in the present and look to the future."

"Sounds like something President Truman would say. But the past can haunt, Mr. Barrington, and there are no exorcisms for some demons."

"You said Nigel drowned," I stated, trying to get Woody back on track.

"Out there, on that lake." He motioned toward the front of the house. "It was a cold, cold experience crossing it yesterday on that steamer, Adam notwithstanding."

"I can imagine."

"They recovered Nigel's body, but his soul still walks. I can feel it, sense it. He'd been in the water several days. I heard he was almost unrecognizable." Woody shivered and wrapped his arms about himself again.

"How did he drown?"

"That's a curious question, Mr. Barrington, Heath. I don't think anyone's ever asked me that before. I don't believe it was an accident."

"Oh?"

He stopped pacing again and faced me head on. "I've said too much. But then, why should I be silent? I've been silent all these years to what avail? Nigel's just as dead and gone. We spent a glorious summer here. We were home from university. Mr. Darkly wasn't around much then. He had business in New York, which is why I think Nigel brought me here. There was a full staff, a housekeeper—oh, what was her name—Mrs. Claggot! And a cook, a groundskeeper, and a maid, all just for the two of us. We laughed and ate and hiked and biked and rode horses over at Cooper's farm, and went into town for sodas at the drugstore and a movie on Saturdays, and we swam. Yes, we swam." Woody fairly beamed as he recollected.

"So Nigel was a good swimmer?"

"Excellent swimmer. Nigel was an excellent swimmer,"

he stated firmly. "He grew up on this lake. He could outswim anyone I know."

"So what happened when the summer was over?" I asked quietly.

Woody sighed deeply. "All good things come to an end, don't they, Heath? Mr. Darkly came home to Dark Point. And he was angry to find me here. Other people on the lake and in town had apparently been talking. He didn't like me much, you know. I didn't come from money, which I think I mentioned. I was at university through the generosity of my aunt and my own hard work. And I wasn't manly enough for Mr. Darkly. I didn't play ball or smoke or drink to excess, and I didn't have a steady girl. That bothered him most of all. Well, at least now I drink to excess. Surviving Prohibition was hell, and yes, I started young." Woody dropped his head back and laughed aloud before continuing. "Anyway, he accused me of being a bad influence on Nigel, and he threw me out of the house. Mr. Darkly forbid Nigel to see me anymore."

"How could he do that?" I asked incredulously. "You were both adults by that time."

Woody laughed again, this time more sharply. "You really don't know Dexter Darkly, do you?"

"I haven't met him yet, as I've said, so I'm just going on what I've heard and read."

"Well, I can tell you all you need to know. I got a letter from Mr. Darkly shortly after I left the lake house, telling me he had forbidden further contact between me and Nigel, and he would seek legal action if I came in contact with his son again. He told me he would seek to have me committed to an asylum if I came near him anymore."

"My God. Could he have done that?"

Woody shrugged his shoulders and shook his head. "Who knows? Probably. Mr. Darkly was and is a wealthy, powerful man. What I am, what *we* are, to put it discreetly, is considered a mental illness by many. I could have fought it had he tried, but it would have been very embarrassing and costly for me and my family, and I may not have won. I'm ashamed to say I was young and afraid. I thought it best if I put some time and distance between us, just temporarily, you understand. So I went to Europe. I thought I'd let Mr. Darkly cool down a bit, and then I'd come home and contact Nigel discreetly."

"And?"

Woody swallowed hard and looked away from me. "I got a letter in Europe from my aunt Sophia that Nigel had died. She read it in the newspaper. I never saw him again."

I walked closer to him and put my hand on his shoulder. "That must have been an incredible shock."

He turned back to look at me, and I saw his eyes were moist. "You have no idea how the world can suddenly implode, yet still go on spinning. I sailed home immediately, but Nigel was already buried, gone. Mr. Darkly refused my calls, my letters were returned unopened. All I had to go on were the newspaper clippings. I never got a chance to say good-bye, to say anything. He's buried here, you know. At the family cemetery up the hill. I didn't even know *that* until recently. I guess I came to say good-bye."

"You can't blame yourself, Mr. Acres."

"Blame? I blame myself every day. Nigel was too sensitive, too afraid of his father, but who could blame him? It wasn't his fault, it was mine for being a coward. I was just as afraid as he was, maybe more so. Well, I'm through being afraid, of hiding. I know some people find me too blunt, too out there, but I can't cower any longer. It was his father's fault, too, though, for being a controlling prude, for wanting Nigel to be something he wasn't."

"I'm sure Mr. Darkly shoulders some guilt, too, Woody."

He pulled away from me, shaking his head. "I doubt it. As I said before, you don't know Mr. Darkly. His shoulders are sloped."

"Sloped?"

"Guilt slides right off them, along with anything of weight or decency."

"I'm sure he tried to be a good parent," I said, not knowing why I was defending a man I'd never met.

"Oh? Why don't you ask Violet Atwater what she thinks of his parenting skills?"

"Mrs. Atwater?"

"Née Darkly. Dexter Darkly's daughter."

"Mrs. Atwater is Mr. Darkly's daughter?"

"And Nigel's older sister, that's right. They weren't exactly a close-knit group. From what I understand, Mr. Darkly wanted a son and was rather disappointed in old Violet. He'd about given up hope when Nigel was born ten years later. From that point on, Violet was relegated to the back, brushed aside, and she clearly resented Nigel and her father."

"Certainly she couldn't have blamed Nigel."

"Logically, no, but emotions are not logical. The way Violet felt about him bothered Nigel quite a bit."

"She was ten years older. That's quite a difference when you're a child."

"Yes, she wasn't around much by the time I met Nigel. I only saw her a few times. She eventually married, of course, and started a family of her own from what I understand, but I don't think she ever forgave her father or Nigel. Rumor has it she didn't even come home for Nigel's funeral, something Mr. Darkly condemned her for, I'm sure."

"Oh my. And so here we all are. Quite the group, I'd say."

"Quite. I'm sorry to have gotten a bit emotional," Woody said, wiping his eyes with his pocket handkerchief.

"No apologies necessary, Woody."

He looked at me again and smiled that sweet smile. "As I said before, pity your friend is joining you tomorrow. I think we could have had a fun weekend. What's his name?"

"I don't recall saying it was a he, Woody."

"No, you didn't. You didn't have to, did you? Not with me. Please, can't you tell by now that you can trust me?"

I looked at him, deciding, before I finally said, "Alan. Alan Keyes is his name. Listen, Woody, as I said before, given the fact that I'm a police detective and all—"

Woody held up his hand. "You don't have to say another word, Heath. I understand, I truly do. Believe it or not, I can be very discreet when I need to be. None of us needs more trouble in our lives."

"Thanks, I appreciate that. If even the slightest hint of anything should get out, I'd lose my job. I could be arrested and worse."

"Remember what Mr. Darkly threatened to do to me nine years ago? I do, so believe me, I'm the picture of discretion, Heath. Besides, I don't even know what you're talking about."

I smiled and relaxed just a bit. "Nor do I. Just rambling, I guess. Though it is nice to be able to talk with someone."

"Lovely, and I agree. Well, perhaps the three of us can compare notes sometime tomorrow night."

"Yes, perhaps."

"You remind me of him, you know," he said softly.

"Who?"

"Of Nigel. It's really rather eerie. Your face, your eyes, your build, your hair—so similar to Nigel's. I got a chill when I first saw you coming up the hill with Bishop. A bit older, of course, and a little taller, but looking at you is like imagining what Nigel would look like if only…"

"If only he hadn't died."

"Yes. The resemblance is striking." Woody stared at me, almost looking through me again.

I shivered, suddenly chilled. "I suppose I should finish unpacking and get out of my traveling clothes," I said, changing the subject.

"Hmm? Oh, yes, I suppose you should. Do you have the time?"

I glanced at my pocket watch. "Just twenty after four now."

"Hmm—several hours to kill before dinner. Can I give you a hand with your unpacking?" he asked with a mischievous smile, our earlier conversation behind him for the moment.

"Thank you, but I think I can manage."

"I was afraid you'd say that." Woody sighed and shrugged his shoulders. "Very well then, I'll see you about."

"It was nice meeting you."

"Likewise. Don't let Mr. Darkly scare you too much."

"I won't. I promise."

"And if he scares me, can I call you? The policeman in shining armor, or at least a tweed traveling suit."

"At your service, sir!" I replied, grinning.

"I'll count on it. Don't forget, just shout or whistle, I'll come running." He walked to the door and then stopped, his hand on the knob, and looked back. "I hope I haven't upset you by saying how you resemble Nigel."

"No, really, it's fine."

"Maybe it's just me, being back at this place, in this house. Maybe it's just me, wishing."

"It's okay, Woody. I'm flattered you think I resemble someone as fine as Nigel must have been."

He smiled warmly at me once more. "Thanks, you're a gem, and a handsome one, too. I hope I haven't made you too uncomfortable with my bluntness, it's just that I don't see the point of pretending anymore, at least to the point that it doesn't get me arrested or institutionalized."

"None of us want that. I'm glad you understand my need for discretion."

"Of course, your job and all. It's a crazy world we live in. Like I said, I understand. Not to worry. See you about, Heath."

"See ya, Woody."

Woody nodded and then turned and went out the door, closing it behind him.

The weekend was turning out to be more interesting than I expected. I found myself attracted to Woody, yet puzzled by him. And of course, Alan was arriving tomorrow, and I was just getting started with him. As I finished putting my things away, I decided to keep it cool and professional with Woody, at least for now. My mind still whirled with thoughts as I changed out of my tweed traveling suit and put on a button-down shirt, red V-neck sweater, and charcoal gray wool slacks with my black cap-toe shoes, freshly polished.

In the bathroom, I lined up my toiletries neatly along the sink, and then stowed my two cases beneath the bed, checking first to be sure it was clean under there. It was—my compliments to Bishop and Nora.

CHAPTER FOUR

I checked my watch again—almost five. With nothing else to do, I picked up my gray fedora, went out into the hall, and made my way down the two flights of stairs. As I reached the bottom, the door to the study swung open, revealing a thin, very tan, frail-looking old man. He peered up at me from deeply set gray eyes and then looked me up and down, a rather startled expression on his heavily lined face.

"How do you do?" I said. However, the old man did not reply but continued to stare at me, his mouth slightly agape. I noticed his neatly tailored clothes hung rather loosely off his shoulders as if they were a size or two too big for him.

"How do you do, sir?" I said again, growing a bit uncomfortable.

"Hmm? What's that?" he replied at last, shaking off the fog he appeared to be in.

I raised my voice. "I said, 'How do you do, sir?'"

"Oh, fine, of course, fine. Forgive me. No need to shout, I'm not deaf yet. You are Mr. Barrington. Or should I say Detective Barrington?"

"Mr. Barrington will do, thank you. I'm not on duty and Geneva Lake is not in my jurisdiction."

"Mr. Barrington, then." His voice was raspy and throaty.

"And you are my host, Mr. Darkly?"

"That's right. You're somewhat older than I expected, Mr. Barrington. A couple of years, anyway. The photo in the newspaper looked, well, younger," he said, wheezing a bit, his breathing rather labored.

"A stock photo, from my early days in the department, sir. I'm thirty two now."

"Stock photo. Still…" He looked me up and down again, appraising me. "You've taken care of yourself. You look good for thirty-two. You could pass for late twenties."

"Ah, thank you, Mr. Darkly," I replied, somewhat awkwardly.

"You dress well, too. Married?"

"Uh, no, I'm single." The older I get, the more people assume I'm married.

"Oh? Nice-looking fellow like you?" He looked deep into my eyes, and I wondered what he was thinking.

"Married to my job, I'm afraid, sir." I managed a smile.

Mr. Darkly snorted. "That's a fool's marriage. A job can be a mistress but should never be a wife. A job won't cook you dinner or keep you warm at night. All settled in, are you?" He asked, changing the subject abruptly.

"Ah, yes, sir. My room is lovely. Very cozy."

"Lovely, you say. I must say I would expect a police detective to use the word *lovely* to describe a pretty young thing *in* the bedroom rather than the bedroom itself."

"The room is very nice, Mr. Darkly." I felt like I was being interrogated under a hot lamp. I shifted my fedora from one hand to the next.

He snorted again and shook his head. "You're an odd fellow. You mentioned in your letter you were bringing a friend along. I arranged the room behind yours for him."

"Yes, thank you. Alan Keyes. He's a fellow officer."

"I recall you mentioning him in the newspaper article. Close, are you?"

"I only just met him a few weeks ago. Nice chap," I responded, feeling a bit defensive.

"I imagine so. Well, welcome to Dark Point. I'm happy you were able to accept my invitation for the weekend." He cleared his throat and swallowed several times, still wheezing.

"The pleasure is all mine, Mr. Darkly. You have a beautiful home here."

"Thank you. Dark Point was built in 1881 by my father, Hugo Darkly, when I was five years old. It wasn't more than a cottage at first, but it was slowly added on to until it became the house you see today. You can still see a bit of the old cottage in the back entry of the kitchen."

"Building a house out here back then must have been quite an undertaking."

The old man's voice softened. "An undertaking of love. My father loved this house, this lake. So do I. Dark Point passed eventually to me, of course, as did our main home in Chicago, but I spent many childhood summers here and have very fond memories. I eventually settled in Milwaukee for business reasons, but I continued to come here every spring." He looked off wistfully down the hall, apparently staring at something I couldn't see.

"You spent all your summers here?" I asked.

He coughed fitfully, and then turned back toward me. "Oh, I did my share of seeing the world. During my college years, I spent a good part of most every summer in Europe, sailing over in June and returning in August. Paris, London, Rome. Those were great times as well. Ever been to Paris, Mr. Barrington?"

"No, not yet. Perhaps someday."

"Don't put it off, son, or someday will never come."

"I'll keep that in mind."

"Paris is wonderful—beautiful women, though we couldn't understand anything each other said. But we managed to communicate, if you follow me," he said, grinning crookedly.

"I've heard the French can be very hospitable," I replied diplomatically.

"Don't put off going, my boy, don't put it off. I loved every inch of Paris. Thankfully the war wasn't as hard on her as it was on London." He shook his head slowly. "War is a terrible thing, Mr. Barrington. I sometimes wonder if Nigel hadn't…well, if he would have had to gone to war. Fate, I suppose, or something like that."

"None of us know what the future holds, sir."

"Some of us do, son, at least I believe so."

"You mean fortune tellers and whatnot? I can't say I put much faith in them, Mr. Darkly," I replied, shaking my head.

He looked me up and down again with those sunken gray eyes. "Sometimes we can be our own fortune tellers, sometimes we need to be. But I digress. We were talking about Dark Point, yes?"

"Yes, sir, that's right. You mentioned you had spent a few summers in Paris and Rome."

"Ah yes, Paris. Giselle was her name—a lovely girl. But my heart remained firmly planted here, and it still does. The Chicago house was sold when I moved to Milwaukee, then I eventually sold that and took an apartment in Chicago, but always Dark Point was here, waiting." His smile faded, and his eyes took on a lost look as he gazed about the entrance hall once more.

"Dark Point is your family home."

He looked back at me. "The one constant in my dark life,

Mr. Barrington. It should have passed to my son in time, but not anymore. I've no one to leave her to."

"Yes, I heard about your son's death. I'm sorry."

He nodded his head slowly. "So am I. He came to me rather late in life, when I was forty-three."

"That would have been 1918, yes?"

"Very good, Mr. Barrington. You are a sharp young man. Yes, Nigel was born in 1918, my only son. He died in '39."

"I'm sorry. An accident?"

He scowled, his tone changing again. "I realize you have an inquisitive mind, Mr. Barrington, but I really don't care to discuss it."

"Oh, of course. Forgive me." My face flushed a bit. "Memories can be painful."

He nodded somewhat stiffly. "Yes. Yes, they can. It was a long time ago. Eight years now. It seems like yesterday in some ways, a lifetime in others." He leaned back a bit, resting himself upon the doorway before continuing. "Nigel was a fine young man—smart, handsome, took after me, if you don't mind my saying so."

"Not at all."

"Well, maybe not so much in the looks department. He got his looks from his mother. She was a fine looking woman. But everything else he got from me."

"I'm sure," I said.

"You remind me of him, actually, Mr. Barrington."

"That's very flattering, sir."

He paused to clear his throat, coughing up some phlegm. "The resemblance is noticeable. I thought so when I saw your picture in the paper, and then just now when I first saw you. Rather startling, to be honest. Like seeing a ghost."

I shivered again. "I can imagine that would be startling."

"It was Acres, you know," he said matter-of-factly as he wiped away some spittle from his mouth with his handkerchief.

"Acres?"

"Harwood Acres."

"Oh, yes. Interesting fellow."

"You know him?" he asked sharply.

"I met him upstairs earlier."

"Oh, that's right, he's across the hall from you. He's the same age as my son. They met in college."

"I see."

"A little younger than you, I expect."

"I'm thirty-two."

"Thirty-two, yes, so you said. Nigel was just twenty when he died, only a month before his twenty-first birthday."

"I'm sorry for your loss, Mr. Darkly."

"Thank you." He stared up at me. "It's your eyes, I think, that remind me of him the most, though his were green. You're how he would look, just a few years older now."

"You were mentioning Mr. Acres," I said, changing the subject somewhat and shifting my fedora again to my left hand.

He coughed once more into his handkerchief, and his breathing again seemed rather labored. "That's right, Mr. Acres. Harwood's different, rather queer, if you get my drift. My son was young, impressionable, easily swayed."

"Easily swayed," I echoed.

"Yes," Mr. Darkly replied. "Nigel was innocent, shy, a handsome lad. Harwood, as I'm sure you've already noticed, is rather brash, forward, and headstrong."

"He does seem rather outspoken."

Mr. Darkly snorted. "To say the least. I'd steer clear of him if I were you," he sputtered, pointing a thin, bony finger at me as if in warning. "Nigel and he became close, too close.

They went to Europe together, shared a room at university. Nigel even brought Harwood here one summer. I was in New York. I never cared for him, for what he did to Nigel. When I returned, I forbid Nigel to see Harwood any longer for Nigel's own good. People were beginning to talk, you know. Nigel had changed."

"You were trying to do what you felt best for your son."

"Exactly. I…I didn't know. I'm glad you understand, Mr. Barrington. It was shortly after that Nigel drowned in that lake out there." His voice had grown quieter.

"I'm so sorry."

Mr. Darkly shook his head. "If it hadn't been for Harwood, I don't believe it ever would have happened. Nigel was a good son, manly, strong yet sensitive. He was just too influenced by Harwood's seductive ways."

"Yet you invited Harwood Acres to spend the weekend with us?"

He looked at me sharply, his gray eyes piercing from rather sunken sockets in his face. "Yes. I invited several people from my past, Mr. Barrington. I don't hold grudges. I'm seventy-two years old. It's time to make peace before it's too late."

"Very admirable, sir."

He coughed heavily again before replying. "I'm rather surprised Mr. Acres came, to tell you the truth, though I paid for his train ticket, so I suppose he figured he had nothing to lose."

"That was very generous of you, Mr. Darkly."

He shook his head, causing the loose flesh on his veiny neck to wobble back and forth like a turkey's. "Acres never had much in the way of money, and I don't imagine he's amounted to much over the years."

"He appears to have done all right," I said, feeling defensive of Woody all of a sudden.

Mr. Darkly laughed. "Oh, I imagine he found someone to take advantage of. It's in his nature. I may have made a mistake inviting him. There's something evil about Harwood Acres."

"Evil?"

"Yes, evil. It's not evident at first, as it's below the surface. I felt it nine years ago. He despised me, you know. I thought perhaps it had dissipated over time, but instead it's gotten stronger. His heart is full of hatred."

"He seems to be a nice enough fellow, Mr. Darkly. He appeared to have genuinely cared for your son."

The old man shook his head vehemently again, and the flesh on his neck went with it. "Appearances can be deceiving, Mr. Barrington, as any good policeman should know."

"I agree, sir, but I think I'm a fairly good judge of character, and a good policeman. Mr. Acres's heart may be broken, but I don't believe it's full of hatred."

"You'll see, Mr. Barrington, you'll see. To be honest, he frightens me. But I invited him and he's here, so I'll make the best of it along with the rest of them."

"Your daughter is here this weekend, too, I understand?"

"Violet? Yes, she's here, and her husband, the doctor. The first time I've seen her in several years. She's changed a bit, aged. Of course, haven't we all?"

"Time goes by."

"Yes, and a few years can be an eternity in some ways, Mr. Barrington." He stopped to catch his breath, coughing up something into his handkerchief again, which he then stuffed back into his pocket. "It's my own fault. I shut her out after Nigel died. She was always jealous of him, you know. She was ten years old when he was born, and used to being the only child. Her mother spoiled her. Violet didn't adapt well to having a younger brother, and she would often be rather cruel to him. To protect him, I sent her away to boarding school, and I think she resented me for it. The last straw was when she didn't come home for Nigel's funeral. I've barely spoken to her since, though she did visit once with her new husband just after their wedding. It was awkward, to say the least."

"Family relations can be difficult."

"Indeed they can." He started coughing again, rather fitfully. "You have family, Mr. Barrington?"

I took a step back from him, wondering if he was contagious. "I'm an only child, but my parents are still alive. They live in Milwaukee."

"Be kind to them. Forgive them their faults, please."

"I will, Mr. Darkly. I have."

"And forgive me, won't you? I need to attend to some paperwork."

"Yes, of course."

He pointed that bony finger at me again, and I noticed his nails had grown rather long and yellow. "I'll see you at dinner, eight sharp."

"Certainly, Mr. Darkly. It was a pleasure meeting you."

"Thank you, and likewise." He retreated slowly into the study, closing the door behind him, which only muffled the sound of more coughing.

CHAPTER FIVE

I stood staring at the closed door in front of me, wondering what to make of him, of everything. Finally, I shook my head and made my way to the front of the house out onto the porch. I put on my fedora at long last, glad I had worn a sweater, as it was getting rather chilly. The wind had picked up, and I could hear the tree branches blowing, some scraping against the sides of the house. Down the porch to my right, I noticed a man and a woman in two of the many white wicker rockers gathered there. He was rocking rather sedately, a book resting on his chest, and she was knitting furiously. As I walked toward them, the man noticed me and got to his feet, momentarily forgetting his book, which thumped to the porch floor.

"Do be careful, dear, that book doesn't belong to you," the woman snapped, not looking up from her knitting.

"I'm sorry, Violet." He picked the book up and placed it on the table next to his rocker. "How do you do?" he said to me.

"How do you do," I replied, tipping my hat. "I'm sorry to intrude. I just wanted to introduce myself. Heath Barrington from Milwaukee. I arrived this afternoon."

The man nodded. "Yes, of course. The police detective.

I'm Dr. Preston Atwater, and this is my wife, Violet." She nodded politely, looking up at me rather distantly with narrow, squinting eyes.

"We're in from Chicago. Arrived yesterday," Preston continued.

"A pleasure to meet you both." The light out here was dim, as the sun had already begun to set, but I gathered them both to be in their early forties. He was clean shaven with a rather thin face and a long nose that rested between two oversized dark eyes. I shook Dr. Atwater's hand, noticing he was smartly dressed in a tweed blazer, slacks, white shirt, and a dark green ascot. I don't think I'd ever seen anyone actually wear an ascot before, except in the movies.

Mrs. Atwater continued knitting away at some unknown article of clothing, perhaps another ascot. She looked rather disinterested in anything else around her, including me. She wore a dark brown skirt, sensible brown shoes, and a light green blouse, probably chosen to coordinate with Dr. Atwater's ascot, I thought. She had a sweater about her shoulders, and crowning her head of brown curls was a nifty brown felt hat with a yellow band.

"Won't you join us, Mr. Barrington?" Dr. Atwater asked politely, indicating a vacant rocker moving back and forth in the breeze next to his.

"Thank you," I replied, "if you're sure I'm not intruding."

Preston glanced at his wife before replying, but she remained emotionless as far as I could tell, the felt hat shading her face.

"No intrusion at all, Mr. Barrington. Violet and I were just passing the time. It's gotten too dark to read very well anyway. Please, join us."

"Thank you," I replied, taking a seat. The rocker was rather chilly, even through the wool of my slacks.

I nodded to his book. "Interesting reading?"

"No, not really. Puts me to sleep, not that it's a bad thing. Not much to do around here, I'm afraid. I borrowed the book from the library."

"The library?"

"Mr. Darkly's library. Not the best selection—mostly Greek literature, historical novels, that sort of thing."

"Preston prefers dime-store novels," his wife interjected, still not looking up from her knitting.

He looked annoyed. "I enjoy the classics as much as anyone, Violet, but that library was put together to impress people, not to entertain them."

"Please, Preston." Her voice was more a command, as in *not now*. She looked past her husband at me, a rather strange expression on her gray, mousy face.

"Anything wrong, Mrs. Atwater?" I asked.

"It's just…it's nothing, really, but you look familiar. Have we met before?"

"No, I don't believe so."

She shook her head. "Then my mistake. Are you enjoying the lake, Mr. Barrington?"

"It's quite a place. This is my first visit, though I used to come to the ballroom in Lake Geneva many years ago."

"I see. I used to go to dances there myself, before I met Preston. Those were fun, gay days. Perhaps I saw you there once."

"Perhaps. You don't dance any longer?"

She looked sideways at her husband. "Preston has two left feet. So I knit."

Dr. Atwater looked pained. "I'm afraid I never got the knack for dancing, Mr. Barrington. Never came easily to me."

"We each have our plusses and minuses, Doctor. I'm sure the medical field would not come easily to me."

He smiled. "You are too kind, sir. Besides, Lake Geneva has many other things to offer besides dancing. The lake is quite beautiful, though it's a little early in the season yet. You really should make a point of doing some boating and hiking while you're here."

"Yes, I'd like to do that. I don't get out of the city often enough."

"It's been many years since I've been back here myself," Mrs. Atwater said, more to herself, I think, than to anyone.

"I understand you're Mr. Darkly's daughter."

She put down her knitting and stared at me. "Did my father tell you that?"

"Ah, no. One of the other guests mentioned it."

"One of the other guests. I can only imagine. People do talk, don't they?"

"Human nature, I suppose," I replied, shrugging my shoulders.

"Human nature leaves a lot to be desired, Mr. Barrington," she said in a rather disgusted tone. Her eyes had narrowed even more.

"I suppose that's true, Mrs. Atwater, but then it can be quite remarkable at times, too. I get the impression you and your father aren't very close."

"Did one of the other guests mention that, too?"

"More or less."

"Mr. Barrington, I don't mean to be rude, but the relationship I have or don't have with my father is rather a private matter and really no concern of yours or anyone else's."

My face flushed. "I beg your pardon, Mrs. Atwater. I didn't mean to pry."

"It's all right," she replied in a tone suggesting it most certainly was not. She turned to her husband. "What time is it, Preston?"

"Quarter of six, Violet."

"I'm going in. It's gotten quite cold. I want to telephone Mrs. Crump and check on the children, and I need to dress for dinner." She gathered up her knitting and put it back into her bag. Dr. Atwater and I rose with her as she got to her feet, clutching her bag in one hand and holding her sweater at the neck with the other. "We'll see you at dinner, I'm sure," she said to me.

"Yes, I look forward to it," I said, tipping my hat once more.

She looked me up and down again. "Indeed. Are you coming, Preston?"

"I'll be along shortly, dear."

She gave him a look I couldn't quite see, and then turned on her heel in those sensible shoes and made her way down the porch and into the house, still clutching her sweater about her shoulders.

When she had gone, Dr. Atwater turned to me, a rather embarrassed expression on his face. "I'm sorry about my wife, Mr. Barrington. She's rather sensitive about her father. I've only met him once in all these years, and she rarely mentions him. I was frankly quite surprised she agreed to come here at all this weekend, given their history."

"It is I who should apologize, Dr. Atwater. At times, the policeman in me comes out too often, and I end up grilling people when I merely mean to make conversation."

"Hazard of the trade, I imagine. Sort of like when I start diagnosing someone who's merely making conversation with me."

I nodded. "Yes, I suppose so. You mentioned you were surprised your wife agreed to come here?"

"At least she was invited. Dexter didn't want me here," he said rather awkwardly.

"Oh? I had heard it was Mr. Doubleday who was the uninvited guest."

The doctor nodded his head. "Yes, that's true. He showed up today—quite a scene—Mr. Darkly and Mr. Doubleday don't exactly care for each other. Violet says she invited him, though she never mentioned it to me. Of course she forgets to tell me a lot of things, intentionally or unintentionally. Mr. Doubleday is her uncle."

"I see. But you say Mr. Darkly didn't want you here, either?"

"The invitation was made out to Violet Darkly, not Violet Atwater. We've been married seven years. Of course, he didn't come to the wedding."

"That's unfortunate."

Dr. Atwater shrugged. "I suppose so. I think it hurt Violet, but she won't admit it. I know she seems harsh, Mr. Barrington, even cold. But inside, she's still a scared little girl."

"Scared of what?" I asked, surprised.

"Of Dexter D. Darkly," he answered, lowering his voice lest he be overheard, I imagine.

"And yet she came."

He nodded his head again. "Yes, and like I said, it rather surprised me. Of course she said she'd only come if I came with her. I don't think she even told her father I was going to be here. We just showed up together."

"That must have been quite a surprise to Mr. Darkly," I replied.

He snorted a laugh through his nose. "I'm sure. I could tell he was annoyed, but what could he do?"

"True."

"I suppose that's why she invited Mr. Doubleday, too," Dr. Atwater continued.

"Why's that?"

"Because she didn't want to be here with her father alone. The more people she could surround herself with, the better."

"It's good she has you," I said.

"Yes, I suppose so. I hope she feels that way. Sometimes I wonder." Dr. Atwater picked up his book from the table and stared at it. "I should be getting in, too."

I nodded. "Likewise. I understand dinner's at eight."

"Yes, that's right. I rather fear you've been invited into a bit of a hornet's nest, Mr. Barrington. You seem to be the only outsider."

"It does appear that way."

"Dinner last night was rather tense, and lunch today was worse. It seems we all, you excepted, have an unpleasant past with Mr. Darkly. Perhaps you will be the referee." Mr. Atwater smiled rather strangely at me and then said, "See you at dinner." With that he strode down the porch much as his wife had done, disappearing into the house.

Chapter Six

The last glimmer of sunlight was on the lake, and the wind had picked up even more. The empty rockers now moved back and forth in unison as if inhabited by a gathering of ghosts. I watched them rock for a bit, then went inside where I found Bishop setting the table in the dining room.

"Might I use the telephone, Bishop? I'll reverse the charges."

"Certainly, sir. Just down the hall in the study. Mr. Darkly said any of the guests are free to use it as necessary."

"Thank you."

I strolled down the hall and knocked on the heavy door before turning the knob. The room was empty and rather dark, so I flipped on the overhead light and glanced about. Boxes were piled along the walls, many marked *important papers*, which I imagined he'd had sent from his Chicago apartment last fall. A padlocked iron box sat beneath a small table on the left wall. Curious. To the right of the table was a door that probably led to a closet. There was a fireplace in the far right corner, kindling and wood neatly stacked for a fire. The two windows to the left of the fireplace looked out at the back of the property and were framed in red silk drapes. Under them was a credenza, with a set of crystal decanters, mostly full, on a silver tray.

In front of the windows was a heavy black leather chair pulled up to a large old-fashioned dark wooden desk, with two smaller side chairs facing it, upholstered in the same red as the curtains. Near the matching desk set was a small lamp with a dark green glass shade, a blotter, ink pen and well, typewriter, notepad, what looked to be a bottle of medicine, and the one and only telephone.

I went over to the desk and set my fedora down as I lifted the heavy telephone receiver, turning the dial all the way around with my finger.

"Operator," a woman said, sounding quite bland and rather tinny.

"Yes, long distance to Milwaukee, please."

"One moment please."

Shortly another female's voice, slightly clearer. "Long distance—number please."

"King's Lake 5-2835 and reverse the charges, please. This is Mr. Barrington."

I heard a clicking noise, a long pause, then ringing before Keyes answered, then the operator again, this time to Keyes, "Long distance from Lake Geneva, Mr. Barrington calling with reversed charges. Will you accept?"

"Yes, operator."

"Go ahead, please."

"Hello, Alan, it's Heath," I said when I heard the operator disconnect.

"Yes, I heard. Calling collect, eh? I thought this Darkly chap was loaded."

"From what I can see he has more than enough, but I hate to take advantage. Hope you don't mind."

"Not at all. You know us policemen are rolling in dough," he said with a laugh. "It's good to hear your voice, though."

"Thanks, yours too, and likewise," I replied honestly,

wishing I could say more, but knowing I could be overheard. "How was work?"

"Nothing special. I had patrol duty with Sheffield. Couple of calls, but mostly just driving around. You know how it is."

"Yeah, I remember patrol shifts. Usually pretty boring. So, what are you doing tonight?"

Alan laughed. "Not painting the town, that's for sure. I just finished dinner, thought maybe I'd go for a walk or something."

"What was for dinner?"

"Chicken soup and a boiled egg."

I laughed. "You need someone to cook for you."

"Know any nice girls?"

"I know lots of nice girls, and some not so nice ones, too, but you wouldn't know what to do with any of them."

"Ha! Nor would you, wise guy. But then you can cook."

"And I'll cook for you anytime," I said.

"Sounds nice. A guy could get used to staying home like that."

"I hope so. I know I could. It's getting cold here. Gonna be a chilly night tonight."

"My landlady's generous with the heat," he said. "I've got nothing on but my boxer shorts right now."

I arched my eyebrows, my mind racing at the mental image of that. "Well, don't go out walking like that." At that point I no longer cared if anyone overheard.

Alan laughed again, a nice, easy, gentle laugh that made me laugh, too. "I'll put a smile on," he said. "So how is the place down there? And more importantly, what's this Mr. Darkly like?"

"The house is big. Eight plus bedrooms, a dining room that looks like it seats thirty, library, study, music room—it pretty much has it all."

"Hmm, I'm picturing a big gothic stone place, elegantly furnished and decorated to the last detail."

I laughed lightly. "Well, get that picture right out of your head. It's a white clapboard with a porch and a green-shingled roof. The house is rather dark and heavy, the furniture gathered, I assume, over many years, perhaps castoffs from the Chicago and Milwaukee houses."

"Interesting. What's he like?"

I looked around, just to be sure I was alone, but I lowered my voice just the same. "Different. He's in his seventies, very tan, very wrinkled, sagging thin skin, bony, with dark hair that's either dyed or a toupée, and he seems rather frail."

"No Cary Grant, eh?"

"Not even close. His voice is very raspy, too, and he keeps coughing into his handkerchief."

"Yuck."

"The rest of the guests are an interesting lot as well. I haven't met them all yet, but I imagine I will at dinner. I'll have to fill you in when you get here."

"I'm looking forward to it."

"Great, just don't expect too much."

"What do you mean?"

"Just that it's a big old house full of character—or characters, anyway. You'll see for yourself soon. I'll see you tomorrow morning."

"Well, you certainly haven't exactly painted a rosy picture, but you've got my curiosity aroused. This butler chap's meeting me at the station, you said, right?"

"That's right. His name's Bishop. Nice enough fellow. I'll meet you at the dock when you land, and pay no attention to the deckhand on the steamer."

"What's that supposed to mean?"

"Oh, nothing," I replied coyly. "Get a good night's sleep."

"Yeah, like that will be easy, now you've got me all wondering."

I chuckled. "My mother always says to keep them guessing. Good night, Alan. Oh and, Alan?"

"Yeah?"

"If I were there with you tonight, I think I'd just have my boxers on, too."

"Yeah?" he replied, his voice deep and husky.

"Yeah."

"I like that idea, and the lights down low. I'll see you tomorrow, Detective."

"I'll see you before that, Officer. In my dreams."

"Careful, Heath. You're always saying walls and telephone wires have ears."

"They can all be jealous tonight, then. Sleep tight, good night."

"Night, Heath."

I replaced the receiver and headed back upstairs to my room to rest a bit and then dress for dinner, whistling softly to myself as I went.

CHAPTER SEVEN

I chose the navy blue double-breasted suit with the cream tie, the black wingtips, and the gold cufflinks. I'd save the black opals for Saturday night when Keyes was here. I checked myself carefully in the mirror and then headed down the two flights of stairs to the dining room. I was the third to arrive. Mr. Darkly and Woody were already there. No sooner had I sat down than Mr. and Mrs. Atwater arrived, followed immediately by a rather portly gentleman with a walrus mustache and eyebrows to match. I guessed he was in his mid to late sixties, dressed in a dark green suit fairly bursting at the seams. I soon learned this was the Mr. Doubleday who shared a bath with Woody, and I smiled remembering that Woody was none too keen on it. I could see now why.

Last to enter was a stunning brunette woman, in her mid to late fifties, I assumed, who turned out to be Lorraine Darkly—Mr. Darkly's second wife, now divorced. She was seated to my right, and Mr. Doubleday to my left. Directly across from me was Woody, and to his left was Mr. Atwater, to his right was Mrs. Atwater. At the head of the table was Mr. Darkly.

The table had been laid in grand style, with candles, linen napkins embroidered with the now very familiar *D*, decanters of red wine, salt cellars, finger bowls, fine china with gold rims, and a dazzling array of silverware on both sides of the plates. I counted no fewer than four different forks, three spoons, two knives, and one instrument I wasn't quite sure of. It looked like the miniature pinking shears my mother had in her sewing basket. All, I noticed, were monogrammed. In addition, each of the twelve chairs around the table had been embroidered with a different month of the year. I happened to be sitting in May, complete with May flowers encircling the word. Along the far wall were extra chairs, and I couldn't help but wonder if they had been embroidered with the days of the week.

After a few misstarts, I soon learned social dinner conversation protocol. You converse with one person during the first course, then change to the person on the other side of you during the second course, and the person across from you during the third, and so on. As there were seven of us at dinner that night, this obviously left someone out, but I noticed Mr. Darkly appeared to be holding court with Mr. Doubleday to his right and his daughter Mrs. Atwater on his left at the same time. So during the appetizer, which I learned was a scrumptious caviar torte, I introduced myself to Mrs. Darkly, since our host had failed to do the introductions himself.

I watched as she selected the fork on her far left, and then I followed suit. "The, uh, caviar torte is excellent, isn't it?" I said.

She nodded in agreement. "Yes, this new cook seems to be quite capable, though I don't understand why he let the last one go."

"Had she been with him a long time?"

Mrs. Darkly shook her head. "No one is with Mr. Darkly for long, Detective, or so it seems." She glanced up the table at him and then back to me. "He's a difficult man."

My mind flashed back suddenly to Mr. Murdoch, the victim in my last case, who was also rather difficult, it seemed. *What is it with wealthy men being so disagreeable?* I asked myself. "Were the two of you married long?"

She glanced up the table at her ex. "Too long. We divorced two years ago. I spent my share of summers here in this awful old house while Dexter chased his ghosts. He's looking rather like a ghost himself these days. At least a ghost of his former self."

I stole a look up the table at Mr. Darkly, but I had no point of reference for what his former self was like. "How do you mean, Mrs. Darkly?"

"Dexter was always a large man, much like our Mr. Doubleday," she said rather loudly, but Mr. Doubleday himself was engrossed in a loud conversation with Mr. Darkly and Mrs. Atwater. "Within the last year Dexter must have lost seventy-five pounds or more. I always wanted him to lose weight, but now I think he looks ridiculous. That tan of his, more orange than anything, and a man of his age dyeing his hair? Really, people must be laughing at him. I'd pity him if I didn't dislike him so."

"I see."

She looked at me point blank. "No, I'm sure you don't. I'm sure you think me rather harsh, but you're an outsider here. I married Dexter after his son died. Dexter's much older than me. I didn't think it mattered at the time. I was in love or thought I was. And I foolishly thought he was in love with me."

"Perhaps he was."

She laughed. "Mr. Barrington, I truly wonder if perhaps you weren't invited here as therapy for us all. People will tell a perfect stranger things they wouldn't dream of telling their families or friends."

"Yes, I believe you're right, Mrs. Darkly," I said, nodding in agreement.

"Of course I am. I just proved my own point a moment ago, didn't I?" She laughed, but I could tell she was also somewhat embarrassed at having shared so much. "Still, a policeman is rather like a priest, isn't he? Bound by a moral code to be discreet and keep secrets."

"I can assure you, madam, I am the very model of discretion, on my honor. And besides, even policemen and priests have their secrets," I replied, somewhat mysteriously.

"Do tell, Detective. I can be very discreet, as well," she said, smiling mischievously.

"Ah, Mrs. Darkly, I do believe that would take all your fun away. Better to keep you guessing."

At that point Bishop arrived at my right to clear the remains of my torte, followed almost immediately by poached garlic soup, which smelled delicious.

As soon as the soup was presented to her, Mrs. Darkly turned her attentions to Dr. Atwater across the table, so I turned to Mr. Doubleday.

"Just a touch of the torte on your mustache, Mr. Doubleday," I said rather quietly.

"Excuse me?"

"There's some of the torte in your mustache," I repeated, a bit louder.

He swiped at it rather unsuccessfully with his napkin before dropping it back in his lap and glaring at me. "You're the policeman from Milwaukee."

"Yes, that's right. Heath Barrington."

"Donovan Doubleday. Heard about you. Expected old Darkly to make proper introductions, but perhaps he forgot since you're the only outsider. Why are you here?"

I was rather taken aback. "Mr. Darkly invited me. He'd

heard about the last case I'd solved. The victim was someone Mr. Darkly was familiar with."

"Curious. The whole damned weekend is curious." He took a rather large spoonful of his soup, spilling some of it down the front of his shirt and rather garish orange and blue necktie. "Can't say I like it."

I tasted mine, finding it just as delicious as it smelled. "You don't care for the soup, Mr. Doubleday?"

"What? What are you talking about?" he snorted irritably.

"You don't like the soup?"

He glared at me. "Of course I like the soup, the soup's fine. It's this weekend I don't care for. I only came because Violet asked me to. Dexter doesn't want me here." He looked to his left at Mr. Darkly, but he was deep in a private conversation with Mrs. Atwater.

"Oh, I see. I misunderstood. About you not liking the soup, I mean."

He looked at me like I was an idiot, and then took another large spoonful. "Fine soup. Dexter always manages to find good cooks. Question is why can't he keep them."

"Yes, Mrs. Darkly was just commenting on that."

"Mrs. Darkly? Oh, you mean her." He pointed with his rather large chin to Lorraine Darkly on my right.

"That's right, she was just mentioning that Mr. Darkly has trouble keeping servants."

"Servants, business partners, children, wives. Constance was his first wife."

"Constance?"

"Constance. What she ever saw in him is beyond me."

"You knew her well?"

"You might say that. She was my sister. My baby sister." He took a rather large drink of wine, followed by more soup. "Wonderful woman, lovely, more than he deserved."

"I understand you're Mrs. Atwater's uncle."

"Yes, that's right. Constance was Violet's mother and my sister, so Violet's my niece," he explained, as if I were a bit slow.

"Yes, I understand."

"Violet turned out okay, though Dexter played havoc with her mental state, I fear. Seems to be a hobby of his."

"She seems all right, rather private," I replied. "We chatted briefly tonight on the porch."

"Yes, she told me she'd met you when I ran into her upstairs before dinner."

I could only imagine what she'd said about me. I'm sure her first impression wasn't a good one, and I didn't seem to be faring much better with her uncle.

"Violet keeps to herself. Don't think she ever got over her mother passing. Constance loved Violet, and when she was gone, Dexter didn't seem to have any time for her. He spent all his attention on Nigel."

"Nigel," I said.

"Nigel was Violet's brother, Dexter's son. My nephew."

I nodded. "Of course. Mr. Darkly was discussing him earlier."

Mr. Doubleday cleaned his bowl dry. "Nigel was a good kid. Not his fault, really. The whole thing was a bit of a mess. Violet was born first, and Dexter made no mistake of being unhappy about it. He wanted a son. He blamed Constance for it all the time. When Violet was ten, Constance got in the family way again, God knows how. From that point on, it was Dexter and Nigel. My Constance and Violet were swept aside like dirt. Pass the rolls, please."

I handed Mr. Doubleday the bread plate. "That had to be difficult for them."

Mr. Doubleday chewed off the end of a roll and continued

speaking before he had swallowed. He reminded me of a large horse. "I told Connie to leave him—to take the children and just flat out leave. She was afraid, I think. Then one night I got a call from her, said she was leaving. Nigel would have been five years old then, Violet fifteen."

"She was taking the children with her?"

"As any mother would, Mr. Barrington. And no court would have stood in her way, no matter how many lawyers Dexter hired."

"So what happened?"

Doubleday glanced back to the head of the table where Mr. Darkly's conversation with Violet had grown more animated and loud. He leaned close to me and I could hear his chair creak beneath his weight. "I got a telegram the next day; Connie had been killed in a riding accident."

Too soon Bishop was there again, clearing the soup, replacing it with a bruschetta salad, and I was forced to turn my attentions to Woody, seated across from me, though I had so many more questions for Mr. Doubleday.

"So, Heath," Woody said, leaning in to be heard across the table, as everyone had become quite animated, "how goes your meal?"

I grinned at him. "The food's delicious, but you were right about the tension. There seems to be quite a bit of angst here among everyone."

"To say the least. At least they're talking tonight. At lunch today, everyone just glared at each other. Maybe tomorrow night they'll be throwing things."

"Maybe," I replied, wondering if I should phone Alan and tell him not to bother coming. This wasn't quite the relaxing quiet weekend I had envisioned.

"Any good gossip on your side of the table?" he asked.

"Nothing you don't probably already know. Does anyone here like anyone else?"

"Oh, sure. I don't know about the rest of them, but there's really only one person here I definitely don't care for." He rolled his eyes in Darkly's direction.

I nodded. "Yes, that does seem to be the consensus, from what I've gathered." I wondered to myself why Mr. Darkly would want to spend the weekend with people who clearly disliked him, and why those people would want to spend the weekend with him.

The salad course flew by and was quickly replaced by asiago and sage scalloped potatoes and lamb with port sauce, and I found myself turning back to Lorraine Darkly.

"So, Mr. Barrington, are you managing to keep up?" she asked, peering at me over her wineglass.

"With all the food or with the conversations?"

She took a large drink and then smiled. "You do almost need a scorecard."

"That would be most helpful."

"I'll see if I can find you one," she said, smiling.

"I must say it's challenging just figuring out which utensil to use with what course," I admitted.

She laughed lightly. "Work from the outside in, Mr. Barrington. It's simple."

I returned her smile. "Thanks. So, I believe you said you were Mr. Darkly's second wife?"

"Yes. He's much older, you know. Dexter's seventy-two."

"Much older," I replied, as I knew I should.

"He's not much to look at now, but there was a time." She picked up her wineglass again.

"People change."

"Yes. In hindsight, I suppose he was never what you

would consider attractive. He was overweight, jowly, and cantankerous. But there was something about him. I can't explain it, really. Well, at least he's not overweight or jowly anymore."

"So you've said. He does look rather thin."

"He's going through his third midlife crisis, I'm sure. That's what this is all about, of course."

"Oh?"

"It has to be. He woke up one day and realized he's seventy-two years old and not getting any younger. His first wife is dead, his beloved son is dead, his daughter barely speaks to him, nor do I, he has grandchildren he doesn't know at all, he has more enemies than friends, and he's basically alone in the world."

"That must be a cold realization."

"Indeed. Like I said, I'd pity him if I didn't think he deserved exactly what he got."

"So, what do you think he hopes to accomplish by bringing you all together?"

She laughed lightly, her wineglass now empty again. "Family harmony, perhaps? Who knows what goes on for certain in his devious mind? If I had to hazard a guess, I'd say he started feeling sorry for himself. So, he had a good look in the mirror, went to Monaco to some fat farm and lost a lot of weight, got a ridiculous tan, had his hair dyed, and then brought us all here to prove to us, if not himself, that's he's still a strong, vital man."

I looked back at the old man at the head of the table, now arguing rather pointedly with Mr. Doubleday. He was coughing in between sentences, and his face was rather red.

"Ridiculous looking, isn't he?" she asked.

"It's hard for me to say, Mrs. Darkly."

"Not hard for me to say. He sent me a letter, you know.

Sent us all letters of invite, except for Mr. Doubleday, of course. I'm sure you've heard about that."

"Er, yes, yes, I have."

"Scandalous, showing up uninvited." She clicked her tongue. "Well anyway, he sent us these letters inviting us here for the weekend, telling us he wanted to put the past behind him, to start anew."

"Is that why you came, Mrs. Darkly? To start anew?"

She set her dinner fork down on the edge of her plate and laughed as she poured herself another glass of wine from the crystal decanter, which was almost empty. "You must be joking, Mr. Barrington. I married Dexter because I was young and in love, or to be brutally honest in retrospect, in love with the prospect of being Mrs. Dexter Darkly. He married me because he had lost one son and he wanted another. Being a younger woman of good breeding, I'm sure he thought I could give him that son. He was in his sixties when we married."

And then there was Bishop again, clearing from the right, serving the dessert from the left, a strange concoction of cherries and some sort of dark chocolate cake, and my attentions were forced once more on Mr. Doubleday. So many unasked questions still reeling in my mind!

"Did you enjoy your meal, Mr. Barrington?"

"Delicious, and you?"

"Satisfactory. Though the portions seemed rather skimpy," he said, looking rather disappointed. "And the company rather hostile, present company excluded, of course."

"Ah, thank you, I guess. I believe you were telling me about your sister Constance being killed in a riding accident."

Mr. Doubleday snorted, took a gulp of wine, and stabbed at his dessert. "If you want to call it an accident. The circumstances, not to mention the timing, seem rather questionable."

"Oh?" I said, picking up the last remaining utensil in front of me, which by process of elimination, I assumed was my dessert fork.

"I was just discussing that very thing with Dexter." He looked up the table at Mr. Darkly.

"I see." I took a small bite of the cake and wondered if I should try to stab the cherries or attempt to scoop them up as they rolled about the plate.

"Some people think money can make everything all right, make any problem just disappear," Mr. Doubleday stated, using his rather chubby finger to force cake and cherries on to his fork. Somehow I doubted that was the proper way to do it.

"Oh?"

He looked at me, his mustache moving up and down as he chewed. "I went to the hearing on the accident, you know, listened to the reports. It was all nice and tidy, just the way Dexter arranged it, I'm sure. You're a policeman. I'm sure you've seen that kind of thing or at least heard about it."

"I've heard of things like that happening, Mr. Doubleday, but I've never witnessed it. I assure you I would insist on the truth being told."

"If you're being up front, you're one unusual cop," Mr. Doubleday retorted, shoving yet another portion of the dessert onto his fork with his finger.

"I've been told I am rather unusual in many ways."

"I bet. Why do you think Dexter asked you here?"

"What do you mean?" I asked, giving up at last on the dessert. I didn't need the calories, anyway.

"You're an outsider," he explained, pointing at me with his fork. "The rest of them," he continued, waving the fork about, "in one way or another, are family or at least acquaintances. I understand he'd never even met you before."

"Yes, that's true. It is rather different. But he invited me here because he'd read about my latest case and was eager to meet me."

"Maybe," Doubleday said, swallowing a mouthful and then reaching once more for his wineglass. "But I bet I know a better reason. You even speak like him. Very proper."

"Like who?" I asked, though I had a feeling I knew what he was going to say.

"Nigel Darkly, of course. He was my nephew. I watched him grow up. There's definitely a resemblance. Violet noticed it, too."

I nodded. "Yes, Mr. Acres and Mr. Darkly both mentioned it as well. I wasn't aware."

"No, how would you be? Dexter's gotten rather squirrelly, I think. Or squirrelier. Is that a word?"

I shook my head. "I'm not sure, but I think I know what you mean."

"He's trying to bring back the dead. I'm surprised he didn't give you Nigel's old room."

"So you were saying Mrs. Atwater asked you here, Mr. Doubleday?" I said, changing the subject and shivering a bit again.

"That's right. After Connie's death, Dexter, as the sole remaining parent, was of course given full custody of Nigel and Violet. Violet was shipped off to Boston to a finishing school. From that point on, she was pretty much forgotten about. So when she told me he was hosting a family get-together, I smelled a rat. She said the invite didn't even include her husband."

"Rather unusual," I replied.

Mr. Doubleday raised his bushy eyebrows so that they met in the center, looking like a ratty squirrel on his forehead.

I definitely think if *squirrelier* isn't a word, it should be. "To say the least. Violet was not going to come here by herself; she wanted Preston and me both here. Preston's her husband."

"Yes, we've met. I'm rather surprised you came, Mr. Doubleday, given what you've said."

"I wasn't going to at first, especially when I remembered all those damned stairs from the dock up to the house. But then I thought it over and figured, why not? If nothing else, it gives me a chance to see Violet a little bit, and to support her. And I guess I really wanted a chance to speak my mind to Dexter, see if I could get him to finally admit the truth."

"And what do you believe to be the truth, Mr. Doubleday?"

But before Doubleday could answer, Bishop was clearing the dessert plates. Mr. Doubleday's had been wiped clean. I noticed that throughout the entire dinner, Mr. Darkly barely touched any of his food. He was indeed watching his weight.

The time according to my pocket watch was quarter after nine. Mr. Darkly got slowly to his feet, officially signaling the end of dinner, and the rest of the guests followed suit. I turned to Mrs. Darkly. "It was a pleasure meeting you."

"Likewise, Mr. Barrington, Detective. I'll be wondering all night about your secrets."

I gave her a sly smile and exchanged similar pleasantries with Mr. Doubleday, then glanced across the table at Woody, who winked at me with his larger eye.

"So what happens now?" I asked him, leaning across the table.

"You thank your host, then the ladies retreat to the music room for tea, and the men wander into the library for smokes and billiards."

I put my napkin next to my plate and walked to the head of the table to speak with Mr. Darkly. As I approached, he looked up at me with a sly smile on his lined, sunken face.

His gray eyes peered out at me from sockets ringed with dark circles.

"Did you enjoy your dinner, Mr. Barrington?" he asked, his voice still rather raspy.

"My compliments to your cook, Mr. Darkly. The food was wonderful."

"Good, good, I'm pleased. The dessert to your liking? I noticed you didn't finish it."

I was surprised, not realizing he had been watching me so closely. "Oh it was fine, just too much food. I'm not used to it, sir."

"Food should be a pleasure. I can't eat the way I used to—don't enjoy it nearly as much."

"I'm sorry to hear that. I did notice you didn't seem to eat a lot."

"Sinus trouble. Can't smell or taste hardly anything anymore. The only pleasure left to me is a good, stiff brandy after dinner."

"A fine ending to any meal," I commented.

"Actually I enjoy a good brandy before every meal, too. Helps the digestion."

"Every meal?"

"Except breakfast, and sometimes even then." I think he laughed, but I couldn't be sure if it was a laugh or a hoarse cough.

"I could use a stiff brandy, Dexter," Mr. Doubleday interjected. I hadn't noticed him come up behind me and was rather startled by his booming voice over my shoulder.

Mr. Darkly glared at him. "You could stand to lay off the booze, and the food, too, Donovan."

"And you could be a little nicer to your guests, but that's apparently not going to happen, either."

"As I recall, you're not one of my guests."

"Your daughter invited me. That's good enough for me, ought to be for you. Or are you going to 'arrange' for me to just disappear?"

Mr. Darkly opened his mouth to reply but instead turned to me. "As one of my invited guests, won't you join me in my study for a brandy, Mr. Barrington? I keep a decanter of the good stuff in there at my ready."

Mr. Doubleday came around to my side and looked at me. "Go ahead, Barrington. Have one for me." With that, he waddled out of the dining room.

As we watched him disappear through the double doors and into the hall, Mr. Darkly looked up at me and said, "Forgive my brother-in-law, Mr. Barrington. He's rather a boor and he tends to overindulge in food and drink, as I'm sure you've surmised. How about that brandy?"

"Ah yes, of course, I'd be delighted."

I followed him into the hall and to the left toward the staircase. Mrs. Darkly and Mrs. Atwater, I noticed, had crossed over to the music room, and Woody and Dr. Atwater were just ahead of us, heading for the library, where I assume Mr. Doubleday had gone.

The two of us walked rather slowly, and I noticed Mr. Darkly held on to the wall here and there, ostensibly for support. When at last we reached the study door, which was still unlocked, I observed, he opened it and stepped inside, turning on the overhead light as I had done previously.

"My study," Mr. Darkly explained, closing the door behind me.

"Yes, I was in here just before dinner to make a phone call. I hope you don't mind."

"No, of course not. My house is your house," he said, suppressing a cough as best he could.

"I reversed the charges."

"Splendid. Not that I can't afford it, you know, but some people take advantage, ruin it for everyone."

"That's unfortunate."

"Very. Damned cold in here. Unseasonable for April, I think, though we usually don't open the place up before Memorial Day weekend."

"It is rather chilly," I agreed.

"The house wasn't really built for year-round use, Mr. Barrington, though we do have the fireplaces. One of Bishop's duties is to clean and rake them every day and always to have a fresh fire ready to go."

I thought to myself that Bishop and Nora were going to be very glad to have this weekend come to a close.

"Do me a favor and light it for me, won't you? I can't bend down like I used to."

"Certainly. Have you a match? I don't smoke."

"There's a box on the mantel," he said, pointing his bony finger with the long, yellow nail.

"Right, I see it." I plucked the metal match safe up and extracted a wooden match. The fire was soon going, and I tossed the burnt-out match into it.

Mr. Darkly came over and stood beside me, holding out his thin, crooked hands to the warmth, his veins bulging like roads on a map. "Better," he said at last. "Have a seat." He motioned me to one of the side chairs in front of his desk, and I made myself comfortable as I watched him move slowly behind the desk to the credenza under the windows. He pulled the stopper out of one of the decanters and set it aside, his hand trembling rather noticeably. From beneath the credenza, he retrieved two crystal tumblers and set them up top. "I can ring for some ice if you like."

"No need, straight up is fine."

He smiled. "Good man. Brandy is a drink best served unencumbered." He poured each of us three fingers, and then set mine on the desk in front of me.

Truth be told, I prefer a vodka martini with a pickle, no olives, but I'm nothing if not a good guest. I lifted the tumbler and sipped the brandy, letting it burn slowly down my throat, feeling it in my nostrils.

Mr. Darkly fairly inhaled the contents of his glass and poured himself another before settling into the black leather chair behind the desk, coughing fitfully again.

"Are you all right, sir?"

"Fine, fine. Never better," he replied dismissively with a wave of his hand.

"You're feeling okay?" I asked, my eyes on the medicine bottle atop the desk.

He followed my gaze. "Oh, that. Awful stuff. Cold medicine, you know. My doctor insists I take it three times a day before each meal, not that it does any damned good. I predict by 1950, they'll have a cure for the cold."

"That would be a tremendous discovery indeed, sir."

"Ah, colds aren't so bad. Scientists should be spending their time researching other things, but I digress. Did Bishop get you all settled in?"

"Oh yes. He's wonderful, really. Good servants are quite hard to find these days, I imagine."

"You have no idea, especially out here. It was better before the war. Nowadays, women all want to work in the factories and offices. Nobody wants to be a domestic anymore."

"It's good that you found Bishop, then."

"He and his wife came highly recommended. I'd never have hired them otherwise—too much at stake."

"Oh?"

"They were alone here all winter, Mr. Barrington, while I was in Monaco. They had to be completely trustworthy. And I paid them plenty for it."

"Oh I see, of course."

"And now that I've given up my apartment in Chicago, all my valuables are here." He gestured toward the piles of boxes along the wall. "Haven't had a chance to find a place for it all yet."

"You brought everything here?"

"Not everything. I sold some off, but the valuable stuff I sent here. That's why I didn't dare let the house sit empty all winter, as has been the custom in the past. There have been break-ins, you know."

"Speaking as a police officer, Mr. Darkly, I can say it's always best not to take chances, regardless."

"Very true. I keep a large amount of cash here in the study, as well. In that strong box there." He pointed to the iron box with a padlock on it, sitting under the side table.

"Is that wise, sir? Wouldn't a bank in Lake Geneva be a safer choice?"

"Don't trust banks, son. Not since 1929. 'Course, you're too young to have been seriously affected by it. You would have been what, fifteen or sixteen years old?"

"Fourteen, sir. I remember it well."

"Good. Then don't forget it."

"You don't use a bank at all?"

He snorted. "Oh, of course I do. I can't keep everything about me, but I use them as little as possible, for writing checks and whatnot."

"I see."

"Did you get a chance to meet all the other guests?"

"Yes, thank you. I met Mr. and Mrs. Atwater on the porch earlier, Mr. Acres upstairs, and Mr. Doubleday and Mrs. Darkly just now at dinner."

"I should have introduced you around, I suppose."

"That's quite all right, Mr. Darkly. I can fend for myself in most situations, even social ones." I smiled.

"Still no excuse for my bad manners. I'm just not myself anymore. Forgive me."

"Of course."

"Strange group, aren't they?" he asked.

"Eclectic, definitely. To be frank, sir, I'm not sure how I fit in."

"Is it important to you to fit in, Mr. Barrington?" he asked, swallowing a good portion of the brandy as if it were water.

"I've never really fit in, Mr. Darkly. But what I meant was, everyone else seems to have a past with each other and with you. I'm a bit of an outsider. I was wondering just why you invited me."

He wrinkled his brow even more than it already was. "I told you why I invited you. I wanted to meet you," he replied, sounding irritated.

"And I'm flattered, sir, really."

"No need to be flattered. I saw your picture in the paper and wanted to see you in person."

"Oh, I thought it was because you were impressed by the way I handled the Murdoch case."

"What? Oh, that. You are rather full of yourself, aren't you? Every bit the eager young detective I figured you would be."

"I don't mean to flatter myself, Mr. Darkly. I'm only stating what I believed were your intentions," I said, rather irritated myself.

"Don't go getting in a snit, son. I invited you and I'm

glad you're here. All the better that you're not like the rest of them."

"Well, thank you, sir," I said, though I was beginning to wonder if I shouldn't have stayed in Milwaukee.

"The rest of them, well, we do all have a history together, even Mr. Doubleday. And we cannot change history."

"That's very true, sir. Nor should we attempt to."

"Quite astute of you. But I don't want to change history, son. Only make amends for it."

"Do you have a lot to make amends for?"

He looked at me over the top of his glass, his gray eyes bloodshot. "You said you've met the other guests. I'm sure they've told you. You can't change history, but you can't forget it, either. I don't think any of them have even the slightest reservation about sharing their feelings of me."

"And yet here they all are, and here you are."

Mr. Darkly smiled to himself. "Yes, yes. Funny that. I didn't really think it possible at first. I didn't think they'd all come."

"But they did, so perhaps they want to make amends as well."

He laughed hoarsely. "More likely, they want to see how close I am to death, want to see if I've left the lot of them anything in my will."

"That seems rather cold, Mr. Darkly."

"They're a cold bunch, and it's a cold world, a cold night." He pulled his suit coat closer together. "Not a lot of love lost between us. Do you believe people can change?"

I looked into his cold, almost lifeless eyes. "Of course, if they really want to and have the ability to, anyone can change for better or worse," I said.

He folded his bony hands together and rested his elbows on the desktop, staring at me. "I wonder. More brandy?"

I shook my head and held up my hand. "Ah, no thank you. I'm good yet."

"Nigel could nurse a drink like that, too. I poured him his first drink right here in this room, you know," he said, and then he got up slowly and poured himself another before sitting back down with a groan.

"You must miss him terribly."

He took a mouthful and swallowed, never taking his eyes off me. "You have no idea."

"I'm sure not," I replied.

"Strange, but in some ways I feel he's never left here. In some ways, he's closer to me than he ever was."

I shook my head. "I'm afraid I don't understand, Mr. Darkly."

"I'm afraid I don't either, Mr. Barrington. Perhaps I never will. Or perhaps it's just a matter of time. But each spring when I return here, I feel as if he's been waiting for me. I wonder sometimes if perhaps he is."

"I'm sure that gives you comfort, sir."

"I take my comforts where I can. Do you like the brandy?"

I looked down at my glass. "Excellent, sir." I could tell it was fine brandy, but it really wasn't suited for my palate.

"You don't have to stand on good manners, son. You can tell me if you don't care for it. It wasn't Nigel's drink either, oddly enough. I can barely taste it anymore, but still I enjoy it."

"Really, it's fine. It's nice that you have things you can enjoy."

"Very true, though I don't enjoy it, or anything, for that matter, like I used to."

I took another sip, waiting for him to continue, still feeling it burn my throat.

"I hoped to have a grandson one day, you know. Hoped the three of us, Nigel, his son, and me, could be here, spending time."

"Your daughter has children, doesn't she?"

"Violet? Yes. Two—a boy and a girl, at least I think that's what they are. I never see them—they don't know me at all, nor I them. Atwaters, you know, not Darklys. I'm the last of the Darklys."

"Still, they're your grandchildren."

"Yes, and Violet and Preston's children. I suppose I should have made time..." His voice trailed off.

"Dr. Atwater seems a nice chap," I offered.

"Eh, Preston's all right. Violet could have done far worse, could have done better. Obviously, she can't go anywhere without him. She resents me still, I can tell."

I didn't say anything, slowly swirling the brandy in my glass, wishing I had opted for some ice.

"My own daughter resents me, resents what I had, or thought I had, with Nigel. And Preston, he thinks everything that's wrong with Violet—and there's quite a list—is my fault."

"I'm sure not everything is your fault, Mr. Darkly."

He laughed again in between coughs. "You are too kind, Mr. Barrington, too kind. Violet resents me, Preston blames me. And then there's Donovan Doubleday. I noticed you two were chatting quite a bit during dinner."

"Interesting fellow."

"Yes, if you can stomach a man who speaks with his mouth full, which is constantly during mealtimes. Donovan is my first wife's brother, my brother-in-law."

"Yes, he mentioned that."

"Constance and I were married when I was in my early twenties. She was a beautiful woman."

"I understand she died."

"A riding accident, though Donovan blames me for Constance's death."

"How sad."

"He has his reasons, though the inquiry clearly stated it was an accident."

"Mr. Doubleday mentioned that, well, things weren't going too well between you and your wife at the time of her death," I said as delicately as I could.

"Mr. Doubleday seems to have managed to say quite a bit while devouring his food."

"He was quite animated on the subject."

"He always is. I find him a crushing boor. I told you I want to make amends for my past, but I have nothing to atone for with that man. That's why I didn't bother inviting him here, though he showed up anyway." Mr. Darkly put his glass down, coughing up some phlegm and what looked like blood into his handkerchief again before continuing.

"I'm sure Doubleday told you that Constance was going to leave me. It's no secret, everyone knows that. In retrospect I can't say I blame her."

"He mentioned that she was going to take the children."

"Oh, such and so forth, nonsense. What if she did? There are such things as custody laws, Mr. Barrington."

And there are such things as getting around those laws if you're rich and powerful enough, I thought, but I wasn't foolish enough to argue with my host.

"Clearly Mr. Doubleday has his mind made up, and I know I won't change it. He's a fat, simple-minded dolt. Did he also tell you Constance and I had reconciled the very day of her death?"

"Ah no, he didn't mention that," I replied, shaking my head.

"Of course not. Because he doesn't believe it, but it's true. I had her buried in the family plot. You know, he took me to court over that."

"Really?"

"Yes. Doubleday said Constance's final resting place should be with her parents, not here at Dark Point. He lost the case. The judge laughed in his face, and so did I."

How charming. "And you eventually remarried."

"Life must go on, Mr. Barrington. Yes, I remarried. Lorraine. I noticed you were chatting quite a bit with her, also."

"Just being polite, sir."

"Of course. You've good manners. I respect that. Lorraine and I married several years after Constance died. It was just a year or so after Nigel passed away, as a matter of fact. I was sixty-five, if I recall correctly."

"Never too old to start anew, I believe."

"A sound philosophy, indeed. We would have been married seven years ago this June. Except we divorced two years ago."

"She seems pleasant and certainly still very attractive."

"She's younger than I, of course. Not as attractive as she once was. I wanted more children. We were only married just shy of six years. Finally it became unbearable, and we divorced, as I said."

"I'm sorry."

"You seem to be sorry about most everything in my life, son, but then, I suppose there's a lot to be sorry about."

"At least from what you've told me," I replied, instantly regretting it.

He looked at me sharply. "Touché. My life has been a sorry lot, it seems."

"And yet you seem to have much to be thankful for."

Mr. Darkly snorted. "Like what? My money, or what's

left of it? What has that gotten me? My son, my only son is gone, that's all that matters. I have nothing left now."

I finished my brandy and set my glass on the desk. "Why did you divorce the second Mrs. Darkly?" I asked, curious to hear what he had to say.

"The second Mrs. Darkly, indeed." He rocked gently in his chair, his eyes on the ceiling. "I divorced the second Mrs. Darkly because at long last Lorraine was going to have a child. And it would have been a boy, another son."

"Would have been?"

"A miscarriage. Lorraine didn't take care of herself. She drank too much, and she lost the baby."

"I'm sor…I'm sure that was difficult."

He coughed fitfully again before continuing. "It was unbearable. We divorced a year later. I saw no point in continuing, as she was getting beyond the childbearing years. She fought me in court for alimony, but she lost." He looked at me as if expecting me to say something, but I remained silent. "It doesn't pay to try and fight me in the courts, son."

"Apparently not, sir."

Mr. Darkly laughed. "Lorraine forgot that I had her sign an agreement before we married that she would receive nothing if we divorced and there were no children."

"She must have been bitter."

"And still is. If she were a beverage, she'd be coffee. Strong, hot, and bitter."

"Maybe she's cooled over time."

"I thought that too, perhaps. I asked her here this weekend to put that behind us. In retrospect, I believe I was too hard on her. But I can see now she still resents me. So that's the lot of them."

"You're forgetting Woody," I said.

"Woody?" Mr. Darkly cocked his head, puzzled.

"I'm sorry, Mr. Acres."

"Woody?" Mr. Darkly asked again, clearly still confused.

"Harwood Acres. He told me to call him Woody."

"Woody," he said once more. "Yes, that's right. I haven't heard him called that since Nigel…well, in a long time. I never knew, didn't know, how Nigel felt about him. I thought I could force him to change his mind."

"Nigel?"

"Yes. Though Mr. Acres rather dislikes me, too. I admit I was a bit unpleasant to him in the past."

That's an understatement, from what Woody told me, I thought.

"Nigel would want him to be here now. Would want me to get to know him, but it's almost too late, isn't it?"

"Too late?" I asked.

"Too late. We can't change history. Mr. Acres blames me for Nigel's death. He holds quite a grudge, I've found out."

"Why does he blame you?"

"My son committed suicide, Mr. Barrington. He swam out to the lake and drowned himself. Mr. Acres believes it's because…" He looked down at the desk, almost unable to continue, his voice a hoarse whisper.

"Because?"

"Because I forced them apart," he said at last, still staring down at the desktop.

"I see."

He looked up at me at last, his sunken gray eyes a bit moist, and then took another drink of brandy. "But Nigel never understood, you see. I told you I sensed evil in Mr. Acres. He has a way about him, like the devil. After Nigel died, he sent me threatening letters over the years, saying horrible things."

"Did you report them to the police?"

"No, I couldn't bear to, knowing Nigel wouldn't have wanted it. And I must admit, I was too ashamed."

"Ashamed?"

"Ashamed at what Mr. Acres said, of what he claimed about Nigel, my son. My only son. It was all slander. He claimed my son was like him. I think he wanted to extort money from me."

I felt my face flush. "Do you still have the letters?"

"I burned them all. I couldn't bear them. Finally, they stopped coming."

"You never responded?"

"No. I had nothing to say to him. What do you say to the devil? More brandy?"

"Ah, no, thank you, I'm fine," I replied, not sure if he was talking to me.

"You're so much like him, you know. It's almost as if..."

"Mr. Darkly..."

He coughed again, and then took another strong drink. "I know, I know." He waved his free hand at me. "Watch your back around that one, Nigel. Don't let him get too close."

"Mr. Darkly..."

A quiet knock came from the door, but Mr. Darkly appeared not to have heard. A short while later the knock came again, louder. This time Mr. Darkly looked toward it and called out, "Come in."

Bishop poked his head around the heavy door. "I'm sorry to intrude, but it's after ten, sir, do you require anything else?"

"What?"

"It's after ten, sir. Is there anything else you require?"

"After ten? Already?" He looked at me, then back to Bishop.

"Time gets away from us, doesn't it?" I asked in general.

"Sir?" Bishop said.

Mr. Darkly shook his head, as if clearing himself from a fog. "Go ahead and lock up, Bishop. Anyone else still up?"

"The ladies have retired, sir, but the gentlemen are still in the library. I'll check with them before I go up."

"Fine, fine. Good night."

"Good night, sir," Bishop replied as he pulled the door closed.

I looked at Mr. Darkly, who was still staring at the door. "It is getting late," I said.

"Hmm? Oh, yes. Very late. Do you believe in an afterlife, Mr. Barrington?"

"As in heaven and hell? I'm not sure, but I don't think so."

Mr. Darkly snorted. "I didn't expect you would, not the type. I never used to be either, but it's strange."

"What is?"

"I don't know. I can feel his presence even now." His voice trailed off as he gazed across the room, and then he shook his head as if to clear it. "I shan't keep you any longer. I'm sure the men are playing billiards in the library if you care to join them."

I stood up, realizing I was being dismissed. "Yes, well, thank you for the brandy, Mr. Darkly. I think I'll pass on the billiards, though. It's been a rather long day." I looked at my tumbler on the desk, its contents now swirling in my stomach.

"As you wish. Rather boring company in there, anyway," Mr. Darkly said, wheezing as he got to his feet once more.

"Yes, good night, sir."

"Bonsoir, Nigel."

"Sir?"

He looked at me, confused. "What?"

"I thought you said, 'Bonsoir, Nigel.'"

He shook his head. "You're hearing things, then. Good night, Mr. Barrington."

"Good night." I walked over to the door. As I left the study, I glanced back at Mr. Darkly and noticed he had poured himself yet another brandy and was now standing rather unsteadily by the fireplace, a lost look on his sunken face as he stared into the flames. As quietly as I could, I closed the door and glanced across the hall to the library. Through the half-open door I could hear Woody, Mr. Doubleday, and Dr. Atwater, and I thought briefly about joining them after all.

I soon concluded, however, that the day and the brandy had been too much, so I headed up the two flights of stairs to the attic. My pocket watch said it was quarter after ten. As I approached the door to my bedroom, I noticed a white piece of paper beneath it, as if someone had left me a note. A similar piece of paper lay partly beneath Woody's door, and I saw one beneath Mr. Doubleday's door as well. *Bit of trouble Mr. Doubleday will have bending down and picking that up*, I thought to myself.

I picked up the note that was left for me and went inside, flicking on the overhead light and closing the door behind me. The note was neatly printed by hand, on medium card stock.

> *Please turn on the water in your taps enough for them to drip, as it is possible it may get quite cold this evening, and the pipes are not insulated.*
>
> *If you have shoes that need polishing, please place them outside your door before retiring; likewise any clothes that need pressing, please hang on the hook in the hall outside your bedroom door.*
>
> *As a reminder, breakfast will be from eight to ten in the dining room, à la carte.*

Should you need anything during the night, please use your call button on the wall next to your bed.

I set the card on the small bedside table and looked about. My bed had been neatly turned down, and the fireplace was stacked tidily with kindling and dry wood. *Do Bishop and Nora ever sleep?* I wondered once more.

I undressed down to my undershirt and boxers, and thought briefly of lighting the fire before bed, wishing I had packed a nightshirt. I decided against the fire, however, noting the thick quilt on my bed and thinking the cool air would help me sleep better. After I finished brushing my teeth and cleaning up, I dutifully turned on the taps in the sink and tub and let them drip slowly. In order not to be disturbed by the noise, I closed the bathroom door, hoping I wouldn't run into it in the middle of the night should I need to get up.

I started to set my black wingtips out in the hall for polishing but took pity on Nora and Bishop, deciding I could polish them myself when I got back to Milwaukee. Besides, I had lots of other shoes I could wear tomorrow and Sunday. So I locked the door, turned off the overhead light, and made my way back to the brass metal bedstead and to sleep.

CHAPTER EIGHT

I awoke the next morning rather suddenly, curled up into a tight little ball. It was freezing, and I was frankly surprised I couldn't see my breath. *Curse this sleeping alone business,* I thought. Grudgingly, I threw back the quilt and stepped gingerly onto the hardwood floor. Damn! I grabbed the quilt off the bed, threw it around my shoulders like a shawl, and then made a beeline for the fireplace and the rag rug in front of it.

On the mantel was a metal match safe, much like the one in the study, engraved with a *D* in the center of it. I struck a match and thrust it into the kindling, blowing gently as the tinder caught fire and slowly spread. Standing before the flames, I spread the quilt out from my shoulders like a magnificent cape, trying to catch the heat rays now billowing forth from the fireplace, along with a fair amount of smoke. I suspect the chimney needed sweeping, but I certainly wasn't going to mention that to Mr. Darkly, as I could just imagine him ordering Bishop up onto the roof that very afternoon to clean them all out.

When at long last I felt the blood circulating again in my fingers and toes, I shuffled over to the dresser and put on a pair of my thickest socks, and then made my way into the bathroom, which was even colder than the bedroom, especially since the door had been closed all night. I turned on the overhead light despite the morning light coming in through the window, figuring it would provide at least some modicum of heat, and I turned the hot water on full in the tub and sink.

When the water had reached at least tepid, I washed up and shaved, and dressed as quickly as I could. Then, feeling a tad warmer and more comfortable, I banked the fire a bit and opened the curtains. It was a gray, overcast morning, gloomy. I sighed and took one last look at myself in the mirror above the small chest of drawers. Satisfied, I opened the door and stepped into the hall, trying to be as quiet as I could in case the other guests were still asleep.

I noticed the notes were all gone from under the doors, and by Mr. Doubleday's there stood a freshly shined pair of his shoes. On the hook above was the suit he had been wearing, neatly pressed. It appeared to have a stain on the lapel that Nora must not have been able to get out. I'm sure Doubleday would raise hell about that. I shook my head and proceeded down the stairs, trying to walk to the side to lessen the creaking.

As the note had said, breakfast was à la carte in the dining room—scrambled eggs, bacon, oatmeal, and toast were laid out in warming trays on the buffet. Next to the warming trays stood a pitcher of orange juice and a large urn filled, I was delighted to find out, with hot coffee. I helped myself to a full cup and drank it down as quickly as I could without scalding my throat. I followed that with a second, this time wrapping my hands around it for warmth. No one else was about yet, except Nora and Bishop, I imagined, and they were probably in the kitchen. Everyone else was apparently sleeping in. I didn't feel like sitting down there by myself, so I made up a plate of eggs and bacon and took it up to my room along with my coffee, managing not to spill any of it on the long trek back.

I made myself as comfortable as I could at the small table by the still-smoking fire and ate, looking out the window at the lake far below. Steam rising off the water made for an eerie sight as I thought about Nigel and the way he died. But I would have time to think of those things later, so after finishing breakfast, I brushed my teeth once more and checked the time—9:55. The lake steamer was due at ten thirty, so I took my empty plate, fork, and coffee mug and wandered back downstairs. I deposited my dirty dishes on the sideboard in the dining room, where I noticed Dr. and Mrs. Atwater had made themselves comfortable, enjoying their breakfasts, along with Woody, who sat with them but apart.

"Good morning," I said to all of them.

"Good morning," Woody and Dr. Atwater replied, looking up at me. "Sleep well?"

"Yes, mostly. Not used to the blackness of the country, nor the quiet. Awfully chilly this morning, isn't it?"

"Always colder in the morning this time of year, but it's quite unusual to be this chilly. Feels like rain, too," Dr. Atwater said.

"Yes, it's quite overcast."

"I see you've already been down to breakfast. I was worried you'd frozen to death in your sleep up there," Woody said.

I smiled. "Yes, I was down earlier. Since no one was about, I took my food back upstairs."

"The attic rooms are always colder than the rest of this place, Heath. There's nothing but a thin layer of wood and some shingles between you and the sky," Woody said.

"I could tell. Glad for the fireplace, that's for sure."

Woody nodded. "Yes, they help a little. I wonder if Mr. Doubleday has frozen solid? He's not one to be late for breakfast, or any meal, I imagine."

"I thought I heard him stirring in there. And he had retrieved his shoes and suit from the hall since the first time I came down," I replied.

"Figures. I should have known he's got too much insulation to ever freeze," Woody joked. Dr. Atwater and I chuckled, though Mrs. Atwater glared.

"I don't find that amusing, Mr. Acres," she clucked.

Woody looked abashed. "My apologies, Mrs. Atwater. No offense meant."

"Have you seen Bishop?" I asked, changing the subject.

"He left a while ago on the steamer to retrieve your friend from the station," Dr. Atwater answered.

"Right, that." I checked my watch again. Nearly quarter past ten. "I think I'll wander down and meet them at the dock."

I had thought of riding along with Bishop and meeting Alan at the train when it got in to Lake Geneva, but I didn't want to appear too eager, and I thought the other guests might find that a bit odd as well. Charades.

I climbed the stairs once more to retrieve my overcoat and hat, and then I made my way back down, out the front door, across the path and down the wooden zigzag stairs to the dock, where I could make out the smoke of the steamer as it approached. When it was close enough, I scanned the windows of the steamer cabin, beaming when I saw Alan's face looking back at me, smiling. I couldn't keep from grinning back and waving like a schoolboy.

I stood back when at last the steamer had stopped alongside the pier, and Adam leapt off to make fast the mooring ropes. He gave me a smile, too, then jumped back on board and lowered the gangplank. I returned his smile. He was certainly as handsome as ever, but somehow the thought of seeing Alan again diminished any thoughts of Adam.

I watched as Adam strode down, Alan's—or Alan's

dad's—suitcase tucked under his arm. Following him was at long last Alan, with Bishop bringing up the rear.

At the sight of Alan, I forgot the deckhand completely, and I didn't even notice him boarding once more, nor the steamer departing. It was just the three of us on the dock, one too many as far as I was concerned.

"Hello, Heath," he said, his breath billowing forth in the chilly air.

"Hi, Alan," I responded, still grinning from ear to ear. I extended my hand, and he shook it firmly, though what I really wanted was to embrace him, to kiss him and hold him tight, letting our bodies warm each other.

"You smell like smoke," Alan said.

"Gee, nice to see you, too." I laughed. "It's the fireplace in my room."

"Great. Nice to see you though, really." He was beaming at me, and I at him, I'm sure.

It felt as though we hadn't seen each other in weeks, when in reality we had had lunch just three days ago, in between our shifts. That's the way of it, I guess, with someone new. We'd really only known each other a few weeks. Hard to believe.

Finally, I tore my eyes away from his, aware that Bishop was watching us. "Just the one bag?" I asked, glancing down at the beat-up leather satchel Adam had placed at his feet.

"Yes. The only one I've got. I figured if I forgot something I could borrow one of yours! You packed enough for three people," he said, only half-kidding. I smiled. I liked the thought of him wearing my clothes.

"Shall we go up to the house?" I asked.

"Yes, of course," he said, as anxious for us to be alone as I was, I'm sure.

Bishop took Alan's suitcase, and we climbed slowly up.

I suspected Alan's case was far lighter than mine, as Bishop didn't struggle nearly as much.

Finally, we reached the top, and we continued all the way up to Alan's room in the attic. His room was a bit smaller than mine, but similarly decorated. I loved watching Alan take it all in, looking about in wonder at everything he saw since he'd gotten off the steamer. I got the impression he didn't get out of the city much.

"Shall I unpack for you, sir?" Bishop asked, breathing rather heavily.

Alan glanced at me, unsure of what to do, but I just shrugged. "Oh, no thank you. I can manage."

"Very well, sir. Your call button is located on the wall next to the bed should you need anything. Lunch is at one in the dining room."

"Thank you, Bishop. That will be all for now," he said, and I was impressed at how mature he sounded.

"Yes, sir," Bishop replied. At long last, we were alone.

"Am I supposed to tip him?" Alan asked, still looking a bit puzzled.

"I don't think so, though I'm not sure, to be honest. I figure maybe we just leave some money in the room at the end of the weekend. Remind me to ask Woody about it."

"Who's Woody?"

"Oh, you'll meet him. He's quite a character."

"Great. I take it he knows about butlers and such."

"He seems to. He's been here before."

"It's kind of strange having a butler waiting on you."

I smiled. "I know, just like in the movies! Takes some getting used to."

We stood there grinning at each other for a moment, and then Alan said, "You look great, Heath. It's good to see you."

"You too. I'm glad you came." Now that we were alone, we were suddenly as awkward as two teenage boys. I reached out and touched his arm, and then he put his arms around my waist, our lips melding together. We stood there for I don't know how long. In some ways, it was an eternity and in others only an instant. Damn, Alan was a wonderful kisser. I pulled back a little so I could gaze into his beautiful eyes, and then I kissed him again on the forehead, lightly. "I've missed you, Alan."

"Likewise, Heath. I was so excited on the steamer I couldn't sit down. I'm not sure what old Bishop must have thought."

I laughed. "He seems discreet enough. But I'm ever so glad you're here. Things have been a little strange."

Alan nodded, looking about. "So I've gathered from what you've said. Where's your room?"

"Next door, in the front."

"Convenient!" He smiled at me, though he looked completely innocent.

"Quite. Mr. Acres and Mr. Doubleday are staying up here as well. Mr. Acres is the Woody I was talking about, Harwood Acres, and he's just across the hall. It's not as private as I'd like. No connecting door between our rooms, unfortunately."

Alan shrugged. "In the wee hours of the night, people are fast asleep."

I shook my head. "And in the wee hours of the night, it's very quiet," I reminded him, kissing his forehead once more. I loved the way he smelled—like spice, hair tonic, sweat, and oil all mixed together.

Alan ran his fingers along the back of my neck. "It's a big house. It must have some private corners somewhere," he said mischievously.

I arched my back, pleased at the sensation of his caress. "We'll have to explore. It is indeed a big house, but give me my apartment on Prospect Avenue anytime. There's some odd stuff about this place."

"Yes, you've been dropping all kinds of cryptic hints since your phone call last night. So, since it's not the wee hours of the night, and we haven't found a private corner yet, tell me everything that's happened." Alan suddenly pulled away and looked at me expectantly, bright-eyed and beaming.

"You'd rather talk then catch up, so to speak?" I said, somewhat disappointed that he'd pulled away.

"You keep holding me and kissing my forehead like that, and I won't want to talk for a week. But…as you're always saying, walls and telephone wires have big ears."

I sighed. "You're right, of course. But something tells me you could be as quiet as a mouse."

Alan laughed. "And you as noisy as a big tomcat. Let's see what tonight brings," he said, a twinkle in his eyes.

"You're on, mouse!"

"All right, pussycat. So in the meantime, tell me what's been going on here."

"There's lots to tell, but why don't we go for a walk? There's some intriguing-looking trails running out from the house and into the woods that I'm sure would give us a little more privacy."

"Why, Detective Barrington, you've been holding out on me!"

I laughed. "I just meant it would be good to get some exercise and fresh air, and besides, these walls have big ears, as you said."

"Oh, I see." Now it was his turn to be somewhat disappointed. Alan walked over to the window and looked out at the dark gray sky, hugging his chest with his arms. "But it's kind of cold and overcast out there if all you want to do is walk and talk. Besides, it looks like rain."

"Aw, come on, it will do you good to get some country air. And who knows? Maybe we'll find a warm, cozy cave."

Keyes turned and grinned at me again, "All right, let's go, Detective. I'll follow you."

We left his suitcase on the bed, grabbed our hats, and headed back downstairs and out on the front porch.

"Which way?" Alan asked, looking to the left and right.

"Into the woods," I replied, bounding down the porch steps and off to the right, where a trail ran along the house and disappeared into the trees. Alan gave chase and quickly caught me, not that I minded, and we laughed like schoolboys beneath the branches before resuming our hike along the trail.

"Where do you suppose it leads?" Keyes asked.

"Only one way to find out."

"I knew you were going to say that."

"Predictable already, am I?"

"Hardly!" Keyes laughed. "Lead on. I'll follow you anywhere."

"I like the sound of that." We walked along, often single file as the trail narrowed, then widened, then narrowed again, Keyes and I ducking under low branches and side-stepping near-frozen mud. Beneath the trees, remnants of the last vestiges of the winter snow still clung on in small piles. Elsewhere, green shoots were pushing up through clumps of old brown leaves. Winter had indeed hung on late this year, and spring seemed to be fighting a losing battle.

We chatted like magpies as I told him all about my trip, Woody and the other guests, and my opinions of them, and of course, Mr. Darkly. Keyes recounted his trip as well, and we both commented on Adam, each jokingly accusing the other of being jealous.

The trail wound through and around the towering pines, maples, and sycamores, which grew so close together they blocked out most of the daylight, making the path below even colder. In full summer, when the trees were completely leafed out, this trail must be dark as night.

"Looks like a clearing," I said, pointing to an opening on the path ahead. We quickened our pace and soon stepped out into the daylight once more, where we stopped abruptly. In the center of the patch of land stood a small square plot surrounded by an ornate rusted black iron fence. I knew at once it must be the Darkly family cemetery Woody had mentioned yesterday.

"Interesting," I remarked. The mood had darkened.

"A cemetery," Keyes said quietly.

"The Darkly family plot, I imagine. Mr. Acres mentioned it to me yesterday."

"Odd place for a cemetery."

"Secluded, private. I can see why the Darklys would want to rest here."

Keyes shrugged and looked about. "I guess so. Only four stones that I can see, but there's room for more."

"Let's go in," I said.

"I didn't mean there was room for us."

"Just to have a closer look, you goof." I nudged him on the shoulder.

He glanced about. "Do you think we should? It seems like an intrusion."

"They're not going to mind, so why not?" I didn't wait for him to answer, but instead walked over to the gate and unlatched it. I looked back at Keyes, still standing at the edge of the clearing.

"Coming?" I asked as I pushed on the gate. Its hinges creaked rather loudly as it swung open.

"Needs oil," Keyes said, striding over to me at last. We stepped inside, and I secured the gate behind me, both of us instinctively removing our hats. The four headstones appeared to have been rather recently cleared of debris, each with fresh spring wildflowers laid upon them. Keyes shivered rather noticeably.

"Cold?" I asked, my breath billowing out like smoke.

"It's gotten chillier, and the wind's picked up," he answered, blowing air into his hands and rubbing them together, his hat tucked beneath his arm.

"Yes." I walked over to the first headstone and paused, Keyes behind me. It was a majestic red granite tribute to *Hugo J. Darkly, 1842–1908. Beloved father and husband.*

"Mr. Darkly's father?" Keyes asked.

"Yes, that's right. He built Dark Point."

We moved on to the second stone, this one black marble and slightly smaller. Its inscription read: *Edith (Collingsworth) Darkly, 1844–1915—beloved wife and mother.*

"Mr. Darkly's mother, I imagine," I said. The third stone was smaller than the other two and stood in a corner, almost alone. I walked over, stooping to read the simple letters upon it: *Constance (Doubleday) Darkly, 1887–1924.* "Ah, that would be Mr. Darkly's first wife. Her brother, Mr. Doubleday, is the man I was telling you about."

Alan nodded his head. "Yes, you mentioned he seemed to think his sister's death wasn't an accident."

"Exactly. I wonder about that."

"It's the detective in you," Keyes suggested.

I shrugged. "I can't help it. Curious," I said more to myself than to Alan.

"What?"

Before I could respond, a sudden gust of wind came out of the trees, and the gate swung open with a loud creak, banging back against the fence. We both turned suddenly.

"I thought you'd latched that," Keyes said sharply, looking from the gate to me.

"I did latch it. Maybe it didn't catch."

"Maybe," Keyes replied doubtfully, staring at the gate again. "We should go. It will be time for lunch soon."

"Yes, soon." I nodded, but instead of walking back toward the gate, I went toward the fourth stone, far grander than the other three, rising magnificently up toward the sky. It was angled in the right back corner of the small cemetery, almost directly beneath a low-hanging evergreen bough that had grown out from a pine at the edge of the clearing. Even from a distance I could read the inscription: *Nigel B. Darkly, 1918–1939.* The stone had a large carved angel upon it, its wings folded across its face, as if it were in mourning.

Keyes followed behind me. "We should go, Heath," he said quietly.

"Soon."

"Tragic. So young," Keyes said.

"Indeed. One must fill one's dash as completely as one can."

"Huh?" Keyes asked, puzzled.

"Just something my aunt says. The dash is the time between our birth year and our death year. It means live our lives as completely and fully as we can. Don't put things off because we never know."

Keyes nodded. "That makes sense. Your aunt's a wise woman."

"My mom's sister, Verbina Partridge, is quite a character, and she definitely strives to fill her dash. You'll have to meet her someday."

"I'd like that. I'd like to meet all your family."

"We'll start with my aunt. My folks are a bit more, uh, traditional."

"Okay, sure. I understand." Alan looked back at Nigel's grave. "There are two sets of flowers here," he observed.

"Yes, I noticed. One from Mr. Darkly, the other from Mr. Acres, I suspect. Early forest wildflowers, probably gathered on the hill behind the house or perhaps brought over on the steamer."

"The wind's blowing them about a bit," Alan said. Indeed, the wind had blown many flowers off Nigel's grave and onto the empty plot beside it, which, I assumed, would probably be Mr. Darkly's final resting spot one day.

"Scattered in the wind. I should like to learn more about Nigel Darkly and the circumstances of his death."

"Sometimes it's better to leave things alone, Heath."

I shrugged. "Sometimes. Sometimes not."

"And with you it's usually 'sometimes not.' Always the detective."

I turned to look at him, his face rosy from the wind, his hair tussled. He looked so handsome. "Do you mind terribly?"

He wrapped his arms about himself, probably crushing his hat. "Not at all. It's who you are, Heath. I wouldn't change a thing."

"I'm glad to hear it. I wouldn't change a thing about you, either."

"Thanks. I'm a pretty simple guy. Not much to change even if you wanted to."

"Don't sell yourself short, Alan. We make a good team. We just need time and luck."

"Look there." He pointed to Nigel's headstone. A white feather, probably from one of the many gulls, had blown down and was caught in one of the carved crevices of the headstone, fluttering back and forth in the wind like a butterfly.

We both shivered as the wind grew stronger, and the trees rustled all around us. "My mom always said white feathers were good luck," Alan said.

"Interesting. It didn't do Nigel much good, but let's hope it brings us good fortune."

"It can't hurt. I'm getting cold, though, and it's probably near lunch."

I smiled at him again. "All right, you. I can take a hint. Let's get back to the house. You'll want to change and freshen up before lunch. And you still have to unpack."

"No arguments from me!"

We walked back and stepped outside the fence, but before I could reach for the gate to close it, the wind shifted again and blew it shut with a loud clang as the rusted metal hit rusted metal.

Keyes looked at me, a strange, startled expression on his face as he shivered in the cold. "Do you believe in spirits, Heath?"

I shrugged once more, looking back at the stone monuments. "I prefer my spirits to be eighty proof."

"You know what I mean."

"Ghosts?"

Keyes nodded, putting his somewhat crumpled hat back upon his head and pulling it low to keep it from blowing off. He turned up his coat collar against the wind, and I did the same. "Do you?" he asked again.

"Yes, I believe in ghosts, though I don't think they can be seen or heard. But they can be frightening, and they live within us all in some form or other." I put my hat back on as well, turned, and started walking toward the trees. "Let's go."

"Why are you going that way? We came from over there," he said, pointing in the opposite direction.

"Yes, but unless I miss my guess, this trail will lead us back to the house, and more directly than going back the way we came."

"What makes you think so?"

"Mr. Acres said the cemetery was just up the hill. The way we came was too roundabout to be that close."

"Okay chief. I just hope you're right. I'm freezing." He started after me, and I waited for him at the edge of the clearing. As he approached, I noticed the wind died down just as suddenly as it had come up. The clearing seemed very still and peaceful again.

I shuddered, from the cold I'm sure, and shoved my hands deep into my coat pockets. Without another word, we followed the path once more, and within ten minutes, we were back at Dark Point, having made a loop up and around, as I had suspected.

As we neared the house, Keyes came up beside me. "You're right again, not that I mind. Let's get inside while I can still feel my toes."

"Definitely. We've just enough time to get changed for lunch. I'm afraid your unpacking will have to wait."

"I'll at least have to unpack something to change into!"

I laughed. "True! Let's go!"

CHAPTER NINE

We hurried up the porch steps and cleaned the mud and dirt from our shoes as best we could using the old iron boot scrape beside the door. Then we pushed on into the front hall, noticing Bishop was putting the finishing touches on the table in the dining room. With a nod to him, we climbed the two flights of stairs to the attic and disappeared into our prospective rooms, only to reemerge fifteen minutes later changed and ready for lunch.

"Well, you look smashing, anyway," Keyes said, looking warmer and more comfortable.

"Thanks, but so do you."

"You are too kind. I only have the one suitcase, and I had to fairly cram everything into it. I'm afraid my clothes got a bit wrinkled."

"No one will notice."

"I wish I would have had time to hang them up or get Bishop to press them."

"There will be time after lunch. You look fine, honestly."

"You're such a good liar!" Keyes laughed. "Come on, I'm too hungry to worry about it."

We entered the dining room at one after one by my pocket watch and found our seats, indicated as they were the night before by handwritten place cards. Today I was seated on July, between Mrs. Atwater and Dr. Atwater, and Keyes was across from me, between Woody and Mrs. Darkly. Alan and I were the last to arrive except for Mr. Darkly. I noticed no one was yet sitting, but rather standing behind their prospective chairs, making idle chatter and fidgeting with their neckties, dresses or what not. I caught Woody's eye and gave him a shrug of my shoulders.

"It's customary to wait until the host is seated before anyone else sits down," he told me, leaning across the table a bit.

I nodded and checked my pocket watch once more. Three minutes after. Keyes, I noticed, had introduced himself to Mrs. Darkly and Woody, and Woody seemed to be wasting no time in chatting him up.

At ten after, people were growing impatient, and some suggested perhaps Mr. Darkly may have fallen asleep and someone ought to go check on him. Others thought perhaps we might give him five more minutes. At quarter after one precisely, Mrs. Darkly summoned Bishop and asked him to please check on the whereabouts of Mr. Darkly as everyone was getting rather hungry and the food would be getting cold.

Bishop went out into the hall and each of us fell rather quiet, except for Woody, who seemed not to notice nor care that Mr. Darkly hadn't arrived yet, and Keyes, who was obliged to listen to Woody and respond to his seemingly unending questions. The rest of them glanced about or drummed their fingers on the backs of their chairs impatiently. As for me, I tried not to look annoyed at Woody, so I concentrated on the view out the windows. It had started to rain outside, and the freezing drizzle pelted the glass panes.

"Maybe he's waiting to make a grand entrance," I suggested.

"Not Dexter. He's always the first one in the dining

room, and he takes points away from anyone who's not here by one minute after the dinner hour. Dexter's fanatical about punctuality," Mrs. Darkly said. "Always has been, and he's only gotten worse."

"Awful weather for April," Dr. Atwater said, changing the subject as he too glanced out the windows at the sound of the sleet.

"Dreadful, simply dreadful," Mrs. Atwater agreed. "Someone ought to turn on the lights, it's gotten so dark outside."

It had indeed gotten dark outside, though it was the middle of the afternoon. Since I seemed to be standing nearest the light switch, I turned and pushed the top button on the switch plate, illuminating the massive chandelier over the table. At that moment, Bishop reappeared at the doorway with an odd look upon his face.

"Mr. Barrington, may I have a word?"

I know it may seem strange, but my first thought was that he was going to scold me for turning on the lights without permission and wasting Mr. Darkly's money. So, somewhat sheepishly, I walked toward him and followed as he stepped back into the hall.

"Mr. Barrington..." he began. "Mr. Darkly..." Bishop's face was an off shade of white, and his voice trembled.

"Yes? What is it, Bishop?"

"Mr. Darkly, sir, I think he's dead!" he blurted out at last, visibly shaken.

"Dead?!" I replied too loudly, as the moment the word left my lips, I knew the others in the dining room behind me had heard. I lowered my voice, too late. "Are you sure?"

"I, I don't know, sir, fairly certain. He looks ghastly. I thought perhaps you, being a policeman, or maybe Dr. Atwater, ought to have a look, sir. He's in the study."

Dr. Atwater was already striding toward us. "Where is he?" he asked, coming out into the hall.

"The study," I said, and the three of us moved almost as one toward the dark door at the end of the hall, now standing wide open as if beckoning us.

I reached the door first, and I gasped in spite of myself at the sight of Mr. Darkly. He was lying facedown in front of the fireplace, his head turned toward us. Vomit spilt from his lips and onto the carpeting. His face was a pale shade of blue, and his body appeared frozen in the middle of a convulsion. I moved over as Dr. Atwater pushed by me and knelt immediately at Mr. Darkly's side. I wondered if I'd ever get used to the sight of death. As he examined the body, I glanced about the room and noticed one of the two windows was open a few inches, making the room very cold. Sleet was collecting on the window ledge and on the floor below. I took the long way around the desk and closed the window behind it, shivering slightly to myself.

"He's dead, all right," Dr. Atwater said, getting back to his feet. "Not that I had much doubt from the look of him."

"What happened?" I asked, coming back toward the door and reaching instinctively for my notebook and pencil in my coat pocket, glad to have brought them.

"Hard to say. Possibly a heart attack, though vomiting is not common with that."

I turned to Bishop, who was standing in the doorway peering in, a rather shocked look on his still pale white face. The others had gathered behind him. Closest was Keyes, who was keeping the rest of them at bay, his excellent police skills kicking in.

I raised my voice to be heard by everyone. "Mr. Darkly has died, and the doctor has confirmed it. That's all that we know at the moment. I urge each of you to return to the dining room and get something to eat. Going hungry won't solve what ails Mr. Darkly." I focused on Bishop. "Under the circumstances, Bishop, perhaps you could set out lunch buffet style and let everyone take what they like."

"Yes, sir, Nora and I can take care of that." He kept his eyes focused on me, trying not to look at Mr. Darkly, I imagined.

"Good, thank you. And perhaps you could bring a sheet to cover the body."

"Of course, sir. There's one in the closet here. We used it this past winter to cover Mr. Darkly's desk, will that do?" he asked, his voice shaky.

"I'm sure it will."

Bishop walked behind the desk to the closet and retrieved the sheet, which had been neatly folded. He handed it to me, his hands trembling ever so slightly.

"That's most helpful, Bishop, thank you." I raised my voice again. "Please, folks, I know this is a shock, but I'd appreciate it if you would return to the dining room and get some lunch, then perhaps retire to your rooms."

"Shouldn't we call the authorities?" Mrs. Atwater asked from the hall, her face a bit ashen. I was sure she couldn't see her father's body from where she stood, but still it had to be distressing.

"I'll take care of that. Until they arrive, I'm assuming authority as a police detective."

"But you've no authority here, Mr. Barrington," Mrs. Atwater said. "You're a Milwaukee police detective."

"First and foremost, Mrs. Atwater, I'm a police detective, period. Now, please cooperate."

"Do as he says, Violet," Dr. Atwater insisted with surprising presence in his voice. "I'll be along shortly. Mrs. Darkly, won't you please?"

"Of course, Doctor," Lorraine Darkly replied. She took

Violet's arm and led her back with the others down the hall toward the dining room, everyone chattering excitedly.

"I'll see to lunch then, sir," Bishop said, following the rest of the group out.

"Thank you, and please try to keep everyone out of here."

"I'll do my best, sir." He turned and walked past Keyes, who was still standing in the hall.

I made eye contact with him. "Keyes, I'll need you here for the moment."

"Yes, sir," he said, walking toward me.

"Close the door behind you. You have your notebook with you?"

Keyes nodded, pulling his notebook from his pocket along with a pencil, then securing the door. "What's happened?"

"Not sure yet. Too soon to tell," I said.

"This is your friend, your fellow officer?" Dr. Atwater asked.

"I do apologize. This is Dr. Atwater, Keyes. Dr. Atwater, this is Alan Keyes, of the Milwaukee Police."

"I saw you earlier in the dining room but didn't have a chance to introduce myself," Alan said.

Because Woody wouldn't give you a chance, I thought to myself.

"How do you do?" Keyes said.

"How do you do?" Dr. Atwater replied.

"Well, Doc, what do you think?" I asked.

Dr. Atwater looked at the body at our feet. "To be honest, something doesn't seem quite right here, Mr. Barrington."

"I agree. I find it odd the window was open."

"Yes, I noticed that—hard not to with the weather we're having. Perhaps Mr. Darkly opened it earlier before it got so cold and started raining."

"Perhaps. Any way to tell how long he's been dead?" I asked.

"Not without a thorough autopsy, though it's curious. Rigor mortis has already set in," Dr. Atwater noted. His demeanor was calm and professional. He was clearly used to this sort of thing and just as clearly dispassionate about his father-in-law.

"What does that mean?"

"Normally, rigor mortis sets in roughly three hours after death, and complete stiffness reaches its peak after about twelve hours. The body will relax again after approximately seventy two hours."

"So that would mean he died around ten this morning."

"It would appear that way, though I spoke with him in the hall only an hour or so ago. So, unless…"

"Unless what, Doctor?" Keyes asked.

"Not sure. I really don't want to speculate until there's been an autopsy, but as I said, something doesn't seem quite right."

"You suspect foul play."

Dr. Atwater looked at me. "It's a possibility here, for certain."

I sighed. "Of course we'll have to question the others, find out who was the last to see him alive besides you, if anyone. That may narrow down the time of death." I glanced about the room again. Not much had changed since last night, except for the obvious fact that Mr. Darkly's lifeless body was now on the floor, and he was wearing different clothes.

Other than that, and the fact that the drapes were open and the fire was out, everything looked about the same. On the desktop still sat the telephone, ink pen and well, typewriter, notepad and pencil, blotter and desk set. The medicine bottle had been opened, though, its stopper resting on the blotter. Beside the phone was an empty brandy glass, but mine had been removed. Still, things didn't seem to add up. Call it instinct.

"I'll call the local police and ask they send a coroner as well."

I walked over to the desk again and lifted the receiver, once more letting my finger turn the dial all the way around for an operator. I waited for the familiar buzzing noise, which meant my call was going through, but instead the line was silent. "The phone is dead."

"What? Try it again." Keyes suggested.

I clicked the bar in the cradle up and down several times. "As dead as Mr. Darkly, I'm afraid, and no other phone in the house, from what I understand."

"Perhaps the weather…" Dr. Atwater said.

"Or perhaps something else." I followed the cord coming out the base of the phone, only to find it ending abruptly a foot or so short of the rest of the cord, which was attached to a phone box on the wall behind the desk, under the credenza. "The cord's been cut."

"Cut? Are you sure?" Dr. Atwater said.

"It's right here between my fingers, Doctor."

"Maybe mice chewed it."

"Awfully clean for a mouse," I said, examining the two ends more closely.

Dr. Atwater looked surprised and puzzled. "But who would cut it? Why?"

"Very reasonable questions to which I have no answers yet."

"Then we can't call the authorities."

"Exactly," I replied, resisting the urge to compliment Dr. Atwater on his gift for stating the obvious.

Keyes looked at me, a puzzled expression on his beautiful face too. "Cut? That's interesting."

"Very," I replied.

"We could send Bishop down to the pier and raise the signal flag," Dr. Atwater suggested.

"Signal flag?" Keyes said.

"It lets the steamer know to stop at the dock. When the yellow flag with the red circle is on the flag pole, it means the steamer is wanted at the dock," I explained, remembering what Bishop had told me. "But the stairs down there must be a sheet of ice right now with all this freezing rain. Besides, I doubt the steamer is running this afternoon."

"I suppose someone could hike the road around and into town," Dr. Atwater said.

"Good luck getting volunteers to do that in this weather." I took out my pocket watch. "It's after two already. It will be getting dark in a few hours. I suspect we'll have to wait until the rain stops and it warms up a bit."

"Good God, man, that won't be until tomorrow," Dr. Atwater said.

"I don't think Mr. Darkly's going to mind. He's not going anywhere. We'll just close and lock the door. Without a fire going, this room will stay pretty chilly even with the window closed. It should be all right for a day or so."

"Seems rather cold to just leave him in here, like that," Keyes said.

"I know, but I don't recommend moving the body or touching it until the authorities can get here."

"I'm afraid I agree," Dr. Atwater said. "As you mentioned earlier, foul play is definitely a possibility."

"I do wish you'd tell me what you're thinking, Doctor. It may be important."

"Well, as I said, something's not right here," he started

doubtfully. "It's the body. I've seen this kind of thing before once or twice."

"Meaning?" Keyes asked.

"Meaning, gentlemen, that Mr. Darkly appears to have suffered convulsions before death. Notice how the throw rug beneath him is bunched up, as if he had been convulsing on the floor. And see how his back is arched, and he looks almost frozen in the middle of a convulsion? As I said earlier, rigor mortis has already set in—all signs of poisoning."

"Poisoning?"

"Afraid so, though I could be wrong. It's impossible to say for certain without an autopsy and toxicology report."

I looked back at the desk at Mr. Darkly's empty brandy glass and at the medicine bottle next to it. "The brandy, or perhaps the medicine."

Dr. Atwater followed my gaze. "Possible, though not typical if it was strychnine."

"Strychnine?"

"Strychnine causes muscular convulsions and eventually death. The body usually freezes immediately upon death, resulting in rigor mortis, as appears to be the case here."

"So someone could have laced the brandy or Darkly's medicine with strychnine."

"Strychnine is a very bitter substance, Mr. Barrington. The taste can be detectable in very low concentrations, so it's not usually added to food or drink."

"But if the victim had pretty much lost his sense of taste or smell, as Mr. Darkly had…"

Dr. Atwater nodded his head. "Then it's very possible, sir." He walked over to the desk.

"Don't touch anything, Doctor," I reminded him.

He looked back at me understandingly. He bent over

and smelled the empty glass, then the medicine bottle. "The medicine would be my guess. The brandy appears normal."

"What kind of medicine is it?"

He bent a little lower, trying to read the label without touching the bottle.

"Myapartium oil. Probably some version of cod liver," he said. "Nasty tasting on its own, I'm sure."

"Do me a favor, Doc. Don't disclose any of this to the others. We need to keep it confidential for now. Even your wife must not know."

"Not to worry, Mr. Barrington," he said, straightening up again and coming toward me. "I can keep a secret. Besides, it's all just speculation at this point."

I nodded. "True, though speculation can often lead to fact. I'll ring for Bishop and ask him to lock this room up and give me the key. And then," I said, turning to Keyes, "I think we should have a word with the others." I pushed the buzzer for Bishop.

"I'll leave you to it, then, unless you need me for anything else. I'm concerned about how Violet is taking this," Dr. Atwater said.

"Of course, but give me a hand with this sheet first, if you don't mind. We'll just lay it over him carefully." I handed him one edge of the sheet, and together we covered the body. "Thanks, Doctor. I know it's difficult, but once you've gotten something to eat, if you could try to stay in your room with your wife that would be most helpful."

"I'll see what I can do. Violet and her father were estranged, you know, but this will still be a shock to her. She may need a sedative."

"Whatever you think best. Did Mrs. Atwater speak of her father to you very often?"

"No, not very. As I said, they were estranged for many years. Still…"

"Yes?"

"I really think she had hopes of reconciling this weekend, Mr. Barrington. I think she believed he wanted it, too."

"I'm sorry."

"So am I. I think it would have helped her a great deal," Dr. Atwater replied. As he started toward the door, a knock came from the other side and Bishop's head appeared as he opened it.

"I thought perhaps you gentlemen would like me to bring you some lunch in the library."

"I was just leaving," Dr. Atwater said. "Mr. Barrington is the one who rang for you." He stepped aside to let Bishop in, and then went out into the hall.

Bishop entered and looked at me, puzzled. "Yes, sir?" He looked at the body, now covered with the sheet.

"Do you have a key to that door?"

"The study door? Yes, Mr. Barrington." Much of the color had returned to his face from earlier, and his voice was fairly normal. "This is one of the rooms we lock up for the winter. I have the key on my ring here," he replied, lifting a ring of keys attached to a chain at his waist.

"Good. Is that the only key?"

"As far as I know, sir."

"Give it to me, then, please. I want to lock this room up, with access to no one without permission from me, all right?"

Bishop looked rather doubtful. "I suppose that would be all right, sir, though Mrs. Atwater—she's Mr. Darkly's closest living relative…"

I shook my head. "Doesn't matter at the moment, Bishop. I'm assuming authority in the absence of the local police."

"Yes, sir, I understand," he said, fumbling with the ring. "My rheumatism's been acting up. Always does when it rains." After some effort, he finally removed the key and handed it to me. "Anything else, Mr. Barrington?"

"No, that's it. Did anyone eat anything?"

"A few people took some food to their rooms, sir."

I looked at Keyes, remembering how hungry he'd been. "You mentioned bringing us lunch. Would you mind fixing us a couple sandwiches and leaving them in my room, Bishop? Oh, and go ahead with dinner plans, at least for now. People will still have to eat, and it's probably good to get back into a routine. Give folks something to do."

"Yes, sir. I will take care of it."

"Thank you, Bishop," I replied, and I knew he would, knowing it would also be good for him and Nora to have something to do.

"Just one thing, sir."

"Yes?"

"Dr. Atwater said you rang for me?"

"That's right, why?"

"I never heard the bell, sir, and I was in the kitchen with Nora."

"Then how did you know I needed you?"

"I didn't. I just took it upon myself to check in with you, sir."

"Curious." I walked back to the desk and found the wire on the call button had been cut in two. I looked at Keyes, and I could tell he knew at once without my having to say it.

"Must be a defect in the button," I lied. "Glad you're so conscientious, Bishop."

"Just doing my duty, sir."

"Good man," I replied. "And a good man is hard to find."

"Yes, sir."

"By the way, you were in here this morning, yes? Before Mr. Darkly?"

"That's right, sir. I got up around four thirty this morning. After getting dressed, I checked the upstairs halls for shoes or clothes that needed attention and took them down to the laundry for Nora. Then I made the rounds of the downstairs rooms, prepared the fireplaces, and cleared the dishes before setting up the dining room for breakfast."

"About what time did you come in here?"

Bishop furrowed his brow. "Oh, let me see. It was about quarter of six, I imagine. I opened the draperies, straightened the papers on the desk, swept the ashes, emptied the wastepaper basket, laid out a fresh fire, cleared the glasses, and put out new ones."

"Was the window open, do you recall?"

"The window, sir? Oh no, sir, both windows were closed. It was quite chilly last night."

"Yes, I know," I said. "And the glass that's on the desk now wasn't there this morning?"

"No, sir. I mean, two glasses were on the desk this morning, but I took them to the kitchen, and replaced them with clean glasses, which I put under the credenza. Mr. Darkly must have had a drink this morning, before…well, before, sir."

"Yes, before."

"Did you reach the authorities, sir?" Bishop asked.

I shook my head. "No. The phone's out of order."

"Out of order?"

"Yes. When it stops raining and it's safe to do so, you'd better run up the signal flag for the steamer."

"I could go now, sir," he offered.

I shook my head again. "The steps are glare ice. I'm sure

you'd break your leg. It can wait till morning, unless you know of another way to get in touch with the rest of the world."

"I'm afraid not, sir. It would take well over two hours to walk around, even longer in this weather."

"I was afraid so, Bishop."

The three of us left the study, and I took one more look around before turning off the light, pulling the door closed and locking it. It did indeed seem cold to just leave Mr. Darkly lying there, but I didn't want to risk disturbing any evidence. After I locked the door and Bishop had gone on his way, Keyes and I climbed the stairs up to my room in the attic. I got the fire going once more and turned on the light by the table.

"What do you make of it?" Keyes asked.

"Things keep getting stranger."

"I noticed you didn't want to tell Bishop about the phone cord and call button being cut."

"I find it's good policy to reveal things only on a need-to-know basis."

"Sure, of course," Keyes said. "Can't give too much away, right?"

"Right. Sometimes people and things are not what they seem."

"So, you think Bishop could be involved? He seems such a nice old guy."

"I think it's possible, certainly. Again, people and things are not always what they seem, remember that. Anyone here could be involved in Mr. Darkly's death."

"So you think Dr. Atwater's right about Mr. Darkly being poisoned?"

"It makes sense."

"But you don't think it was accidental?"

"Not likely. Hard to accidentally drink strychnine, even

if you can't taste it. And where did it come from? More importantly, where did it go?"

"Where did it go? In the medicine!"

"Yes, but where's the rest of it, Keyes? How did it get in the medicine?"

Keyes looked thoughtful. "The room was unlocked. Anyone could have slipped it in there."

"Definitely. And Mr. Darkly told me he took the medicine three times a day, before each meal."

"So it could have been put in any time after dinner last night or before breakfast this morning."

"Makes sense to me."

"Well, at least we can cross Dr. Atwater off our list of suspects," Keyes said.

"Why?"

"If he poisoned Mr. Darkly, he wouldn't tell us it was poison. He'd let us believe it was a heart attack or something, right?"

I pointed my finger at him. "But Dr. Atwater's an intelligent fellow. He knows I'm a detective and you're a policeman. He would have to be aware that an autopsy would be ordered and the real cause of death would be found out. If he told us it was a heart attack and we then found out it was poison, it would seem suspicious."

"Oh, I see," Keyes said thoughtfully. "But if he tells us from the start that it's poison, it actually makes him seem innocent."

"Precisely."

"Wow, he's pretty clever," Alan said, shaking his head.

"Clever if he did indeed poison Mr. Darkly. He could be completely innocent, but we can't rule him out as a suspect."

"Oh, sure. Of course," Keyes agreed sheepishly. "But if he is innocent, who do you think might have done it?"

I laughed. "As I said before, if ever there was a houseful of suspects, this is it. I think everyone here had a motive except us."

"Not Mrs. Atwater, though, surely. Her husband said she really wanted to reconcile, and he seemed sincere."

"People say a lot of things they don't mean, Keyes. She may have said things to him to lead him astray, or he may have said that to us because he didn't want us to suspect her."

"Isn't anyone honest?" he asked, disheartened.

I smiled at him. "I am, but you'll have to take my word for it. And I know you are, but beyond that, I'm not at all sure. As I said, everyone else in this house is a suspect."

Keyes nodded. "Yeah, I got that impression, too, from what you told me. It's kind of sad, don't you think?"

"What?"

"Mr. Darkly. I mean, I never actually got to meet him, but from what you've told me, he was trying to right wrongs, make up for his past."

"So he said, yes."

"He invited everyone here hoping to start fresh, and yet it seems someone couldn't let go of a grudge, couldn't let the past rest."

"As you said, sometimes it is best to leave things alone."

"Not that you'd ever follow that advice," Keyes said.

"In the right circumstances I would."

There was a knock at the door. "Come in," I called out, loud enough to be heard throughout the house, probably.

Bishop opened the door and came in bearing a tray laden with sandwiches, a pot of tea, cups and saucers.

"Goodness, how did you manage to carry that up all those stairs?" I asked, taking it from him and setting it on the table.

"There's a dumbwaiter in the corridor, sir, down by the servant bedrooms."

"Well, I'm glad to hear that. Thank you, and tell Nora everything looks wonderful."

"Yes, sir, she'll be pleased. Anything else you two need, Mr. Barrington?"

I looked over at Keyes, but he shook his head. "No, I think we're set."

"Very well. When you're finished, just set the tray out in the hall. I'll pick it up before dinner. And if you do need anything else, just press your call button."

"Got it. Thanks again."

"You're most welcome. By the way, sir, if I may…"

"Yes?"

"It's just that, well, Nora was asking me all kinds of questions, sir. She fancies a word with you if you're willing."

"Of course. I'd be happy to speak with her. I haven't actually even met your wife yet."

"Most of the time she's content to stay in the kitchen, sir. She's not much for the rest of it. I'm just the opposite. That's why we make such a good pair."

"Undoubtedly. Please tell her I'll stop by the kitchen after we're finished here, unless she'd like to come up."

"Oh, the kitchen would suit her much better, if you don't mind."

"Very well. We shouldn't be more than a few minutes."

"Thank you, sir, I'll let her know." He let himself out, closing the door behind him.

We ate every bit of the lunch, both unaware of how hungry we actually had been. When the teapot was drained as well and I'd set the tray outside, I turned to Keyes. "Well, not exactly the weekend I had in mind."

"Me either!" He smiled at me. "But it's okay. It's kind of nice, working on another case with you."

"I'm glad you don't mind."

"Not at all. There's never a dull moment with you, Heath!"

"I'll try to keep it that way." I smiled back at him and rubbed his shoulder gently. "And I hope you know you can trust me."

"I do know it, I can feel it. I did from the very start."

I smiled warmly at him. "Shall we see what Nora has to say?"

"If you're waiting for me, you're wasting your time," he said, heading for the door.

CHAPTER TEN

I took one quick look in the mirror, smoothed out my hair, and followed Keyes. We made our way to the kitchen, finding Bishop and a small, elderly woman cleaning up. They both turned to us as we entered.

"Ah, Mr. Barrington, sir, Mr. Keyes, may I present my wife, Nora. Nora, this is Mr. Barrington, the detective I was telling you about, and this is Mr. Keyes, the police officer. They're from Milwaukee."

She gave a slight bow of the head, drying her hands on a worn gray dish towel. She was rather frail, looking more like a librarian than a housekeeper with small wire spectacles perched on her nose, and her gray hair curled into a bun atop her small head. Her narrow ruddy face was lined and creased, giving her a serious but warm look.

"It's a pleasure to meet the woman behind such good and hearty food, Nora," I said.

"Oh, thank you, sir. I enjoy cooking." She looked quite pleased as a blush warmed her cheeks and her expression softened.

"And you keep a very clean and orderly kitchen, I must say."

"A place for everything and everything in its place is Nora's motto, sir," Bishop said.

She looked up at her husband, and I felt she seemed rather embarrassed. "Well, it does help to have things tidy."

"Oh I quite agree," I said. "Bishop was telling me you wanted to have a word with us?"

"Go on, dear. It's all right. Tell them what you told me," Bishop said encouragingly.

I could tell she was deciding whether or not to trust us. I'd seen that kind of a expression many times in my line of work, questioning witnesses and the like. "Shall we sit down?" I suggested, indicating the kitchen table.

"Oh, well, all right. I'll just wipe it down a bit first."

Bishop shrugged while Nora flitted about with a cloth, sweeping invisible crumbs into a dustpan, which she shook into a bin. Finally she wiped her hands once more and lighted softly on one of the old brown spindle chairs. Bishop, Keyes, and I did the same, though perhaps not so lightly.

I looked at the woman across from us, her hands folded in her lap. "Now, Nora, what is it you wanted to tell us?"

She looked nervously again at her husband and he nodded his head.

"Well, sir, it's about last night."

"Yes? Tell us everything and anything, please, Nora. Even if you don't think it important. Officer Keyes will take some notes."

She looked at both of us, perhaps still a little uncertain, but then she continued. "Well, we'd finished down here and had gone up to our rooms, just above the kitchen here, my husband and me, I mean." She looked up to the ceiling and then back at Bishop.

"I was in the bathroom," he said.

Nora nodded her head. "That's right, he was. And I was turning down the bed in our room. Oh, it was just past ten thirty when all of a sudden, I heard the bell in the box."

"The bell in the box?" I asked, taking note.

"The call box, sir. The indicator box. There's one in our room and one here in the kitchen, just there over the hall door. Mr. Darkly was ringing for us from the study."

"How did you know that? How does it work?"

"When someone rings from there, a little disc drops into the slot that says 'study,' sir, and a bell rings. And no one but Mr. Darkly would ring for us from there, I imagine. There's bells for the dining room, the drawing room, the library, Mr. Darkly's bedroom, each of the guest rooms—"

"All right, so the bell rang," I said.

She nodded her gray little head again. "That's right, sir. So I went into the hall and called for Henry."

"Henry?"

"That's me, sir. Henry Bishop."

"Oh, yes, of course. Go on, please."

"I asked him through the door of the bathroom if he'd heard the bell."

"I told her I hadn't heard anything, but I had the water running and was brushing my teeth," Bishop said.

"Well, normally Henry answers Mr. Darkly's calls, but since he was busy, I told him I'd go and attend to him."

"And?"

"I went down the stairs, the back stairs there." She pointed with her chin to the stairs just off the hall entrance. "When I got to the bottom, I saw the light was on here in the kitchen. Mr. Doubleday was standing there, eating a turkey leg. I hadn't met him formally, but I knew instantly it was him from the description Henry gave. He was standing just there, looking a bit guilty." She pointed again, this time with her small bony hand, to a place in front of the icebox. "Then I saw Mr. Acres emerge from the back entry, which I thought was a bit odd."

"Had Mr. Acres been outside?"

"Oh no, sir. I didn't get that impression. He didn't appear cold or anything, and he wasn't wearing an overcoat."

"Good observation, Mrs. Bishop," Keyes said, making notes.

Her lined, wrinkled face beamed, and she smiled again. I noticed she had surprisingly nice teeth, very straight, though yellowed. "Thank you, sir. I notice things, you know. Like the time Reverend Osgood shaved off his mustache—nobody else noticed, but I did, right away."

"You could be a detective, Nora," I said.

She gave me a broad smile. "Oh, go on, sir. I'm just observant, that's all. I hadn't officially met Mr. Acres yet, either, though I did run into him upstairs earlier and saw him coming out of his room. He matched Henry's description, too. Henry's good that way."

"Being observant and being able to describe people and things are big parts of being a detective. So, what happened after you saw Mr. Acres come from the back entry?"

"Well, sir, I asked the two of them, Mr. Acres and Mr. Doubleday, if everything was all right or if they needed something."

"And what did they say?"

"Mr. Acres said he was all set, thank you. So polite, he was, a nice young man. And Mr. Doubleday said he was fine. It was pretty apparent that Mr. Doubleday was raiding the icebox, not that I minded. But if Mr. Darkly knew, he'd be quite upset, I'm sure."

"Oh?"

She tsked and shook her head. "Well, Mr. Barrington, it's not my place to say anything, but Mr. Darkly doesn't much care for Mr. Doubleday, or for Mr. Acres from what he's said. He told us to let him know if Mr. Doubleday asked us to bring him any food or liquor."

I smiled to myself. "I see."

"Yes, sir. Mr. Darkly's funny about things like that."

"So I've gathered. What happened then?"

"Nothing much, sir. Mr. Acres said good night, and he left."

"And what did you and Mr. Doubleday do?"

"Well, I asked him if I could fix him something, as he was obviously hungry, or at least he was before eating that turkey leg, but he said again that he was fine." Nora glanced about before continuing, as if making sure no one was listening in. "Then he told me that Mr. Acres had taken something from the shelf in the back entry."

"He told you that?"

"Yes, sir," she said, nodding. "He said Mr. Acres told him he needed to get something from the back entry. That seemed curious indeed, so I went to have a look, and Mr. Doubleday followed."

"Did you notice anything missing?"

"Oh, right away, sir. Right away. Like I said, I notice things."

"What was it?"

She paused, for dramatic effect I imagine, and then said quietly, "It was the bottle of rat poison."

I raised my eyebrows. "Rat poison? You're certain?"

"No doubt about it, sir. I put a saucer of milk out to the back porch right after supper—there's a stray cat's been coming around, poor thing. And I thought to myself Mr. Darkly should keep cats, then he wouldn't have need of nasty poisons, and I remember looking up at the shelf just then, and there it was."

"Do you remember what kind of poison it was, Nora?"

She looked at me as if I was a bit daft. "Rat poison, sir. Mouse and rat. Nasty things, they are. The bottle was nearly gone, it being a long winter. I was planning on getting another bottle next time we went to town. No point now, I suppose."

"Yes, but do you remember what kind of rat poison?" I asked gently.

"Oh, oh yes, sir. Strychnine, in a green bottle with a white label, big skull and crossbones. I don't like poisons, sir. Cats is what you need."

"You're certain?"

"Very certain, sir. Never a mouse problem when you have a cat or two about."

I smiled. "I'm sure, Nora, but what I meant was, are you sure it was strychnine?"

"I can vouch for that, Mr. Barrington," Bishop interjected. "I used it far more than Nora. It was strychnine all right, in a green bottle just as she described. The mice tend to come inside out of the cold, you know, and I think they were used to having the place all to themselves in the past when the house was vacant off season."

I looked at Keyes, and then back at Nora. "Are you sure Mr. Acres took the bottle?"

"Well, no, not a hundred percent, but that was the only thing missing back there. And it was there after supper, like I said."

"You said Mr. Doubleday followed you back there. Did he know the poison was missing? I mean, did you tell him?"

"Well, yes, sir. I said the bottle of rat poison was the only thing missing."

"I see. Do you recall exactly what you said?"

She scratched her chin and gazed up at the ceiling. "Yes, I said, 'Why, he's taken the bottle of rat poison! What would he want with that?'"

"And what did Mr. Doubleday say?"

"He said Mr. Acres said it was a secret. Very strange, I

thought. I made a mental note to mention it to Mr. Darkly, and then I remembered that Mr. Darkly had rung for me. I'd plumb forgot!"

"Understandable under the circumstances, Nora. What happened next?"

"Well, Mr. Doubleday told me Mr. Acres had probably heard mice up in the attic, was all, and I shouldn't worry about it. Then he said he was just going to have a glass of cider, and that he'd clean up and turn out the lights, so I went on down the hall to the study."

"And what did Mr. Darkly want you for?" I glanced over at Keyes to make sure he was getting all this down; he was scribbling furiously in his notebook.

"Rather strange, sir. He just wanted to ask me if I'd turned on the taps in the kitchen and let them drip, as he was afraid the pipes might freeze. I assured him Henry and I had taken care of it."

"That was all?"

"Well, I did mention to him about Mr. Acres and the rat poison, sir."

"And?" I wondered if Nora wasn't perhaps relishing this attention, her time in the spotlight, and dragging it out as long as she could.

"He said that seemed odd, but I shouldn't worry about it. He told me I should ask you about it in the morning."

"Me?"

"Yes, sir. To see if you noticed any mice up there in the attic, you know."

"I see. But you didn't mention it to me this morning."

Her face flushed a bit. "Well, ah, no, sir. It slipped my mind, I guess, until earlier. And I hadn't met you, of course. I was going to have Henry mention it, but then with all that's happened, I thought I should tell you now."

"Of course, and I'm glad you did. Anything else, Nora, anything at all?"

She moved her right hand softly across her face and looked thoughtful. "Well, the whole thing struck me funny, sir, but not my place to question, you understand. I feel I did my duty in telling Mr. Darkly what I'd seen."

"Though you didn't actually see Mr. Acres take the poison."

"Well, no, sir, that's true. But I did see him coming from the back entry, acting kind of funny. And Mr. Doubleday did tell me Mr. Acres said he had to get something from back there."

"I see."

"And the poison was the only thing missing. Just seems funny to me, sir. If you know what I mean. And now poor Mr. Darkly found dead, sir, all of a sudden like."

"Yes, circumstances do seem unusual, I agree. Anything else, Nora?"

She shook her head and a wisp of her gray hair came loose. "No, sir, not that I can think of right now." She pushed the hair back into place. "It's just all so odd. But that Mr. Acres seems a nice fellow. I'm sure there's a good explanation for it all."

"There generally is, Nora. Did you tell Mr. Darkly you'd also seen Mr. Doubleday in the kitchen?"

Nora's pale little face flushed again behind her glasses as she shook her head once more. "I know I should have, sir, as he had asked us to let him know, but technically he said to tell him if Mr. Doubleday asked us to bring him anything."

"And Mr. Doubleday hadn't asked, he just helped himself."

She nodded, biting her lip. "Yes, sir. That's true. I was going to mention it anyway, but I was a bit distracted by this thing with Mr. Acres and the poison, you know. That seemed more important."

"Of course. What did you do this morning?"

"This morning, sir? Just the usual. Henry got up earlier than me to check the hall for shoes to shine and clothes to press. I got up around five or so. Henry had put a pair of shoes and a suit in the laundry for me, with a note saying they were Mr. Doubleday's. I shined up the shoes and pressed the suit, but I just couldn't get out one stain on the lapel of his jacket— probably turkey grease, darned near impossible to get that out."

"I can imagine."

"I did my best, though I couldn't get it out completely. I'm sure he won't be happy about that."

"No, I'm sure not, but it's certainly not your fault, Nora."

"Thank you, sir. I hope he agrees."

"I'm sure he will. What did you do then?"

"After I tried to clean them? I took them upstairs and hung the suit outside his door and put the shoes on the floor. Then I came back down and started getting things ready for breakfast. Out of curiosity, I checked the shelf in the back entry. The poison was still missing."

"Have you checked recently?" I asked.

"Just before you came in, sir. Not there."

"Thank you, Nora. You've been most helpful."

"Just thought I should let you know, sir, you being a police detective and all. It just didn't seem right."

"You did exactly the right thing. Please keep me posted if you think of anything else."

"Oh, yes, sir, I will. I'm sorry I forgot to have Henry mention it this morning." She nodded her little gray head again, pushing her glasses back up her nose.

"Not to worry. Better late than never, as they say. Well, we'll leave you two to your work, then. Let me know if you think of anything else." We left the kitchen and walked out into the side hall, closing the door behind us.

Keyes turned to me. "What do you think, sir?"

"I think it's curious how you can switch from calling me Heath to calling me sir just like that."

Keyes blushed. "No different than you switching from Alan to Keyes, sir."

I laughed. "I suppose. We have our private roles and our work roles, and we try not to mix them up."

"Exactly, sir. Sometimes it's hard to call you Heath when I'm used to calling you sir."

"We're like Nora and Henry, I suppose, in a way."

"I get to be Henry, sir."

"Not a chance, Keyes."

"But I'm a lousy cook." He laughed.

"Let's call it a draw for now. So tell me what you think."

"It seems to me, sir, that we should have a chat with Mr. Acres."

"And with Mr. Doubleday," I added. "Let's see who we can find first."

CHAPTER ELEVEN

We walked down the side hall to the main hall and crossed to the library, where we came across Mr. Doubleday ensconced in an overstuffed red and green floral print chair by the fireplace, perusing a book on horticulture. A slowly dying fire crackled in the hearth, and wisps of smoke hung in the air.

"Good afternoon, Mr. Doubleday," I said, closing the hall door behind us. He appeared to be alone.

"Oh, Mr. Barrington, and ah…"

"Keyes, sir."

"Yes, Mr. Keyes." He set his book on a small side table and started to get to his feet, which was a bit of a struggle for a man his size.

"Please don't get up, Mr. Doubleday. May we join you?" I asked, indicating two vacant red chintz chairs opposite him.

"Be my guest," he replied, sinking back down into the chair. "What's been going on around here?"

"Going on?" I said as Keyes and I took our seats, careful not to crease my pants.

"Yes. It's four thirty in the afternoon. Are we supposed to just go about our business as if nothing's happened?"

"That, Mr. Doubleday, is exactly what I would prefer you to do."

He shook his large head. "It doesn't seem right, what with Dexter lying in there dead on the floor. Seems disrespectful and rather creepy, I might add."

"Do you have any suggestions?"

"Suggestions? Yes, of course. Why doesn't someone go for help? Get the authorities? Seems obvious to me."

"The phone's out of order," I said matter-of-factly.

"Yes, I heard. I wanted to get into the study to phone my office, and Bishop told me about it."

"The study's off-limits for now, Mr. Doubleday."

"Doesn't matter if the phone's not working. I've no business with a dead man. Though I could use a drink."

"I'm sure you could. Were you in the study at all last night, Mr. Doubleday?"

He glared at me. "Yes, what of it? I went in before dinner. Darkly was still upstairs, getting dressed, I imagine."

"You went in for a drink?"

"That's right. I helped myself—no point in denying it, I guess—Lorraine saw me come out of there. I poured myself a short one, drank it, then rinsed out my glass and put it back. If you want to arrest me for stealing liquor, go ahead."

I ignored the statement. "I understand you were also in the kitchen late last night, having a snack."

His plump face shone red. "You are quite the detective, aren't you? So, you got me on liquor and food theft. Take me away."

"I'm merely trying to ascertain everyone's whereabouts at different times during the evening, Mr. Doubleday," I said, somewhat annoyed.

"Well, ascertain all you want. I was hungry, thought I'd have a quick bite before I went upstairs. Couldn't make it through the night on the skimpy portions Dexter served at dinner. Who told you I was in the kitchen, Acres? He came in and scared the hell out of me. People shouldn't sneak up like that."

"Was Acres after a midnight snack, too?"

"No, he said something about wanting to get something from the back entry, said Mr. Darkly wanted it. Then he walked back there, looking back at me once or twice. Seemed rather peculiar to me, but then Acres is a peculiar guy. Bit of a pansy, if you ask me, a poof."

I bit my lip angrily. "I'm not asking your opinion of Mr. Acres, Mr. Doubleday. I just want to know what transpired between the two of you last night."

"Nothing transpired between us! And I resent the implication." His voice fairly squeaked. "He came in, surprised me, said he had to get something from the back entry, went and got it, I assume, and then the housekeeper came down."

"What did she want?"

"She said something about Mr. Darkly ringing for her. Acres came back just then. We talked, let her know everything was fine. Then Acres said good night and he left."

"Out the door to the hall?" I asked.

He nodded, his jowls bouncing up and down. "Yes, that's right. It looked like he'd gotten whatever it was he was after, because I saw a bulge in his pants he didn't have before."

"Did you mention it to Nora?"

"The housekeeper? Yes, yes, I did. She walked over to the back entry to check what Mr. Acres was after, and I followed her. Curious, you know."

"Of course. And what did she find?"

"She noticed a bottle missing from the top shelf right away."

"A bottle? Did she say what it was a bottle of?"

"Poison, Mr. Barrington," he said, his eyebrows arching up again into that bushy squirrel or perhaps a caterpillar.

"What exactly did she say?"

"She said, 'Why, the rat poison's missing. What would he want with that?' Or something to that effect, anyway."

"And what did you say?"

"I said I didn't know. Maybe he has rats in his room."

"Do you think he does?"

He shook his head irritably, his jowls now shaking back and forth. "How should I know? Mice, perhaps. I've never seen any, though. Clearly poison has other purposes, as you certainly must be aware."

"Did you mention to Nora that Mr. Acres had said he was getting the poison for Mr. Darkly?"

"I don't recall. I know it seemed strange to me that Mr. Darkly would out of the blue ask Acres to fetch him a bottle of poison. Those two don't exactly get along, you know."

"Neither do you and Mr. Darkly, from what you've told me."

Doubleday snorted. "Dexter doesn't, or rather didn't, get along with anyone, really. But he seemed to especially dislike Mr. Acres, so why would he ask him to fetch a bottle of poison?"

"Why indeed?"

"Why is he writing down everything I say?" Doubleday asked irritably, pointing his chubby index finger at Keyes. I noticed he was wearing a green emerald ring that clearly hadn't been off his finger in years; the fat had nearly engulfed it.

"He's just taking notes so I can sort things out later. Do you mind?"

He snorted again. "I've got nothing to hide."

"Glad to hear it. So, what happened next, Mr. Doubleday?"

Doubleday let out a loud sigh and rolled his eyes. "The housekeeper seemed all worried about the poison being missing, but I told her not to let it bother her. Then she asked if she could get me anything."

"And?"

"And I told her I was fine, but that I could do with a glass of cider I'd seen in the icebox. She offered to get it for me, but I told her I could help myself, and that I'd clean up and turn out the light."

"And is that what you did?"

"Well, she fussed about a bit, went back once more to the back entry—I think to make sure the poison really was gone, then she said good night and went out the hall door in a bit of a hurry. Said she'd completely forgotten that Mr. Darkly had rung for her."

"So, you were alone in the kitchen at that point. Do you recall the time?"

"Somewhere around eleven or maybe a bit later. I'm not really sure." He drummed his fat fingers on the arm of the chair.

"So, you were going to have some cider."

"Yes. I poured myself a glass and was just tidying up when Nora came back in."

"Did she say anything?"

He paused and looked up at the ceiling, as if trying to remember. "She looked rather troubled, I recall. I think she was surprised I was still there. She asked me if I needed anything else, but I assured her once more I was fine. She nodded, said 'good night,' and then went back upstairs. Bit of a busybody, if you ask me."

I ignored his last comment. "And what did you do?"

"I really don't see what difference this all makes, Detective."

"Just answer the questions, please, Mr. Doubleday."

He sighed again, still drumming his fingers. "The cider

was a bit bland, and I rather thought a nightcap sounded better, so I went down the hall to the study. I was hoping Dexter had gone up to bed, but the light was on under the door, so I knocked. He called out for me to come in, and I did."

"Was he alone?"

"Yes."

"You said you'd hoped he'd gone up to bed."

"Only because I know he can be stingy with his brandy, so truth be told I thought I'd just help myself."

"Like you did earlier."

Doubleday looked even more annoyed. "It's not like Darkly couldn't afford it, and it's not like I drank the whole bottle."

"True," I replied. "So, you were hoping to get another drink only Mr. Darkly was still up."

Doubleday nodded, his chins moving up and down again. "Dexter can be a bit of a night owl. He doesn't sleep well. I should have remembered that."

"What did you two talk about?"

"We didn't talk much at all, but then we never do, never did. He was at his desk, I asked him for a nightcap, he turned me down."

"Did he seem himself?"

"You mean did he seem disagreeable and cranky? Yes, he did. Very much himself."

"Did everything else appear normal?"

"What do you mean?"

"Was everything the way it was when you were in there earlier last night?"

He shrugged. "Pretty much. The drapes were closed, of course, and a fire going, oh and Acres had left a big fat book sitting on the chair by the door, but other than that, I didn't notice anything."

"Did you notice the bottle of poison anywhere?"

"No, I didn't. It might have been there, but I don't recall seeing it. I don't really know what it looks like."

"Did Mr. Darkly say anything to you about Mr. Acres? About asking him to bring him anything?"

"No, he didn't mention him at all. He didn't say much in general, except that I couldn't have a nightcap and good night. Pretty much what I expected, as I said."

"I see."

"So I said good night, closed the door behind me, and went up to bed."

"You didn't go back down later for the nightcap, after Mr. Darkly had gone up?"

"I considered it, but once I got up all those damned stairs, I didn't really want to go back down again, so I just went to sleep."

"Well, thank you, Mr. Doubleday."

"Don't you want to know what I did once I got to my bedroom? What I wore to bed, what I read, how I slept?"

I smiled politely. "That won't be necessary." *And I certainly don't want to envision what you wore to bed or how you slept*, I added to myself.

"So why all the questions, Detective? Are you naturally curious or just trying to pass the time?"

"Just trying to sort things out, piece things together, Mr. Doubleday. And yes, I am naturally curious. Were you planning on telling anyone else about the incident with the poison and Mr. Acres?"

"The authorities, once they arrive."

"Until the local police do arrive, Mr. Doubleday, I am the authority, and I must insist you tell me anything you think of that may be relevant to this case."

"What case? Are you suggesting Dexter was murdered? You think Acres poisoned him? Wouldn't surprise me."

"Mr. Darkly is dead, cause unknown, by person or persons unknown. That, Mr. Doubleday, makes a case for the police. Do I make myself clear?"

"Clear enough, Mr. Barrington, though my money's on Acres sure as icing on a doughnut," he replied, folding his arms across his ample stomach.

"You're entitled to your opinion, of course." Keyes and I stood up. "We'll see you at dinner, if not before."

"Not sure I'll have much of an appetite for dinner," he said, stroking his mustache.

I opened the door to the hall and looked back at him, still firmly wedged into the chair. "That, Mr. Doubleday, doesn't seem likely."

Keyes followed me into the hall and pulled the door closed. "What next?"

"I think a trip upstairs to Mr. Acres's room is in order. I suspect we'll find him there."

"Lead on!"

CHAPTER TWELVE

As we climbed the many stairs, I turned to Keyes. "So if Woody denies taking the poison from the back entrance, either he's lying, or Doubleday's lying," I said, my voice lowered so as not to be overheard.

"What do you mean?"

"I mean, Doubleday and Nora both said Acres appears to have taken it, but only Doubleday has said Acres told him he got it for Darkly, presumably."

"So if Acres denies taking the poison?"

"Then either he or Doubleday is lying. Maybe Doubleday took it from the back entry before Nora and Acres came in, then Doubleday somehow persuaded Acres to go to that area knowing it would arouse Nora's curiosity."

"Wow, I hadn't thought of that. But what if Acres admits he took it?" Keyes said, his tone of voice matching mine.

"Then things get a little more complicated," I sighed.

When at last we reached the top of the stairs we walked over to the door to Woody's room and knocked.

"Yes?"

"It's Heath, Woody. And Mr. Keyes."

"Come in," he responded, sounding a bit more chipper.

I swung the door open and we stepped inside, looking

about. Woody was lounging on the bed, still in the clothes he'd had on this morning. His feet were splayed out to either side like a mermaid's tail.

"I'd offer you two a seat, but I'm afraid there's just the one chair," Woody said, sitting up on the bed and indicating a wingback near the fireplace.

"That's all right. I don't mind standing," I replied. "You've met Mr. Keyes?"

"Yes, at lunch, or should I say before lunch?" Woody replied. "We had a nice little chat."

"That's what I'd like to do now, chat a bit."

"Oh?"

"Informally, though Mr. Keyes will be taking some notes, if you don't mind."

"Doesn't sound too informal or friendly to me, Heath. What's this about?"

I glanced at Keyes, then back to Woody. In a way, I dreaded this conversation because I liked Woody. Besides, he knew things about me that could make my life very difficult if he chose to disclose them. Still, the policeman in me had to pursue every angle. "Woody, you know Mr. Darkly's dead, and as of yet we can't confirm a cause of death. The phone is out of order, so before facts start getting muddled up in people's minds, I thought I should get some statements from everyone so I can present things to the local police when they arrive."

"I see. First and foremost a police detective, eh?"

"Afraid so," I said, nodding my head.

"I'm afraid, too. Well go ahead, ask away."

"What did you do last night after dinner?"

"Nothing I wanted to." He looked at me with a mischievous smile on his face.

"So, what did you do?" I said again, ignoring his implications. I sincerely hoped our earlier conversation wouldn't interfere or come to the surface, and I made a mental note to be more careful in the future.

Woody sighed and rolled his eyes. "After dinner I went into the library to play billiards with Dr. Atwater and Mr. Doubleday. I lost, no surprise there, Dr. Atwater won. Around ten fifteen or so, Bishop came in and asked us if we would be requiring anything else. We told him no, and he said he and Nora were going to retire, but he reminded us that we should ring if we needed anything. He told us the house was locked up, our beds had been turned down, and if we could turn out the library lights when we were finished, he would greatly appreciate it. We told him we would. We finished one more game. I lost again, but this time Doubleday won, and Dr. Atwater and Mr. Doubleday said they were tired and were also going to retire."

"Then what?"

"Well, Dr. Atwater and Mr. Doubleday left and I was in there by myself. It's no fun playing billiards by yourself, even if it does make it easier to win, so I perused the shelves for a good book, found a somewhat passable one, though God knows who picked out the selection in there—boring! Anyway, I turned out the lights and stepped out into the hall when the study door opened, and there was Mr. Darkly. It startled me, I must say. It was almost as if he was waiting for me to come out of the library."

"And the time was?"

"Just ten thirty."

"Did Mr. Darkly say anything to you, Woody?"

"Yes, he said 'good evening' or something like that, and asked if Bishop and Nora had gone up to bed. I told him they had, but Bishop was emphatic that we ring for him if we needed something. Mr. Darkly replied, somewhat uncharacteristically I thought, that he didn't want to disturb Bishop or Nora, as they'd had a long day. I agreed, and then he asked me if I might do him a favor. My first thought was why on earth would I do him any favors, but instead I asked him what he needed. I was curious, I guess."

"And what did he say he needed?"

"He told me he'd heard mice in the walls gnawing at the woodwork, and he asked me if I'd fetch the rat poison from the shelf in the back entry off the kitchen. He said it was on the top shelf. He couldn't reach it on his own, and he wasn't steady enough to use the stepstool."

"And?"

"Well it seemed odd, to say the least. But I should have liked to have seen him try and get it himself. He would've fallen off that stool and broken his neck."

"So what did you say?"

"I figured if I didn't do it, he'd have to ring for Bishop. I hated to see him bother old Bishop after the day he'd had, and anyway it wasn't like I was tired or anything, so I said I would get him the bottle."

"Oh?" I asked, arching my brow.

Woody shrugged. "I know. I think it surprised him, too. He started coughing and all. Whatever he had, I hope he wasn't contagious. It did seem silly to ring for Bishop just to fetch a bottle from down the hall when I was right there, and Bishop had already gone up to bed, as I mentioned. Besides, I reminded myself I was a guest in Mr. Darkly's house."

"So you went and got the bottle."

"He told me exactly where to find it and what it looked like. Then he asked me not to mention it to any of the other guests, as he didn't want them to know the house had a rodent problem."

"And then what?"

"I asked him if I could leave the book I'd borrowed from

his library there, damned heavy thing. He stepped back inside and motioned to the chair closest to the door, so I put the book down, and then walked down the side hall to the kitchen."

"Did you have any trouble finding the poison?"

"Well, first of all, the kitchen light was on, which I thought strange, until I noticed Mr. Doubleday, or the backside of him anyway, in the icebox. I think I startled him as he fairly shrieked, slamming the icebox door with one hand, holding a turkey leg with the other."

"So Mr. Doubleday was having a midnight snack?"

"Yes, apparently so. Guess he thought he'd have a bite to eat before going up to bed. That man can certainly eat." Woody chuckled.

"And?"

"I told him Mr. Darkly had asked me to get something from the back entry. I suppose that aroused his curiosity, especially when I told him it was a secret. I left him standing by the icebox, gnawing at his turkey leg, and I went back and slipped the bottle of poison into my pants pocket. When I came out from the back entry, I saw that Nora had come down. She said Mr. Darkly had rung for her, which I thought was odd as he'd said he didn't want to bother them."

"Did you tell Nora that?"

"No, I figured Darkly had just changed his mind or forgot. Who knows?"

"And you didn't mention that Mr. Darkly had asked you to get the poison from the back entry?"

"No, of course not. I told Darkly I wouldn't say anything. A man's only as good as his word, Mr. Barrington."

I nodded. "I agree. So what did you do?"

"I said my good nights and left the two of them in the kitchen. I returned to the study and gave Mr. Darkly the poison.

He told me to leave it on the desk, then I said good night to him and went up to bed. I will say he wasn't looking so good."

"Did you retrieve your note from Bishop under your door when you went up?"

"Yes. Very thorough, he and Nora are. I noticed the paper right away. One was under Doubleday's door, too, but not one under yours."

"I'd already picked mine up by that time."

"I figured."

"So did you go right to sleep?"

"I wasn't tired, really. It was eleven by that time, so I should have been, I guess, but I wasn't. I fussed about for a bit, tried to get the fire started in the fireplace, which I finally gave up on, and turned the faucets on in the bathroom, since I figured Doubleday wouldn't bother. I did come back downstairs, though."

"Oh?"

"I'd forgotten that damned book in Mr. Darkly's study, and I figured reading it would put me to sleep. So I went down again. The light was still on under the door, so I knocked, but no one answered. I thought perhaps Mr. Darkly had fallen asleep, so I knocked again, but still no answer. I quietly opened the door and peeked in."

"The time?"

"Oh, about 11:25 or so. I'm not sure exactly."

"And what did you see?"

"Nothing. No one was in there, which is strange because I thought I heard noises when I was waiting in the hall, but then I figured it must be the mice. I just picked up my book and left."

"Did you turn out the lights?"

"No. I was going to, but then I thought perhaps Mr. Darkly

had just gone down the hall to the lav, so I left the light on, closed the door, and went back upstairs."

"Anything else?"

"Not really. Just that when I went back down, I noticed Mr. Doubleday's note was still under his door. I figured he didn't see it or was too fat to bend down and pick it up. Either that or he was still up and about somewhere."

"All right. Thank you, Mr. Acres."

"Woody. You can still call me Woody, can't you, Heath?" he asked imploringly.

I smiled at him. "Of course. Woody."

"Thanks. That means a lot."

"By the way, our earlier conversation, you know…"

"Don't worry about it, Heath. I gave you my word I wouldn't say anything, and as I said, I'm a man of my word, right?"

"Right. Thanks. See you later," I replied, somewhat relieved.

Keyes and I went out into the hall and I closed the door.

As we crossed to our rooms, Keyes looked at me with his brow furrowed. I knew he was curious about what Woody had meant. "Remember I told you about Woody and I talking earlier—and me being a little too open?"

"Oh, yeah. He said he's a man of his word, though."

"Yes, Alan, so he said. I hope he's also an honest man. Time will tell."

"So, what about everything else?"

I shook my head. "I don't know, Keyes. The whole thing is very curious. Curious and puzzling."

"I agree. I don't understand why Acres would admit taking the poison if he actually used it to kill Mr. Darkly."

"I don't know. Perhaps he means to throw off suspicion, or perhaps Mr. Darkly never asked him to get the poison at all. Remember, Nora said Mr. Darkly thought the whole thing about Woody getting the poison seemed odd, as if he really didn't ask him to get it. So perhaps Acres made that scenario up to cover himself since Nora and Doubleday both seemed to have their suspicions that he'd taken the poison. Or perhaps he's telling the truth and it's something else entirely. There are more pieces to this puzzle to be found."

"I suppose you're right. So, now what?"

I checked my pocket watch. "Nearly time for dinner. I suggest we dress."

"With all my clothes still wrinkled?"

"I don't think anyone will notice tonight, Alan."

"Always nice not to be noticed," he replied sarcastically.

"I'll notice you, and it doesn't matter what you're wearing or not wearing," I said with a wink.

"I guess that counts for something, but you're not the one with wrinkled clothes."

"Want to borrow something of mine?"

"Tempting, but I'll manage. See you in a bit." With that, he disappeared into his room, and I went into mine.

Thirty minutes or so later, we reemerged, he looking dashing, despite the slightly rumpled look about his clothes.

"You look swell to me, Alan."

He smiled. "I try. But next time I'm unpacking immediately, no matter what you say. Nice links, by the way."

I glanced at the black opal cufflinks on my shirtsleeves and smiled. "I happened to recall a certain someone admired them."

"I admire a lot about you," Keyes said, smiling back. "Shall we?"

"We shall," I replied, and together we went down the many stairs to the first floor.

CHAPTER THIRTEEN

We entered the dining room last, everyone else already at their places. The room fell quiet, and I felt all eyes upon me as we took our seats on the window side of the table. I was between Keyes and Mrs. Atwater, with Dr. Atwater on her other side. The table was set for eight, with the eighth place setting at the head of the table, closest to the door.

Keyes leaned over and whispered in my ear. "Why is there a place setting for Mr. Darkly?"

"It's a custom in some families—shows respect for the dead," I said. "My father's side of the family always did that during the mourning period and on special occasions."

"Ah," he replied, nodding.

The mood was somber, quiet even as Bishop appeared from the pantry and began serving the soup, which tonight was tomato bisque.

I turned to Mrs. Atwater as I felt I should, beginning the ritual of making conversation with people on either side of me between alternating courses. "That's a striking dress, Mrs. Atwater. It suits you."

The look she gave me cooled my soup. "Thank you, Mr. Barrington. I understand we have no way of contacting the outside world, is that correct?"

I glanced about, noticing that no one else was talking. All

eyes and ears were upon me. So much for social customs. I raised my voice and addressed the table.

"Yes, that's correct, for now. I'm hoping the weather will clear tomorrow and we'll be able to get the steamer's attention."

"I see. And in the meantime?" she continued.

"In the meantime, Mrs. Atwater, everyone, I suggest we each stay in our rooms as much as possible, in between meals, of course."

"Mr. Barrington, the fact that my father has died is indeed a sad occasion, but just why exactly is it a police matter, may I ask? Why are you suddenly in charge here? I feel like I'm under your authority in my own family's home."

"It's unfortunate, Mrs. Atwater, but it is in fact a police matter, at least for now. Your father died under suspicious circumstances."

"What do you mean, 'suspicious circumstances'? My own father died this morning and no one has allowed me to see his body, or to be in the room where he died, or tell me anything that is going on, and frankly I'm getting rather irritated by it all."

Apparently, Mrs. Atwater had elected not to take that sedative, I thought to myself. I raised my voice again and addressed the table at large. "I'm sorry to have kept you all rather in the dark, but circumstances deem it necessary. Dr. Atwater believes that Mr. Darkly did not die of natural causes." Mrs. Atwater gave her husband a look that could curdle milk as collective murmurings went round the table.

"What do you mean? I thought he had a heart attack. We were told it was a heart attack," Lorraine Darkly said loudly.

"For someone of Mr. Darkly's age and condition, a heart attack is a natural assumption, Mrs. Darkly, but the facts do not hold up to that as the cause of death."

"Then what do they hold up to?"

"Poison," Woody said quietly.

I looked at him, surprised. "Excuse me, Mr. Acres?"

"Well, it would have to be, wouldn't it? You said it wasn't natural causes. If it was a gunshot or a stabbing, the cause of death wouldn't be in question, would it? Then there's the matter of the poison."

"Yes, well that is one theory, Mr. Acres, thank you," I said briskly.

"Are you suggesting that Dexter was murdered?" Mrs. Darkly said.

"I'm suggesting that the evidence we have so far points to the fact that either someone from outside the house or someone inside, someone in this room right now, killed Mr. Darkly. I would like your permission to search each of your rooms this evening if necessary."

"For what?" Doubleday said, spitting tomato bisque across the table. "If anyone here did it, I think it's pretty clear who it is." He glared at Woody.

"Nothing is clear right now, Mr. Doubleday, and I'm not sure what I'm searching for. I won't be until I find it, if I find it. It may not even be necessary to search your rooms, but I'd like your permission nonetheless."

"I can't speak for the rest of them, but I must say certainly not," Mrs. Atwater said. "You have no jurisdiction here, Mr. Barrington, as I keep having to remind you."

I nodded in her direction. "That's quite true, Mrs. Atwater. However, if you refuse to cooperate, I will be forced to share that information with the local authorities when they arrive."

"Why don't you do that, then?" She threw her head back defiantly and gripped the edges of the table with her hands.

"I'm afraid I'll have to. And they may wonder why you

refused to cooperate. They may speculate that you needed time to hide evidence."

"That's ridiculous!" Her voice rose several octaves, and a vein on her forehead began to throb.

Dr. Atwater placed his hand on hers atop the table. "Oh, let him have a look, Violet. We've no evidence to hide. We've nothing to hide whatsoever, and I rather suspect Mr. Barrington's not the least bit interested in your unmentionables."

"I didn't come here this weekend to be subjected to this kind of treatment!"

"Why did you come, Mrs. Atwater?" I asked quietly.

She glared at me, the throbbing vein even more pronounced. "That, Mr. Barrington, is none of your concern."

"I'm sorry, but I believe it is. You got a letter from your father, did you not?"

"What if I did?" I could see she was now squeezing her husband's hand.

"A letter inviting you, not your husband, or your uncle, for the weekend. Just you."

"That's right, but I don't go where Preston's not welcome, nor my uncle, so I invited them both to join me."

"How did you think your father would feel about that?" I asked.

"It doesn't matter, it didn't matter. I came here to see my father. What difference does it make if I came alone or with my husband and uncle?"

"No difference to me, but it made one to your father."

"He said he wanted to mend fences, put the past behind us. No reason he couldn't do that with Preston here." She squeezed his hand harder, and a pained look crossed his face.

"How did you feel about mending fences?" I asked her.

"No one, Mr. Barrington, including the infamous Dexter

D. Darkly, could hope to smooth over thirty plus years of bad feelings and neglect in the course of a weekend."

"And yet you came," I pressed.

"Brilliant deduction, Detective. Yes, I came. I came out of curiosity, if nothing else. And who knows? Maybe it was time for a new beginning. Now, it's actually the end, isn't it?" She stopped softly all of a sudden.

"Death is rather final, Mrs. Atwater."

"And so that's it. No more hard feelings, no regrets. It's over." She stared down at her soup bowl.

"No regrets?"

She shook her head. "No, no regrets. If anyone did have them, should have had them, it was my father, but we'll never know now, will we?"

"Perhaps, perhaps not. By the way, where were you this morning, Mrs. Atwater?"

"What do you mean?" She looked up at me, her eyes rather moist, her face flushed.

"I mean, what time did you wake up, and what did you do from that point until lunch?"

Bishop brought the salad, fresh pear with bleu cheese, but no one was eating much, except Mr. Doubleday. I wasn't surprised.

"I feel like I should have my attorney present, Mr. Barrington, if you're going to continue to interrogate me like this."

"Just making conversation, Mrs. Atwater."

"Well, the salad has arrived. Perhaps you can turn your attention to someone else and let me eat in peace. If you want to search our room, search it."

Dr. Atwater looked down the table at me. "Yes, Mr. Barrington, please. My wife's had a very trying and stressful day."

I shook my head. "My apologies, madam. Just one more thing, however. Did you go into the study at all last night or this morning?"

"No."

"No?"

"No, I did *not*," she said, picking up her fork and stabbing about at her salad.

I shrugged and turned my attentions across the table to Lorraine Darkly. "What about you, Mrs. Darkly?"

"What about me?"

"Did you have reason to go into the study last night or this morning?"

"No, though I know others who did," she said, glancing at Mr. Doubleday.

"And do you have any objections to me and Officer Keyes searching your room?"

"I never object to handsome men in my boudoir, Mr. Barrington. Search away, including my unmentionables. Try them on for all I care!"

I blushed. "Ah, thank you, Mrs. Darkly, but that won't be necessary."

"I've nothing to hide, though this whole thing seems ridiculous."

"What seems ridiculous?"

"This whole thing. Not that I'm surprised someone would want to murder Dexter. After all, he was an evil man. But still, the fact that you actually believe someone has…"

"I'm not ruling anything, or anyone, out at the moment, Mrs. Darkly."

"Then search away, by all means." She looked down at her salad plate. "I've lost my appetite. I don't know why, but I find this whole thing rather upsetting."

"I would encourage you and everyone else to eat, Mrs.

Darkly. It won't do anyone any good to go hungry." Though I myself wasn't feeling particularly in the mood to eat, either. "What about you, Mr. Doubleday? Any objections to a search of your room?"

He had made a fair effort at his salad, but not up to his usual standards. "I don't see what for, but go ahead."

"Search mine, too," Woody said. "Doesn't matter."

I looked at him and smiled. "Thank you, Mr. Acres." I looked across the table at Mrs. Darkly. "Mrs. Darkly, you mentioned to me last night that you disliked your ex-husband."

She laughed lightly. "That's right. It's no secret."

"Why?"

"There isn't much about Dexter Darkly to like, Mr. Barrington. If he'd lived a while longer, you would have realized that on your own."

"Yet you married him. You must have felt differently at one time."

She laughed again, this time bitterly. "I was young and foolish. Too late I realized Dexter married me because he wanted another son to replace Nigel after he'd drowned. When I finally did become in the family way, he was overjoyed until I lost the baby. He blamed me for it and eventually tossed me out like yesterday's mashed potatoes."

"You had alimony, of course."

"I should have had alimony. Dexter had me sign an agreement before we were married. As I said, I was young and foolish at the time, and I signed it. His army of lawyers made sure it stuck."

"So he left you with nothing?"

She glanced about the table. "I suppose it doesn't matter now. We have no secrets here anymore, do we? Dexter left me a small allowance, a pittance, really. It was very humiliating. I had to get a job, go to work at the five and dime just to pay my rent. There's the ex–Mrs. Darkly, they'd say, working the perfume counter at the five and dime."

"You never re-married," I said.

She laughed again, even more bitterly. "Not yet, anyway. Are you asking?"

I blushed. "Ah, well, no…"

"Pity. Anyway, since I know you want to know, I got up around seven this morning, cleaned up, dressed, and came down to breakfast. Afterward, I went to the music room and wrote some letters. I have them in my room if you'd care to see them."

"That won't be necessary at this point, but I'd suggest you hang on to them until the investigation is finished."

"I'll do that," she replied, finishing off her glass of wine.

I turned to Mr. Doubleday. "Mr. Doubleday, I know you came because of Mrs. Atwater."

"My turn again, is it? Well, that's right. Dexter and I didn't see eye to eye. He was a cold, cold man capable, I'd say, of anything. He was cruel and mean, and he not only held a grudge, he embraced it. I don't believe he invited Violet here to 'mend fences,'" he said, looking across the table at his niece.

"Why do you think he invited her, then?"

"I couldn't say, but he was up to something no good. He may have been having money problems."

"Oh, uncle, that's ridiculous!" Violet said.

"I'm not so sure, my dear. Selling the Milwaukee house, taking an apartment in Chicago, then giving that up, shipping boxes here, selling off his furniture…"

"He did that because he travels every winter," she explained.

"So he told us. But he's always traveled every winter, and he's always maintained a winter residence as well as Dark

Point. Why give it up all of a sudden? I think he invited you here, Violet, because he was in need of money."

She shook her head. "You think he wanted me to give him money? That's absurd. Then why would he invite Lorraine or Mr. Acres? They don't have any money!"

"How nice of you to point that out, dear," Mrs. Darkly said sweetly, helping herself to more wine.

Mrs. Atwater looked at Mrs. Darkly. "No offense, of course, Lorraine. But my father was a very wealthy man. I'm not sure what his motives were for inviting me or any of us here, but I'm certain it wasn't to borrow money."

Mr. Doubleday shrugged. "Just a theory. But you're right about Mrs. Darkly and Mr. Acres. It doesn't make sense why they'd be invited, or why they'd come, unless they were looking for a handout or something else."

"Dexter invited me because he wanted to make amends," Mrs. Darkly said. "That's what he said in his letter. And I came out of curiosity, not a handout. Though for the record, Dexter owed me."

"Owed you, Mrs. Darkly?" I asked.

"Well, not according to the courts, but a gentleman doesn't just toss his wife out onto the streets without enough money to support herself."

"Sounds like you're still holding a grudge," Mr. Doubleday said.

"What if I am, Donovan? You said yourself Dexter was a cold, cold man to everyone. I hate to say it, but if someone did murder him, I think he got exactly what he deserved."

Bishop entered to clear the salad, mostly untouched, and serve the main course of salmon with rice.

"So, Mr. Acres, why are you here?" Mr. Doubleday asked.

"I thought Detective Barrington was asking the questions, Mr. Doubleday," Woody said.

"Just saving him the trouble, isn't that right, Detective?"

"I really don't need your help, Mr. Doubleday, and I'd hate to have you miss a bite," I replied, somewhat annoyed.

"It's all right," Woody said. "I don't mind saying why I came. The same reason as Mrs. Darkly."

"Because you feel Darkly owed you something? And you came to collect?" Doubleday continued, his mouth now full of bits of salmon and rice that sprayed onto the table when he spoke.

"I never said I came to collect anything, Mr. Doubleday," Mrs. Darkly said tersely.

"But Mr. Acres did," Doubleday said.

"No! I mean I got a letter from Mr. Darkly saying he wanted to make amends," Woody said.

"I can't imagine why he would want to make amends with you, Mr. Acres. He seemed afraid of you, and with good reason, apparently," Doubleday replied. He dove into the salmon again with gusto, his appetite apparently back to normal.

"Why would Mr. Darkly be afraid of me?" Woody asked.

"Don't deny it. He told me about the threatening letters you sent him after Nigel died," Doubleday said, still more small bits of salmon clinging to his mustache.

Woody looked shocked. "I don't know what you're talking about. I never sent him any threatening letters. I sent letters, but they weren't threatening in any way."

Doubleday shook his head. "That's not what Darkly said, and it's not that hard to believe, is it? Everyone knows you hated him, and everyone knows why. And why don't you tell everyone what you took from the back entry last night?"

"You don't need to answer him, Mr. Acres," I said, even more annoyed at Doubleday's manner.

Woody's face flushed bright red, and he raised his voice. "I don't mind answering this blubbering walrus. So what if I didn't like Mr. Darkly? Who did? I don't think any of us are exactly grieving."

The rest of the table was silent, all eyes on Doubleday and Acres.

"Perhaps not," Doubleday said, "but he at least never said he was afraid of any of us. No one else here ever threatened him."

"And neither did I. If he was so afraid of me, why did he invite me? I don't recall you being on the guest list."

"And yet here I am. And there you are, being rather defensive, and you still haven't answered my question. How do we know he really invited you? Maybe you blackmailed your way here."

"That's absurd. What would I have to blackmail Darkly about?"

"Good question," Doubleday replied, picking bits of fish from his mustache and popping them back into his mouth.

"I didn't murder Mr. Darkly, Doubleday, *if* he was murdered. And I didn't come here to get anything from him." He dropped his head, staring at the plate of salmon before him. "I came here this weekend to say good-bye to Nigel, to visit his grave and bury some ghosts, not create new ones."

I looked at him with great sympathy, and then I stood up, raising my hands, Keyes following. "Please, Mr. Doubleday, everyone. It's not going to help to toss about accusations or unkind comments. If everyone's through here, please go up to your rooms."

"I'm quite finished," Mrs. Darkly said, getting to her feet and dropping her napkin onto her plate.

"So are we, aren't we, Preston?" Mrs. Atwater said, also rising.

Dr. Atwater stood up as well. "Yes, dear, of course."

"I think I've had enough," Woody said, standing next to me.

"What about dessert?" Doubleday asked, still sitting at his place, staring down at his empty plate.

"I think you can do without for one night, Mr. Doubleday."

He glared at me but got to his feet, throwing his napkin down upon the table.

"I'll be in my room, then. If you want to search it, you'll have to do it around me," he said. Without another word, he waddled out into the hall and off toward the stairs.

"The same with us," Mrs. Atwater said, and Dr. Atwater and the others followed suit out the door.

"You really know how to clear a room, Heath," Keyes said.

"I wasn't all that hungry anyway. You?"

"Nope, not me."

Bishop entered from the butler's pantry, a somewhat surprised look upon his face as he glanced about at the nearly empty dining room.

"No one was in the mood for dessert tonight, I guess," I said.

"Apparently not, sir."

"Bishop, if Nora can manage without you for a bit, I'd like to see you upstairs."

"Now, sir?" He looked at me with a puzzled expression.

"If you don't mind."

"I suppose not, Mr. Barrington. I'll just let Nora know not to bother cutting the cake or pouring the coffee." He disappeared back into the pantry, only to reemerge a short time later. "At your service, sir."

CHAPTER FOURTEEN

Bishop dutifully followed me and Alan out into the hall and up the stairs to the second floor. At the top of the stairs, the three of us paused. "What's in that room, Bishop?" I asked, looking at one of the doors.

"Oh, that's unoccupied, Mr. Barrington."

"I'd like to see it."

Bishop sighed. "I suppose it would be all right, what with Mr. Darkly gone now."

I looked at him. "What do you mean? Why would he care if we look in an empty room?"

Bishop wrung his hands somewhat nervously. "That room was his son's room. Mr. Darkly told us about it last fall, asked us to clean it regularly. He gave us special instructions that none of the furniture was to be covered up, nothing removed, nothing added. Everything was to remain the same. He even asked we bring in fresh towels once a week and change out the bed linens regularly."

"But no one stays in this room?"

He nodded. "That's my understanding, sir. A bit odd, especially the towels and bed linens, but not our place, you understand."

"Of course."

Bishop looked up at me before continuing. "He wanted the

room locked at all times unless we were inside cleaning. It's the only room that was to be off-limits this weekend, besides his own room and sitting room, of course."

"How curious. How very curious, and more than a little odd, I'd say. Let's have a look."

Bishop looked from me to Keyes and then back to me, a tired, somewhat troubled expression on his face. "Yes, sir. Like I said, I suppose it will be all right, since you're in charge." He fumbled with the keys on his ring until he found the right one, then opened the door, stepping aside for us.

I glanced at Keyes, but he shook his head and gave me one of his *after you* looks, so I stepped inside, not sure what to expect. I turned on the light and glanced about the rather large room. Green silk striped wallpaper made it rather elegant, while on the floor warm wool throw rugs in shades of cream and green covered the wide-planked dark wood floor. Two windows faced the front of the house, and a curved bay with a window seat was on the other wall, above where the front porch wrapped around the side.

A beautiful double bed with a carved wooden headboard stood along the wall opposite the window seat, and two closets flanked the red brick fireplace opposite the front wall. A chair in green damask stood in the corner, seating a rather worn-looking teddy bear with a little pine green scarf around its neck. I opened one of the closet doors and found it full of suits, coats, and shirts. The many pairs of shoes on the floor were all lined up neatly, polished and shined; on the shelf above were hatboxes and sweaters, all stacked by color. The other closet, I found, held more of the same, and the chest of drawers contained socks, underwear, undershirts, shirt collars, and dress gloves. On the top of the chest was a grooming set, a box containing several pairs of cufflinks, a silver pocket watch, a gold school ring, and a penknife.

Next to the window seat was a door to Nigel's private bathroom containing pretty much what I expected; toothbrush, dressing gown, assorted bottles of aftershaves, razor, soap and brush, towels neatly folded on a small green stool next to the tub.

"It's as if he's just downstairs…" I started.

"And could come up any minute," Keyes finished.

"It is indeed a bit peculiar," Bishop added, clearing his throat.

"He must have kept this room like this since the day Nigel died." On one of the nightstands flanking the bed, I noticed a silver framed picture of a rather portly man and a young boy. Mr. Darkly and Nigel, I presumed. The other nightstand held another framed photograph, this one clearly torn in half, leaving just a photo of a young man. I picked it up and examined it.

Bishop glanced down at the picture. "That's Nigel Darkly from what I understand, sir. Mr. Darkly said it was the last known photograph taken of him."

"It looks like it was taken here at the lake."

"Yes, sir. Apparently, the summer before he died."

"The summer he spent with Woody," I said, more to myself than anyone. "I imagine that was the other person in the photograph."

"And Mr. Darkly ripped Woody out of the picture," Keyes suggested.

"It would appear that way, literally and figuratively."

"I can see the resemblance," Keyes said, looking from the photograph to me.

"You think so?"

"Yes. Definitely there. It's like looking at an old photo of you."

I set the frame back on the nightstand, next to the lamp

and turned to Bishop. "You keep the curtains open in here all the time?"

"No, sir. Mr. Darkly instructed us to open and close them regularly. We took them down for cleaning just the week before all of you arrived and hung them up again just a few days ago."

I walked over to one of the front windows and moved the curtains aside so I could peer out into the darkness. From this floor, the lake would be just visible through the trees. I wondered to myself what must have been running through Nigel's mind the day he took that final swim.

"You all right, sir?" I heard Keyes ask, coming up behind me.

"Yes, fine." As I turned toward him, something caught my eye on the window ledge. I picked it up and held it out before me. A white feather.

"What's that?" Keyes asked.

"A feather. It was on the window ledge."

"It must have blown in when we had the windows open for airing last week, sir. Funny I didn't notice it, though."

"It's just a small white feather, easily missed. Keyes believes they're good luck."

"Oh yes, Nora believes white feathers are from angels' wings, sir. She says they definitely bring good luck. 'From an angel's wing it was plucked and placed before you to bring you luck.'"

"Let's hope she's right," I said, placing the feather in my coat pocket.

"Was there anything else you wished to see in here, sir?"

I glanced about, suddenly feeling rather melancholy, as if I was saying good-bye to a friend, and then I shook my head. "No, Bishop. I think we're through here, time to move on. You can lock it up again, if you want to."

I strode over to the door and out into the hall, purposefully not looking back, as Keyes and Bishop trailed behind. "I want to have a look outside, Keyes."

"Outside? Now?" Keyes said, obviously surprised.

"Yes, but not now. First thing tomorrow morning before breakfast. I'm sure the rain will have stopped by then. Right now, I think we ought to have a look in Mr. Darkly's bedroom."

We went across the hall and waited while Bishop unlocked the door for us and ushered us in, turning on the overhead light. It was larger than Nigel's room, with a corner brick fireplace surrounded by a white painted mantel, a writing nook, bathroom, and two large closets on either side of his bed, which was covered with a custom-made coverlet, embroidered with a large *D* in the middle. I opened one of the closets and rifled through some of his suits and shirts. Most were indeed of a much larger size than Mr. Darkly would now have worn. Odd that he wouldn't have updated his wardrobe.

I closed the closet door again and then glanced about the room once more, taking it all in. "Where does that door go to?"

Bishop followed my gaze. "The sitting room, sir. Mr. Darkly tells me it's the old nursery, above the entry. The first Mrs. Darkly had it converted to a sitting room. There's a door to it from the hall as well."

I strode over and opened it, flipping on the overhead light so that I could look about. An old oak rolltop desk sat against the far wall with one of those banker's chairs on rollers in front of it. A red leather camelback sofa and matching chair were against the other wall. A couple of oak bookcases were opposite them, filled with heavy-looking leather-bound books, much like those in the library below. Amongst the books were also some framed photographs. Most, I noticed, were of Nigel, but some were of a very young-looking Dexter

Darkly, in Paris, Rome, and other exotic places. Next to the desk sat a large globe on a metal stand. "Is the door from the hall locked, Bishop?"

"Yes, sir. Mr. Darkly kept his bedroom and the sitting room locked at all times."

"But you and Nora had access?"

"That's right, sir, to clean."

I tried to open the desk, but the rolltop was locked. "Do you have a key for this?"

"No, sir," Bishop replied, shaking his head.

"Pity. Locks aren't any good without keys." I looked over at Alan and smiled. "And neither are police detectives." He smiled back at me.

"Mr. Darkly kept a key ring on his watch chain, Mr. Barrington," Bishop volunteered.

"Which he probably had on him when he died," I said.

Bishop nodded his head solemnly, a rather grim expression on his tired old face. "Yes, I'm afraid so."

I shrugged my shoulders. "Well it looks like a trip down to the study is in order."

"Oh dear, sir. Do you really think that's necessary?"

"Believe me, Bishop, I wouldn't suggest it if I didn't." We went back into the bedroom, out the hall, and down the stairs. This time it was my turn to unlock the door, as I held the key to the study. I flipped on the light. Everything was just the same as it was, except for the fairly strong odor hanging heavy in the room. I looked back at the little manservant. "Perhaps you should wait in the hall, Bishop. This won't take long."

"As you wish, sir," he replied with obvious relief.

I closed the door to block his view and knelt down next to the body, glancing up at Alan. "You ready, Keyes?"

He shrugged. "Sure, I guess. Ready as I'll ever be."

I pulled back the sheet, trying not to look at Darkly's face. "Get the keys from his chain."

Keyes knelt beside me. "Are you sure this isn't illegal, Heath?"

"We can't reach the local authorities, so I'm the acting official."

"But shouldn't we maybe just wait until we do reach them?"

"In a murder investigation, every second counts. You should know that."

"Yes, I suppose so," he said, though his voice was doubtful. "Here, I've got his key ring."

"Good." I pulled the sheet up over the body once more. We stood up, and I took the key ring from him. I looked at the boxes stacked along the wall. "You know, Keyes, there really aren't that many boxes here, all things considered."

"What do you mean?" he asked.

"Just that a wealthy man like Mr. Darkly must have accumulated quite a bit of stuff over the years, maintaining two residences and all. If everything he kept from his Chicago apartment is here, what happened to the rest of it?"

"Didn't you say he told you he'd sold some of it off?"

"Yes, but from the looks of it, he must have sold *most* of it off. And if he was going to downsize, why not clean out some of the old stuff from here and keep his Chicago things?"

Keyes shrugged. "Maybe this stuff was nicer."

"Doubtful. It looks like mismatched castoffs, things that were brought here from the city over many years. No, I think perhaps Doubleday was on to something."

"You think Mr. Darkly was hard up?"

I shook my head as I spotted the strongbox beneath the

table. "I don't know for sure. He did mention that he kept a lot of cash in that box."

"Not very wise."

"He was a victim of the stock market crash in '29. Didn't trust banks much," I said. "But he claimed he made a full recovery. Let's have a look."

I ignored Keyes's troubled expression and bent down next to the strong box, trying various keys from Darkly's key ring on the padlock until it popped loose. Gently I removed the lock and swung the door open. Inside were indeed stacks of bills, but they were mostly tens and twenties. "Not much more here than two or three hundred dollars."

"Maybe he's got other hiding places," Keyes suggested, as he paced about nervously. I noticed he kept glancing toward the hall door, as if he expected the Lake Geneva police to come bursting in at any moment.

"Perhaps. And please stop pacing, Keyes. You're making me nervous."

"Sorry." He stopped in his tracks but I could tell he was still very anxious. "Say, maybe someone else got here before we did and took most of the money. Maybe they just left some stacks so it wouldn't be obvious some were missing."

I smiled at him. "That's definitely a theory," I said, putting the money back inside and securing the lock. As I did, something shiny next to the table leg caught my eye. I picked it up, careful not to disturb any fingerprints that might be on it.

"What's that?" Keyes asked, walking over to me and bending down.

"A pearl-handled pocketknife with the initials H.A. on it."

"HA?"

"Not a laughing matter, Keyes," I joked, making light of it. "H.A.—Harwood Acres."

"How did that get there?"

"He must have dropped it. He told me he was looking for it," I replied.

"Pretty careless."

I cocked my head, still staring at the knife. "It probably didn't make much noise when it landed on the rug, and if he was in a hurry when he dropped it…"

"And the room's been locked up, so he couldn't get back in to look for it."

"True." I got to my feet, putting the knife carefully into my pocket. "Let's go back upstairs. The smell in here is getting to me."

"Me too," Keyes replied, rising up next to me.

I opened the door to the hall to find Bishop waiting there dutifully. I'd almost forgotten about him. "I don't think we'll need you anymore for the moment, Bishop."

He looked doubtful. "I don't mind staying, sir, if you need me."

"It's fine, Bishop. I'll make sure everything is locked up and secure. Trust me."

He nodded his small gray head. "As you wish, sir. I'll just give Nora a hand in the kitchen, then. Please ring if you require anything at all."

"I shall." After he'd gone down the side hall, I turned out the light and locked the study door once more. Then Keyes and I climbed the stairs back up to Mr. Darkly's quarters. Everyone else in the house must have been ensconced in their rooms, for no one was about, which was just as well for the time being.

We entered the sitting room and crossed once more to the rolltop desk. "I think this small key is probably the one," I said, holding it up for inspection.

"Seems likely, sir." Keyes glanced about the room and eyed the door to the hall.

"Don't be so nervous, Keyes. We're police officers doing police work."

"Yes, sir," he said, but again he didn't sound convinced.

I turned the small key in the lock and was pleased to hear a small click. I slid back the roll top to reveal a large desktop with multiple drawers and cubbyholes behind it.

"Well," I said aloud.

"What exactly are you looking for, Heath?"

I shook my head. "Not sure. Maybe nothing, maybe something."

"Shouldn't we have a search warrant before we do this?"

I turned in the chair and looked at him, so sweet, so innocent. "Keyes, sometimes we just have to get things done, okay? I promise if any implications or accusations arise from this, which I doubt, I'll take the blame for it. You were in your room the whole time, okay?"

He stood there staring at me, and I couldn't tell if he thought I was mad or just a little crazy. Finally he spoke, slowly and deliberately. "No. We're in this together. Whatever happens or doesn't happen, I'll support you."

I was taken aback but couldn't help but smile. "Okay bud, have it your way, and thanks." I swiveled back around in the chair as Keyes hovered nearby, glancing from the door and back to me. I started going through the various and assorted papers and curiosities stashed throughout the desk. I came across old letters, newspaper clippings, business cards, check stubs, photographs, his checkbook, canceled checks, postcards, receipts, and some novelty pin-up pictures from Paris, apparently many years old. I looked at each, dutifully putting them back where I found them when finished.

In the top left drawer, I noticed a small cobalt blue bottle. The label looked like it was from a pharmacy, made out to Dexter D. Darkly.

"What's that?" Keyes asked.

"Arsenic trioxide, prescribed by a Dr. Kingsly."

"Arsenic?"

"Arsenic trioxide. Medicinal purposes."

"What kind of medicinal purposes would require arsenic?" Keyes questioned.

"I'd have to confer with Dr. Atwater to be sure, but I have a hunch, if I remember a few things our friend Fletch, the coroner back in Milwaukee, told me." I set the bottle back into the drawer and took out a neat blue folder embossed with the name *Eagle Insurance Company, Chicago, Illinois.* I turned on the green glass banker's lamp to better see it. I opened it up and examined the document inside. "Life insurance policy. Interesting."

"Oh?"

"Mmm. It's a policy taken out on Dexter Darkly three months ago."

"Three months ago? That would be January."

"Thursday, January 9th, 1947, to be exact. Curious. I wonder when exactly Mr. Darkly returned from Monaco."

"I wouldn't think he'd come back in January. Not to Illinois or Wisconsin, anyway."

I shook my head. "I wouldn't think so either, unless he had affairs to settle." I read farther down on the insurance policy, letting out a low whistle.

"What?" Keyes asked.

"Violet Darkly Atwater and Lorraine Darkly are named the primary beneficiaries—five hundred thousand dollars each."

Keyes echoed my whistle. "Tidy sum. They'll be happy."

"Hard to say. Interesting."

"You really can be cryptic at times, Heath," he said, exasperated.

"Sorry, I was just reading the fine print, you know. It says the policy is null and void if death is caused by any pre-existing illnesses or conditions. And under that, Mr. Darkly said he had no pre-existing illnesses or conditions. Apparently, a Doctor Kingsly gave him a clean bill of health on December 18th of '46—four months ago—there's a copy of it attached."

"Fat lot of good a clean bill of health did Mr. Darkly."

"Indeed. Dr. Kingsly, Kingsly—the name rings a bell."

"Sure, he's the doctor who prescribed the arsenic."

"Yes, I remember, but there's something else, too. Let me see that checkbook again," I said, more to myself than to Keyes, as I reached up to the top cubby where the checkbook was. I flipped through the register. "December 18th, 1946—Dr. Adam Kingsly—one thousand dollars. Curious."

"That's quite a bit of money for a medical exam," Keyes said.

"I agree. Maybe Dr. Kingsly is a specialist."

"In what?"

I smiled at him. "That remains to be seen. This is notable too. The balance in the checkbook is just $2,657.00."

"Just?" Keyes replied. "That's more than I make in a year."

"True, but not all that much if you're Dexter Darkly."

"Well, you said he didn't have much faith in banks. Wouldn't surprise me if he's got gold coins stashed all over this old house."

I shrugged. "Stranger things have happened. My old high school friend George Carpenter's dad supposedly kept several thousand dollars in gold inside an old tree in their back yard. George and I tried to find it once but couldn't." I put the checkbook back in its cubby again and continued my search through the depths of the desk. In the bottom left hand drawer, I came across Mr. Darkly's passport.

I looked it over and then handed it to Keyes. "Take a look at this."

"My goodness, that's Mr. Darkly? He really did lose a lot of weight."

"Yes, he's rather heavy in that picture. You'd hardly recognize him. He looks like a different man."

"I'll say. I mean, I only saw him after he died and in those old pictures, but still—"

"Notice anything else unusual about that passport?" I said, interrupting him.

Keyes looked it over front to back. "What?"

"Look at the last stamp."

"Ireland, March 1946."

"Exactly."

Keyes shook his head. "I'm sorry, I don't get it. What's so important about Mr. Darkly going to Ireland?"

"The fact that he didn't go to Monaco this past winter, as he told everyone. He said he spent last winter in Monaco, yet his passport clearly shows he didn't. He hasn't traveled abroad since March of '46, just over a year ago."

Keyes furrowed his brow. "But why would he lie about something like that? Who cares where he went or didn't go?"

"More importantly, I think, if he didn't go to Monaco, where was he?"

"Well, we know he was back in the States by January."

"That's true. I think we'll need to question this Dr. Kingsly when we find him."

Keyes handed me back the passport, and I put it back where I'd found it.

"Anything under the pencil tray, sir?"

"Hmm?"

"The pencil tray. That's where I always stash things in my desk."

"I'll have to remember that," I said with a grin. I lifted up the tray in the top drawer and found papers beneath it. "Good call, Keyes."

"Glad I can be of some help. What's there?"

"Let's see." I took out the first several documents. "Looks like receipts, bills of sale and the like from his Chicago place. From what these say, he apparently did sell off almost everything. Furniture, dishes, jewelry, artwork, even his automobile."

"Wow."

"Looks like most of it went to an auction house—Allegrie Auctions, Michigan Avenue, Chicago. The rest went to various consignment and antiques dealers."

"He must have done pretty well selling all that off."

I nodded my head in agreement. "Apparently so. Wonder what he did with the cash or where it is."

"Maybe it's here in the house somewhere, like we said. That would certainly be a motive for someone to bump him off—if they knew about it. Mrs. Atwater and her husband knew about him selling stuff off, and they stand to inherit the house, I imagine. It would give them free rein to search the place. And maybe Darkly got rid of all his old servants because he wanted the place to himself to give him time to hide it."

"I like that you are open to possibilities, Keyes. You've presented a good theory. To find the answers, I think we need to discover exactly what he did with the cash and why he sold in the first place."

"All good questions, sir."

"And all good questions need answers. This is interesting."

"What is it?" Keyes asked, leaning over my shoulder.

"A ticket stub for the Canadian Pacific Railway."

"For where?"

"Chicago to Toronto, Ontario, Canada, dated November 18th, 1946, with a return ticket dated December 20th."

"Canada? No one goes to Canada for the winter, sir."

"Not without good reason, I suspect. And I doubt Mr. Darkly was a skier, so what was it?"

"Another good question." Keyes scratched his chin.

"We seem to be stocking up on them, but we're in short supply of answers."

"I have another idea, Heath."

I swung around in the chair to face him. "Excellent. Let's hear it."

"Well it's just another theory, a possibility."

I shook my head. "Doesn't matter. I'm open to all ideas, you know that."

"Well I was just thinking, Mr. Darkly hadn't been seen by anyone in several years, right?"

"Yes, that's right, I believe. I think Mrs. Darkly was the last one to see him before this weekend, and that was a few years ago."

"Exactly. And everyone remarked about how much he had changed, how much weight he'd lost, how different he looked."

"Go on."

"And as you said, even Bishop and Nora were new, hired just last fall."

"Correct."

"So I was thinking, sir, what if the body in the study isn't Mr. Darkly?"

I raised my eyebrows. "Then who is it?"

"Another good question. But it makes sense, don't you think? Maybe Darkly was being blackmailed by somebody. This person forced Darkly to sell off his things and raise a large amount of cash to pay him off. But that wasn't enough.

He killed Darkly and assumed his identity, knowing no one close to him had seen him in several years. Then he fired his staff, probably via telegraph or letter, and set up house here at Dark Point with Bishop and Nora."

"For what purpose?"

"Because he wanted to be Dexter Darkly. How better to get his hands on everything Darkly owned than to become him? And if our previous theory of him hiding the money here is correct, what better opportunity to search for it?"

"But why would he risk inviting Darkly's daughter and Darkly's ex-wife for the weekend?"

Keyes furrowed his brow again. He was so cute when he did that. Of course, he was cute when he didn't do that, too. "Hmm. Maybe the real Darkly had arranged the weekend before the fake Darkly bumped him off, so the fake Darkly had to go through with it."

"Seems a bit out there, but I suppose it's possible. So who killed the fake Darkly and why?"

"Obviously, whoever killed him thought they were killing the real Darkly."

"So, we still have a murder to solve regardless."

"Well, yes," he said, his brow furrowed even more. He did indeed look adorable.

"Good creative thinking, Keyes, well done. But I don't think it will hold water."

"Why not?" Keyes asked rather defensively.

"I think Lorraine Darkly and Violet both would be able to spot an imposter before too long, if not immediately. And if someone wanted to impersonate Mr. Darkly, don't you think they'd try to look as much like Dexter Darkly as possible, not the opposite? According to all accounts, Mr. Darkly was heavy and pale his whole life, so an imposter would try to gain weight and use makeup to appear pale."

Keyes shrugged. "But the dead man downstairs is rail thin and very tan. Like I said, it was just a theory."

"Curious."

"There you go again," Keyes said, sounding slightly exasperated.

I smiled. "Sorry, but when we were downstairs in the study before, getting the keys…"

"Yes?"

"When I pulled back the sheet, there was a brown smudge on it where it had touched Darkly's face."

"A smudge?"

"Hmm. I didn't think much about it at the time, but in retrospect it's curious."

"How so?"

"I think if we examine Mr. Darkly closer, we'll find he may have been wearing face paint. What you said about someone altering his appearance made me think of it."

"But why would he want to do that?"

"To give the appearance of having just returned from sunny Monaco, when in fact he'd spent the winter in Canada and Chicago."

"Seems a lot of work to go through for what purpose?"

"That remains to be seen."

"Hmm. So what about my other theory, about Dr. and Mrs. Atwater? That's still possible, isn't it? I mean if they did know he'd hidden his money here, and they did have access to the study…"

"Yes, Keyes, that theory is still possible. But for now, I think we've seen all there is to see here. Let's call it a night and get a fresh start in the morning."

"What about the other bedrooms?"

"They can wait. It's been a long day and I'm tired, I'm

sorry to say. I imagine the others have turned in anyway. Might as well let them sleep."

"No arguments from me, sir."

"Let's go, then." We left the sitting room via the bedroom, turning off the lights and locking things up as we went. Out in the hall all was quiet. We climbed up to the attic floor, stopping outside the door to Alan's room.

"I'd light the fire in the fireplace if I were you. It's still pretty cold."

Keyes looked at me with those gorgeous blue eyes. "I can think of other ways to stay warm, but I guess the fire will have to do."

"Unfortunately. Murders have a way of killing my romantic side, so to speak," I said.

"My luck to date a police detective," he said quietly, careful not to be overheard.

"I'm sorry, Alan. I'll make it up to you," I said, putting my hands on his shoulders.

He grinned. "We've only just begun, Heath. We've got time."

I glanced about to make sure no one was near, then I leaned in and kissed him lightly. "I like the sound of that." I gazed into his eyes and touched his cheek lightly.

"So do I, and the feel of that."

"Sounds like the rain has stopped," I said, turning my ear to the roof.

We both listened quietly. "Yes, I think so."

"Sleep well, Alan. I'll see you in the morning," I said, smiling at him warmly.

"Good night, Heath. I'll see in you my dreams. You sleep well, too."

"I will. Lock your door, okay?"

"Why?" Alan cocked his head, looking adorable again, like a great big puppy.

I shrugged. "No reason, but you never know."

"Okay, you too."

"I will, I usually do." I walked the short distance down the hall to my door and looked back at him, still standing outside his door, a smile on his face.

"See you in the morning, then."

"Right. What time?"

"Early. Before breakfast. I'll knock on your door."

"Don't think I'll get much sleep."

"Me either, despite being tired."

"Lots to think about."

"Lots," I replied. Then I turned the knob and went inside to bed.

CHAPTER FIFTEEN

As predicted, I didn't sleep very well. The fireplace was smoky and something dripped constantly somewhere outside the windows. Plus, as Alan said, I had much to think about. I must have drifted in and out, though, because before I knew it, dawn had broken. I climbed reluctantly out of bed and onto the cold floor, scurrying over to the fireplace to breathe life into the smoldering embers, noticing the room smelled heavily of smoke. I did my best to wash the smell off me, but my clothes reeked of it, too. Oh well, off to the cleaners when I got back to Milwaukee. I dressed as quickly as I could, grabbed my fedora, and went quietly out into the hall and down to Alan's door, knocking softly.

A rather groggy-eyed figure greeted me, tousled hair and unshaven, but still so damned attractive. "Sleeping in, Keyes?"

He looked sheepish. "Sorry, won't be but a minute." He let me in, and I watched as he disappeared into his bathroom, clothes in hand. I sat on the edge of his bed and put my hand where his body had been, feeling the warmth and picturing in my mind him lying there. Too soon he emerged, dressed, shaven, and combed.

"Looks like you cut yourself," I said, getting to my feet and reaching out my hand to his face.

"Just a nick. I was trying to hurry. You still smell like smoke."

I smiled at him. "I know. It's six thirty. The day awaits. Come on," I said, and I went out the door, down the stairs to the first floor, and out onto the porch. The sun was shining, and it had warmed up, but was still considerably cold for April. As the day went on, the temperature would rise back to normal levels. The fresh, crisp air was a welcome change from the stale, smoky odors of the house, and I breathed in deeply.

"What are you after?" Keyes asked, catching up to me.

"Not sure," I replied, putting my hat on.

"Something new has been added," Keyes commented, looking at my fedora.

"You'll make a first-rate detective after all," I said, beaming. "I thought the white feather made a snappy contribution to my hatband."

"I agree," he said, smiling. "So what are we doing out here?"

"The window."

"What window?"

"The window in the study was open when we first found Darkly dead. Bishop said it was closed when he went in there yesterday morning, so someone opened it after Bishop was in there."

"But it was freezing cold and raining yesterday. Why would someone open the window?"

"The rain didn't start until lunchtime, but you're right. It was very cold in the morning, colder than it is now. So, why would someone open a window, and leave it open? And, perhaps more importantly, who? I can't imagine Darkly opening it. He was very susceptible to the cold."

"So you think whoever poisoned him opened it," Keyes said.

"It would seem logical, but why? To escape without being seen? If so, why not close it all the way behind you? It was open just a few inches. The same with gaining entry. If someone opened the window to get into the study unseen, why leave it open a few inches after you're in?"

"Why indeed, sir?"

"One opens a window to let something in, let something out, get fresh air, throw something in, or throw something out. Let's have a look around back."

We went down the steps and around to the back of the house, the ground soggy beneath our feet. "Our shoes are going to be a mess, Keyes."

"Yes, sir."

"The sacrifices we make, I suppose, in the name of the law," I said resignedly.

The back of the house was fairly plain compared to the front, and it was easy enough to ascertain which two windows belonged to the study. "The one on the right is the one that was open, Keyes. It would be the one on the left if we were inside the study looking out."

"Yes, sir, that makes sense."

I left Keyes staring up at the window while I poked about the sodden ground beneath it. I didn't find any footprints or marks on the clapboards that would indicate someone had climbed in or out of the window, though it was possible the rain had erased them.

"Anything?"

I turned to look at him and something caught my eye, glinting in the sunlight. "Nothing here, but perhaps there," I replied as I walked over to whatever it was.

"What is it?" Keyes asked, coming to my side.

"Let's have a look." I knelt down to examine it, careful not to get my trousers wet. "It's a bottle, missing its stopper."

"So I see."

"Not just a bottle, but *the* bottle, I suspect, though the label's been nearly washed away in the rain." I reached into my coat pocket and took out my pencil, inserted it in the neck of the green glass bottle, and lifted it up from its resting place. I was careful not to let anything inside it spill out.

"The poison bottle, sir?"

"It fits the description," I replied, getting to my feet, "and it doesn't appear to have been out here long. If I had just poured poison into Mr. Darkly's medicine and wanted to dispose of the evidence, what would be the quickest way to do it?"

"Throw it out the window."

"Exactly, though I must say not very creative or even very smart. Still, the bottle lay pretty much where it would if someone had tossed it out that window," I said, looking back at the house. Keyes followed my lead.

"Wonderful discovery, I'd say, Heath."

"I'd say so, too. Curious, though. Why not retrieve the bottle after the fact before someone else found it? And if one did panic and throw it out the window, why not close the window afterward?"

"Maybe they wanted to wait until it stopped raining to retrieve it. Or maybe once they threw it out, they didn't want to take a chance on being seen retrieving it or leaving footprints."

"Perhaps," I replied.

"And maybe they left the window open because they couldn't close it all the way. Some of these old windows stick pretty badly, especially when it's raining."

"An astute observation, Keyes. Well done."

He beamed at me. "Thank you, sir."

"Though it did close effortlessly when we were in there after Darkly was killed."

"Oh. Yeah, that's right."

"We'll have to have the bottle dusted for fingerprints, of course. I'll take it up to my room for safekeeping until the police get here."

"Yes, of course. I noticed you used your pencil to pick it up."

"Can't destroy any evidence, though I suspect we'll find Woody's prints on the bottle."

Alan cocked his head again in that adorable puppylike way of his. "Why is that, sir?"

"He admitted taking the bottle from the kitchen. If he poisoned Darkly, why bother wiping his prints off it? And if someone else did it, they'd want to leave Woody's prints."

Alan shrugged. "Makes sense."

"Undoubtedly. Just one thing, Keyes."

"Yes, sir?"

"Remind me not to lick the tip of my pencil this afternoon."

He smiled that ice-melting smile at me. "Yes, sir."

With the bottle held out in front of us, we walked back around and into the house, careful to scrape the mud off our shoes on the boot scrape before entering. Bishop was in the dining room, preparing for breakfast.

"Good morning, gentlemen," he said.

"Good morning, Bishop," I replied. "Sleep well?"

"I suppose so, sir, under the circumstances. What's going to happen?"

"I'm not really sure, but I suppose you'd better run up the signal flag for the steamer as soon as you're able to. I imagine the sun has melted most of the ice off the stairs by now, but tread carefully just in case."

"Yes, sir, I'll tend to it straight away. May I take that for you, sir?" Bishop asked, indicating the bottle I was holding out in front of me.

"No, thank you. Police evidence. After you put up the

flag, I wonder if you'd ask everyone to join me and Mr. Keyes in the library."

"Before breakfast, sir?"

"They can bring their breakfast along, if they want. I have a few questions for everyone before the local authorities get here."

"As you wish, sir."

"Oh, and I'd appreciate it if you and Nora would be present as well, Bishop."

"She's not much for crowds, Mr. Barrington, but I'll ask her."

"She can stay in the background, but it's important she be there."

"Yes, sir. I'll make sure of it, then, if it's important."

"Thank you, it is. I'll leave you to it, then." I turned and headed toward the stairs, Keyes next to me. When we got up to the attic, I unlocked the door to my room, and we went inside.

"Smells like you," Keyes said with a grin.

"Maybe you'll think of me every time you smell smoke from now on."

"I think of you enough as it is, Heath."

"Nice to hear," I said, carefully putting the poison bottle down on the table and removing my hat, the white feather still erect. I stole a quick glance in the mirror and smoothed out my hair, noticing Keyes was watching me.

"So you have it figured out?" he asked.

"Possibly. Still some more answers needed."

"I have another theory, if you're interested."

"Always."

Keyes smiled at me. "Well I was just thinking, suppose they all did it, sir?"

"Meaning?"

"I mean, nobody liked him, did they? Everyone had a

motive, everyone had the opportunity. What if they all got together beforehand and discussed it? I read a book like that once, where all the suspects each took a turn killing this chap."

I shook my head. "I do like the way you think, Keyes. You keep an open mind, inventive. Although it seems to me that was one of your theories on the Murdoch case, too." I grinned at him.

He smiled back rather sheepishly. "And you don't think it's a likely scenario this time, either."

"Well, no, but I wouldn't rule it out. I make it a point not to rule anything out until it's proven to be impossible."

"So what's your theory?"

"My theory is that we go down and have something to eat and then see what we can find out in the library. It's just after eight already."

"All right, I know that tone. Let's go."

CHAPTER SIXTEEN

Strong cups of black coffee, juice, and eggs inside us, we walked down the hall to the library. We were the first to arrive, but we didn't have long to wait. Mrs. Darkly and Woody came in shortly after, each balancing a coffee cup and saucer.

"You wanted to see us?"

"Yes, actually. Make yourselves comfortable," I replied, standing next to the fireplace. Keyes was by my side, his notebook and pencil at the ready.

No sooner had the two of them settled in the overstuffed chairs in front of the billiards table than Doubleday squeezed through the door, followed by Dr. and Mrs. Atwater.

"What's this all about, Barrington?" Mr. Doubleday asked gruffly, a plate of doughnuts in one hand, coffee in the other.

"Just a few things I hope to clear up. Please take a seat, everyone, won't you?"

Dr. and Mrs. Atwater took a place on the settee, Mrs. Atwater to the right of Woody. They both looked rather worn and tired but still smartly dressed in more or less coordinating outfits. Doubleday positioned himself at the table, spreading out his food before him. The small wooden chair creaked beneath his weight. Bishop and Nora were the last to arrive, finding spots just inside the door. Nora looked quite uncomfortable, and I noticed Bishop held her hand.

"Well, it looks like we're all here," I said, looking about at the assembly.

"Where else would we be?" Mrs. Darkly inquired. "There's nowhere to go, and you did order us here. And apparently when you say something, we all jump."

"Were you able to raise the signal flag, Bishop?" I asked, ignoring Mrs. Darkly for the moment.

He nodded in the affirmative, shifting as all eyes fell upon him. "Yes, sir. The steamer runs fairly often on weekends, so it should be here shortly. The ice has mostly melted, and the steps are clear."

"Excellent," I replied. "By the way, how will we know when it's seen the flag?"

"Three short blasts on the whistle, sir."

"And we'll be able to hear that in here?"

"Most definitely, sir. You can hear the *Mercury*'s whistle from anywhere in the house."

"Excellent. Then I'll get on with things."

"Get on with what exactly, Mr. Barrington?" Mrs. Atwater asked, rubbing her temple as if she had a headache. "It's awfully early for theatrics, and I didn't sleep at all well. I'm sure none of us did. What are you getting on with?"

"With the case at hand, as it were, Mrs. Atwater. All of you know that Mr. Darkly is dead, and I can say quite certainly he was murdered." I paused for effect but everyone seemed rather nonplussed.

"If that's your big news, Mr. Barrington, I'm afraid we've already surmised that."

"Yes, you pretty much said that at dinner last night."

"He did say it, didn't he?"

"But," I looked at each of them in turn, "I didn't say who did it."

"You mean you know?" Mrs. Atwater gasped.

"I mean to say all the evidence points strongly to one person in this room now." There. *That* was the dramatic pause I'd sought, as everyone looked around at each other and then back at me, eyes wide.

I strode about the room amongst them as I spoke. I'd seen a detective do that in a movie once. "The murderer put poison into Mr. Darkly's cold medicine, which he kept on his desk in the study. Each of you had a motive, and each of you had opportunity."

"I take issue with that."

"Regardless, Dr. Atwater, it remains that all of you did have motive and opportunity. But only one person admitted taking the poison, and that person was seen coming from the back entry where it was kept."

"Wait a minute. I only took that poison because Mr. Darkly asked me to!" Acres exclaimed.

"A likely story," Doubleday snorted, glaring at him.

"Please, Mr. Doubleday," I said reproachfully. "Now then, according to other witnesses, Mr. Darkly never said anything about asking Mr. Acres to get him poison, isn't that so, Nora?"

"Me, sir?" she said, her voice cracking.

"Go on. Tell them what you told me about what happened Friday night."

"Oh dear, sir," she said rather quietly as she shifted her weight from one foot to another and squeezed her husband's hand tighter.

Bishop looked at her and smiled. "It's all right, Nora. Just tell him again what you told him before."

"Yes, Nora, please. You said Mr. Darkly rang for you from

the study after you and Bishop had gone up for the night," I prompted.

She glanced about nervously, all eyes upon her, and then she slowly nodded her head. "Yes sir, that's right. He rang from the study."

"And what happened next?"

"Well, Henry was indisposed, so I went down to see what Mr. Darkly needed. When I got to the kitchen, I noticed Mr. Doubleday and Mr. Acres, sir."

"And Mr. Acres had just come from the back entry where the poison was kept."

"That's right, sir." She fiddled with the neckline of her dress, grasping and ungrasping the fabric nervously with her free hand.

From across the room, Acres spoke up rather loudly, his voice off pitch. "I told you I took the poison, that's no secret. Darkly asked me to get it!"

I looked at him, as did everyone else. "That's true, Mr. Acres. You did tell me you'd gotten the poison." I turned to Mr. Doubleday. "And Mr. Doubleday, you and Nora noticed the bottle missing from the back entry after Mr. Acres had gone?"

"That's right. Acres told me he had to get something from back there, and it was a secret. He was real strange about it, so the housekeeper and I went and had a look."

"I was secretive about it because Mr. Darkly told me not to tell anyone. He didn't want everybody to think the house had mice!" Acres exclaimed.

I looked over at Nora again. "And Nora, did you mention any of this to Mr. Darkly that night?"

She nodded. "Yes, sir. After Mr. Doubleday and me noticed the bottle missing, I went to the study to see what Mr. Darkly needed. Well, I did mention to him then about Mr. Acres and the rat poison, sir."

"And what did he say?" I asked.

"Oh my," she said, a worried tone in her voice. "He said that seemed odd, but that I shouldn't fret about it. He told me I should ask you about it in the morning."

"I see," I continued. "So, it didn't appear he had any knowledge of Mr. Acres taking the poison, and he never told you he had asked him to get it?"

She shook her gray little head. "Oh no, sir. In fact I thought it odd, if I may say so, sir, that if he had wanted the rat poison, he wouldn't have asked me or Bishop to get it."

"He told me he didn't want to disturb you as you'd already gone up to bed!" Acres fairly shouted.

Nora looked ashen. "But he did disturb us, Mr. Acres, or rather I should say he did ring for us." She clutched Bishop's hand and grabbed at her dress even more now.

Woody looked exasperated. "Well I can't explain that. Maybe he thought of something after he'd asked me to get him the bottle."

Her face looked even paler as all eyes were upon her. "Yes, maybe so, sir. He did ask if we'd turned on the water in the kitchen for the night."

I turned to face Woody once more. Everyone's eyes were going back and forth from Nora to Woody like a ping-pong ball. "Or maybe," I spoke slowly and deliberately, "or maybe, Mr. Acres, he never really asked you to get him the poison at all. Maybe you made that up after going to the kitchen to get it and finding Mr. Doubleday there."

"That's ridiculous!"

"Is it? You also admitted you went back down to the study later and no one was there. You could have slipped the poison into the medicine at that point, and then tossed the bottle out the window."

"I went back down to get my book, which, I might add, I left in the study when Mr. Darkly asked me to get him the poison."

"Did you?" I was pushing him hard, wondering if he'd break.

"*Yes!*" His face was red, and beads of sweat had popped out on his brow.

"Your fingerprints will no doubt be on the poison bottle, which we found out back beneath the window."

"Well, I don't know how it got there. The last I saw, it was on Mr. Darkly's desk, and he was sitting right there." His voice had risen several octaves, and he was starting to sweat even more. A small rivulet ran down his nose. "If I killed him, why would I admit taking the poison?"

I walked closer to him but kept my voice loud enough so that everyone could hear. "Perhaps because you knew others knew you took it, so the best defense is a good offense."

"I don't even know what that means," Woody cried.

I kept pushing. "It's not hard to figure out. Mr. Darkly also confided to me, Mr. Acres, and apparently also to Mr. Doubleday, that you had sent him threatening letters over the years."

"That's right, Darkly told me they were nasty, hate-filled letters," Doubleday added, his wooden chair creaking as he leaned forward.

"Actually he told me the same thing," said Mrs. Darkly.

"He mentioned the letters to me and my wife, too," Dr. Atwater put in, looking askew at Acres.

"I tell you I didn't murder Mr. Darkly!" Woody's coffee cup fell to the floor, shattering as the coffee splattered.

I faced him point-blank and stared at him hard. His eyes were huge and dilated as he stared back at me, waiting for what I was going to say next. The room was completely silent. "No," I said finally. "No, I don't believe you did murder him. Not at all."

"What?" A collective gasp all around.

Bishop had started to come forward to pick up the pieces of the cup.

"Leave that for now, Bishop, please."

"Yes, sir," he said, moving back to his place next to Nora, who took his arm. She looked rather faint.

"What do you mean you don't think he killed Darkly? You just told us he did."

"Actually, Mr. Doubleday, I said all the evidence appeared to point in his direction, a fact which I think was intended."

"What are you saying?" Dr. Atwater asked.

"I'm saying someone intended to frame Mr. Acres for Mr. Darkly's murder."

Woody, I noticed, had slumped back into his chair, his face white but obviously overcome with relief. He took out his handkerchief and mopped the sweat from his brow. "Jesus Christ, Heath, why did you put me through that if you didn't believe I did it?"

"I'm sorry, Woody. I had to play out my theories, test reactions."

"And your theory now is that someone framed me?" he asked, incredulous but clearly calmer.

"That's preposterous. Why would anyone do that to this poor boy?" Mrs. Darkly exclaimed.

"Why does anyone frame someone else for murder, Mrs. Darkly?" I asked.

"What evidence do you have to support this nonsense?" Doubleday snorted.

"For starters, I found a life insurance policy taken out on Mr. Darkly four months ago. The primary beneficiaries are Violet Darkly Atwater and Lorraine Darkly."

"Me?" Mrs. Atwater said, surprised.

"I don't believe it," Mrs. Darkly said, a shocked look upon her face.

"That's right. Five hundred thousand dollars each."

"I don't believe it, either."

"It's true, Mrs. Atwater," I said. "Perhaps it was his way of making amends after all."

"But what does that have to do with Mr. Acres being framed for murder? Wait a minute. Are you suggesting Violet had something to do with this?" Dr. Atwater asked, his voice rising to match the color in his face.

I looked in his direction. "Calm yourself, Doctor. Mrs. Atwater, I do not believe, is the murderer."

"I should say not," he said, patting his wife's arm. Both of them appeared quite shaken.

"Surely, then, you don't think I did it," Mrs. Darkly said, her voice fairly screeching.

"Do I?" I said, arching my brow just a bit.

"How dare you insinuate such a thing. Dexter was a cad, but I most certainly did not poison him."

"No, Mrs. Darkly, I don't believe you did, either," I answered, a wry smile on my face.

"Oh, for goodness sake, get to the point, man. If you don't think Lorraine or I did the deed, Mr. Barrington, what then is so important about a life insurance policy? Aside from the fact that it existed at all, that is."

"The important fact, Mrs. Atwater, is that under pre-existing conditions on the policy, Mr. Darkly had checked 'None.' He even had a certificate of a clean bill of health from a Dr. Kingsly."

"Bully for him," Mrs. Darkly said, fanning herself with her handkerchief.

"Mr. Barrington," Dr. Atwater said, "you're being rather cryptic about all this. First you suggest Mr. Acres killed Mr. Darkly, then you say he was framed because of some insurance policy. As my wife said, get to the point, won't you? My wife's nerves, and mine, can't take all this."

I smiled. "My apologies, Doctor. By the way, are you familiar with arsenic trioxide?"

He looked surprised. "Arsenic trioxide? Why yes. It's often used in cancer treatments, why?"

"A bottle of it, prescribed by the same Dr. Kingsly, was found in Mr. Darkly's desk drawer."

"Who is this Dr. Kingsly?" Dr. Atwater asked.

"A physician in Canada, I suspect, though I don't know for certain."

"Canada?"

"Yes. You see, Dexter D. Darkly was dying a slow death before he was ever poisoned. I believe he had terminal cancer."

"What?!"

"He didn't spend last winter in Monaco, but rather seeking alternative treatments in Canada."

"How do you know that?"

"His passport, along with train tickets and other documentation, Mrs. Atwater. He spent the majority of his money from selling off his assets, his home in Milwaukee, his apartment in Chicago, his cars, everything, hoping to be cured. Clinging to life, he shipped what remained of his possessions here, still hoping for a cure."

"So that's what happened to the money," Keyes said aloud, but mostly to himself.

"That's ridiculous. Are you saying my father was broke?"

"Not entirely, but it does appear there wasn't too much left."

"I knew it! I told you I smelled a rat!" Doubleday said.

"A very sick rat, Mr. Doubleday. His bankbook shows he made cash deposits to his account to cover large checks he had written to various clinics, doctors, and specialists over the last two years or so."

"I don't believe it!"

"It will be easy enough to prove. I intend to wire this Dr. Kingsly as soon as I get back to Milwaukee, and I'm sure the local authorities will back me up on getting a court order for Mr. Darkly's medical records. And of course, an autopsy will be done."

"Even if Dexter was dying of cancer, what does that have to do with him being poisoned?"

"I'm getting to that, Mrs. Darkly." I walked back over to the fireplace and turned to face them all. "You see, I think when he accepted his fate, he decided to make amends with his family, with people from his past. To right wrongs, shall we say. He came back here to a place he loved, to the last place Nigel was."

"And?"

"Yes, Mr. Barrington, get to the point, as we keep saying. Stop being so theatrical!"

"Sorry, Doctor. But the whole thing is rather theatrical, almost unbelievable. Knowing he was dying and realizing he had very little of his fortune left, he decided to take out an insurance policy so he had something to leave to his daughter, his grandchildren, and his ex-wife, whom he must have felt he did indeed owe something to after all."

Mrs. Darkly looked ashen as I continued.

"But the insurance policy required that he have a clean

bill of health and no pre-existing conditions, so he bribed, for lack of a better word, this Dr. Kingsly while he was still in Canada to say he was in good health at the time the policy was taken out."

"Highly unethical," Dr. Atwater said.

"Highly," I agreed. "Then Mr. Darkly made up the story about going to Monaco and used face paint to make himself appear tan and healthy, even going to the extreme of wearing a wig."

"And the weight loss…"

"Exactly, Mrs. Darkly. He didn't go to a fat farm in Monaco, but was instead wasting away from cancer."

"Oh my God."

"I knew he didn't look well, but even I didn't realize…"

"Nor did he want you to, Doctor. That, I suspect, is the reason you weren't invited here this weekend. Knowing you were a doctor, Mr. Darkly was afraid you would realize he was far more ill than he let on. That's also why he stayed by himself much of the time, keeping his distance."

"But surely he must have realized an autopsy would reveal he had cancer. You said so before."

"Yes, but not if cancer wasn't suspected, Doctor. Not if the autopsy was searching for traces of poison, which they most certainly would find if that's what they were looking for."

"You mean he wanted someone to murder him?"

"Not exactly. He wanted it to appear as if someone murdered him."

Mr. Acres stood up suddenly. "And he wanted it to appear as if that someone was me!"

"I'm afraid so, Woody," I said softly.

"That son of a bitch!" His face was red with anger. Keyes went over to him, his hand on his shoulder.

"I know it's a bit of a shock," I said, "but it's true. Mr.

Darkly intended to commit suicide by poisoning himself, making it look like he was murdered by Mr. Acres."

"Why?" Woody asked, slumping once more into his chair with the help of Keyes. "Why would he do such a thing?"

"You can probably guess as well as anyone can. Mr. Darkly blamed you for Nigel's suicide and always has."

"I loved Nigel," he said softly, burying his hands in his face.

"I think Mr. Darkly knew that, which only made him hate you more. You never sent him threatening letters after Nigel died, did you?"

"No! I told you I didn't. I wrote him, certainly, asking what had happened, asking where Nigel was buried, but my letters were all returned unopened. I still have them in a box back home."

I shook my head sadly. "I'm afraid he really invited you here this weekend not to make amends but to frame you for his own murder. He told everyone, including me, you had sent him threatening letters. I hate to admit it, but he was convincing, at least at first. I think he invited me partly because he had read that I was a young, hotshot detective. Perhaps he felt he could plant the seed in me and everyone else that you hated him, and he believed that I, anxious to solve another murder and put another feather in my cap, so to speak, would be only too eager to point the finger at you to the authorities when they arrived."

"Oh my God."

"Really, Mr. Barrington, this sounds almost too unbelievable."

I turned to her and nodded my head. "I agree, Mrs. Atwater, but the facts we have support my theory, and I believe the facts we'll gather will, too."

"So my father poisoned himself and framed Mr. Acres

because he was dying of cancer and didn't have any money left? Because he wanted me and Lorraine to have some insurance money?"

"Basically, yes. He had some money left, I believe. Enough for basic expenses, to cover his burial, but not much. He's probably even borrowed on Dark Point."

"And he invited you here because he wanted you to suspect Mr. Acres?" Dr. Atwater asked.

"That's one theory I have."

"Beside the point that you're a dead ringer for Nigel, pardon the expression," Doubleday added.

"So I've been told. Apparently there is a resemblance."

"But why drag us all into this? He could have thrown himself down the stairs, or drowned himself, or any number of other things and made it look like an accident. The insurance company would have to pay on that."

"I don't think those ideas would have appealed to Mr. Darkly. Swallowing poisoned medicine is easier than any of those things. It's fairly painless, at least in theory, and it's hard to make that look like an accident. I think, too, the insurance company would investigate an accidental death more than they would a murder, especially if a police detective gave testimony that it was indeed murder. And besides, he wanted revenge against Woody."

"So, he planted all the evidence against me?"

I turned back to Woody. "Mostly, yes. He waited until everyone else had gone up to bed, and then got you alone to ask you to bring him the poison bottle. He knew your fingerprints would thus be on it, and no one would believe you when you said Mr. Darkly asked you to bring it to him. And he rang for Bishop after he'd sent you to the kitchen, knowing they would probably find you in the kitchen. Since you'd promised not to tell anyone you were getting the poison, he probably figured you'd act suspicious. Then, when Nora mentioned it to him, he pretended not to know anything about it and told her to be sure and tell me about it the next day, knowing I would find it odd. He stashed the bottle of poison in his desk drawer, only to retrieve it the next day and add some to his medicine. Then he tossed the bottle out the window, knowing we'd find it, and just to make sure we did, he left the window open a bit."

"What about the phone being out of order?" Mrs. Atwater asked.

"Ah yes. And the servant bell cord was also cut," I added. "Cut?"

"Yes. The phone and bell cord were both clearly and intentionally cut. Mr. Acres, did you ever find your pocketknife?"

He looked at me, his face still drained of color. "What?"

"Your pocketknife. Did you ever find it?"

"My pocketknife? No, no, I didn't. Why?"

"Because I found it on the floor of the study, as if you dropped it there in your haste."

He looked confused. This had been a very trying morning for him. "How would it have gotten there?"

"I believe, Mr. Acres, that it was planted, with your fingerprints on it and probably fragments of the phone and bell cords on the blade."

He shook his head slowly, uncomprehending. "But how, why?"

"Sometime yesterday morning while you were out of your room, Mr. Darkly made his way up there. Bishop saw him in the attic, but innocently believed he was double-checking my room to make sure it was cleaned satisfactorily. Instead I think he was looking for something, something of yours, something he could no doubt plant in the study as evidence. When he saw your pocketknife, with your initials on it, no less, I'm sure he felt he'd hit the jackpot. He purloined it and used it sometime this morning to cut the phone and bell cords, and then stashed it on the floor to be found by the authorities."

"Why bother cutting the cords?" Dr. Atwater asked.

"Just a theatrical touch," I explained. "He wanted it to appear as if Woody cut the cords, effectively cutting off any means Mr. Darkly might have had for summoning help when he realized he'd been poisoned. And, perhaps, making sure that he himself wouldn't be able to summon help if he changed his mind after drinking it.

"So, finally, knowing he'd planted seeds of a motive with everyone with his stories of the hate-filled letters, knowing Woody's fingerprints would be found on the poison bottle and the pocketknife, and knowing Nora strongly suspected Woody took the poison from the kitchen, he took his final dose of medicine along with a brandy, most likely, and settled back for the end."

"Cold and calculating," Woody said, finally.

"Dexter was always cold and calculating, but this is too much!" Mrs. Darkly said. "I could use a drink."

"Really, Lorraine, it's not even noon yet."

"It is in my world, Violet. By the way, Mr. Acres's coffee splashed on your skirt when he dropped his cup."

Mrs. Atwater looked down at her cream wool skirt and noticed for the first time the splotches of brown on it, the remnants of the cup still scattered about her feet.

"It's all right, Violet. We'll have it cleaned when we get back home," Dr. Atwater said.

"My apologies, madam," Woody said softly, his head clearing a bit. "And make mine a double," he added, still looking visibly shaken.

"A double, Mr. Acres?" Violet asked reproachfully, dabbing at her skirt with her handkerchief.

"Yes, what of it? I was almost arrested for a murder I didn't commit, framed by the dead man. Your father," Acres muttered.

"So the old coot was dying anyway?" Doubleday said. "Jesus, I could use a drink, too. How long did he have?"

I shook my head. "Impossible for me to say, Mr. Doubleday. Any opinions, Dr. Atwater?"

Dr. Atwater scratched his chin thoughtfully. "Difficult to determine, of course, without knowing exactly what kind of cancer Mr. Darkly was suffering from and exactly what treatments he was undergoing, but given what you've said, he probably had six months, maybe more, maybe less."

"Obviously, Mr. Darkly knew time was running out for him, so he had the house opened early."

"That bastard. So he takes the cowardly way out," Acres said, the color slowly returning to his face.

"Not cowardly, Mr. Acres. He was trying to help me and Lorraine," Violet said quietly, still fruitlessly dabbing at her skirt.

"Help you by framing me for murder, when he was going to die in six months anyway!"

"Well done, Detective. Good job. I'm glad we can put all this behind us now. The son of a bitch should have swallowed that strychnine twenty years ago and saved all of us a great deal of trouble," Mr. Doubleday said.

"Really, Mr. Doubleday, your language," Mrs. Darkly said reproachfully.

"Hardly a time to stand on manners, Mrs. Darkly. Bishop, how about that drink? God knows Darkly's not going to care now if we drink his liquor or not."

"The brandy's in the study, Mr. Doubleday, and I'm afraid that room is still off-limits for now," I stated matter-of-factly.

"But there are extra bottles in the cellar, Mr. Barrington, or at least there used to be." Mrs. Darkly offered.

I looked at Bishop, and he nodded. "That's true, sir, the reserve supply. Along with the wine."

I shrugged my shoulders resignedly. "Well, have at it, then. Bring a bottle and some glasses."

"Yes, sir."

"Do you still need me, sir?" Nora asked, quietly.

"I'm afraid I do, Nora, for just a while longer. Do you mind?"

"No, sir," she replied, though I knew she did.

Bishop went out, only to return a few minutes later with a rather dusty bottle of brandy and a tray of tumblers.

"Anyone need ice?" I asked.

"Not me," Doubleday said. "I don't even need a glass, just give me the bottle."

"Ladies first, Mr. Doubleday. Would you like ice, Mrs. Darkly?" I asked.

"Thank you, no. Just pour."

"Yes, madam," Bishop answered.

"While Bishop is attending to Mrs. Darkly, perhaps you could answer a question for me, Mr. Doubleday."

"Depends on the question," he replied gruffly, his chair still creaking beneath him.

"How did you know the poison the medicine was laced with was strychnine?"

He looked up at me, his pudgy cheeks growing red. "What do you mean? Everyone knows that, we all know that."

I shook my head. "No, I don't believe so."

"Of course they do. You said it, didn't you? Didn't he say the medicine had strychnine in it?" Doubleday sputtered, his mustache bouncing up and down as he glanced about at the others in the library.

The room fell silent and Bishop stopped serving as everyone turned toward Doubleday.

I deferred to Alan. "Keyes, you've been taking notes. Perhaps you could review?"

"Ah, yes sir," he answered, flipping back through the pages of his notebook. "No sir, no mention of strychnine was ever made."

"He just didn't write it down, then. I'm sure someone said it."

"Anyone?" I offered, looking about the room. Each shook their head or said "no."

Doubleday gave a grunt. "Well, so what? You said Darkly was poisoned. How many different kinds of poisons are there?"

"Hundreds, I'm afraid, Mr. Doubleday—arsenic, hemlock, cyanide, mercury, and aconite, just to name a few," Dr. Atwater answered.

"Yeah, so? Strychnine is fairly common, isn't it?"

"Not particularly. Not enough that you'd just pull that name out of a hat. You'd have no way of knowing it was strychnine if you hadn't seen the bottle," I said.

"Lucky guess, then. What's your point? You already said Darkly committed suicide. What difference does it make if I somehow guessed it was strychnine?"

"Actually, I said Mr. Darkly intended to kill himself and frame Mr. Acres for his death. Whether or not he actually did kill himself is uncertain."

"What's that supposed to mean? You are an infuriatingly cryptic son of a bitch."

"Then let me clarify. It was something else you said yesterday, when we were having our conversation right here in this room."

"What? What did I say?" He looked at me suspiciously, his face red, eyes bulging.

"It was when I had asked you if the study appeared normal when you admitted you went to talk to Mr. Darkly after leaving the kitchen. Do you recall what you said?"

"Yes, of course. I said everything looked about the same as it always did."

"And that was after Nora had been there and back."

"Yes, that's right. I hadn't really thought about it. So what?"

"And yet what you actually said was…if I may, Keyes?"

Keyes flipped back the pages of his notebook again, once more scanning the lines until he found the ones he was looking for. He cleared his throat and began reading. "The drapes were closed, of course, and there was a fire going, oh and Acres had left a big fat book sitting on the chair by the door, but other than that I didn't notice anything."

"Thank you, Officer Keyes. Your note taking is remarkable." I looked back at Doubleday, still seated at the table, remnants of his doughnuts scattered about the plate before him. "That is what you said, is it not?"

He shrugged. "Yeah, I guess so, what difference does it make?"

"Mr. Doubleday, how exactly did you know the big fat book on the chair by the door belonged to Mr. Acres? You said Mr. Darkly never mentioned his name or discussed him in any way that night."

"Well, who else would it belong to?" He threw up his hands, doughnut crumbs flying about.

"Oh, any number of people, I would assume. Dr. Atwater, Mrs. Atwater, Mrs. Darkly, me, Officer Keyes, perhaps even Mr. Darkly himself."

"It looked like the kind of book Acres would read," Doubleday said.

"Really? What kind of book was it?"

"I don't know! A big, fat book!" His face was quite red now, almost crimson.

"Just as I thought. Since you feel I'm being cryptic, let me elaborate. I suspect, Mr. Doubleday, that after Nora left you in the kitchen and she went back upstairs, you did go down the hall to the study, not on the hopes of having a nightcap, though I'm sure you wouldn't have turned one down, but because an idea was forming in your head. You blamed Darkly for your sister's death, certain that he had murdered her or had her murdered, and had gotten away with it because of his money and his name. You hated him for that. You weren't even invited for this weekend, probably, as you suspected, because Darkly felt you knew the truth. Isn't that right?"

"Darkly did murder Connie. All the evidence was there, but it was conveniently swept under the carpet. They made me look like a fool for even suggesting it!"

"And you believe he murdered her because she was going to take Nigel away from him, the one person he loved more than life itself."

"He didn't care about anyone else, including Connie and Violet."

"That's not true, uncle!" Mrs. Atwater said.

"It is true! I'm sorry, Violet, but it is!"

"Certainly you believe it to be true, Mr. Doubleday. So, when Nora told you Acres had taken a bottle of poison, a thought occurred to you. Acres had a bottle of poison, and that must have been what Acres had said he was getting for Mr. Darkly. That meant the poison was probably in the study, and no one knew it except for Acres, Darkly, and you. And Nora believed Acres had taken it. How simple it would be to poison the old man's medicine, especially since he couldn't taste or smell very well. And if fingers were to be pointed, they'd surely be pointed at Mr. Acres, wouldn't they? After all, you'd be careful not to disturb his fingerprints on the bottle."

"Acres is a pansy. He'd probably *enjoy* some prison time," Doubleday snarled, his eyes narrowing.

The hair on the back of my neck bristled at this. "That, Mr. Doubleday, is completely inappropriate."

"Inappropriate things are often true," he snorted.

"You want the truth? Then let me continue without rude comments."

"Fine, by all means continue with this ridiculous story. I'm sure we're all greatly amused."

"I, for one, am not laughing, Mr. Doubleday. Next, you walked down to the study to look things over, but Darkly was still in there, so you used the nightcap as an excuse. Darkly turned you down, so you said good night, went across the hall to the library, and waited until Mr. Darkly left the study and went upstairs for the evening. Then you went back in, turned on the light, and searched through the drawers until you found the poison. I'm sure it wasn't hard to find. Mr. Darkly wouldn't have taken much trouble to hide it."

"Then what did I supposedly do?" His tone was sarcastic, his eyes now just slits, staring coldly at me.

"Then, Mr. Doubleday, you carefully took the stopper out and started to pour it into the medicine bottle. But a knock on the door startled you, causing you to spill some of the poison on your jacket. You panicked, grabbed the bottles, and hid in the closet. Peering out through the crack of the door, you saw Acres come in, take his book from the chair, and leave."

"Interesting theory," he muttered, his arms folded across his ample stomach. "And ridiculous, as I said."

"Is it? I think not. When the coast was clear, you came out of the closet, returned the poison to the desk drawer, put the medicine back on the desk, and went upstairs to bed. At that point, you retrieved the note from under your bedroom door. Mr. Acres told us that when he went back upstairs after retrieving his book, the note was still under your door, but according to your testimony, you had gone right up to bed after being turned down for the nightcap."

"Maybe I forgot to pick it up until later."

"Maybe you didn't pick it up until later because you never went upstairs until after Mr. Acres had come down a second time and had gone back up again."

"Says you. Maybe I picked it up this morning before breakfast."

"And what time would that have been?"

"I got up around seven."

"Bishop, when you were in the attic this morning picking up Mr. Doubleday's suit and shoes for cleaning, was the note still there?"

"No, sir."

"And what time was that?"

"Around quarter to five, sir."

Doubleday shrugged. "He probably didn't notice. Maybe it slid all the way under."

"And maybe, as I said, you didn't go upstairs until after Mr. Acres had gone up the second time with his book."

"Maybe. There seem to be an awful lot of maybes in your so-called theory, Detective."

I ignored him and continued. "And so the next morning Mr. Darkly came along, retrieved the poison bottle from the desk drawer, and added still more poison to the medicine, not realizing you had already put some in there. When he was finished, he opened the window, tossed the bottle out and took his fatal dose of medicine both he and you had poisoned. He knew that by leaving the window open, someone would eventually search the yard and find the bottle."

"As I said, an interesting theory but impossible to prove," Doubleday said, unfolding his arms and fiddling with the buttons on his shirt, which was stretched tight over his protruding stomach.

I nodded. "Interesting and accurate, I'd say. There's no other way you could have known the poison was strychnine, and there is no other way you could have known the book on the chair belonged to Acres."

"Doesn't make for a very strong case, Detective."

"Just one other thing." I turned to the elderly housekeeper who still stood silently by, fidgeting with her apron. "Nora, you cleaned Mr. Doubleday's suit, did you not?"

"I tried to, sir. But there was a rather nasty stain on the lapel I couldn't get out."

"Indeed. Please retrieve that suit from Mr. Doubleday's room for me now, won't you, and lock it away for safe-keeping?"

Doubleday struggled forward in his seat. "What for? You've no right to take my suit."

"I have a feeling, Mr. Doubleday, that the boys in the lab will be able to ascertain traces of strychnine in the fibers of your suit where you spilled it on yourself."

Doubleday rose with some effort to his feet, his face contorted with rage and indignation. "That suit is private property. You touch it and you'll have a lawsuit on your hands!"

"Really, Mr. Doubleday, awfully possessive about it, aren't you? If you're innocent, what's the harm in having your suit examined?"

Doubleday opened his mouth to protest, but clearly couldn't think of anything to say. Instead he dropped back down into his seat and fiddled with the remaining doughnut crumbs on his plate. "All right, Barrington, so what if I did put a little poison in his medicine? Not that I'm saying I did, but so what if I did? So what? Is it murder if the victim was going to commit suicide anyway? If he was dying anyway? If he was trying to frame someone else for his own murder? And who's to say which dose of the poison killed him? Maybe it was his own dose."

"That's for the courts to decide, I'm afraid, Mr. Doubleday. And by the way, it will be duly noted that you assisted in the attempted framing of Mr. Acres as well."

Three short blasts sounded throughout the house just then, causing all of us to jump.

"The steamer, sir."

"Yes, of course. Go, Bishop. Tell them to radio for the local police."

"Yes, sir, right away."

"And, Nora, if you'd be so kind as to retrieve that suit and lock it up for me."

"Yes, Mr. Barrington, if it's all right?"

"I don't think Mr. Doubleday has any further objections, do you?"

"Pour me a drink."

"Pour it yourself, Doubleday. And make it a tall one. It may be the last you have for quite a while."

CHAPTER SEVENTEEN

Keyes and I reached the dock in time to see the *Mercury* pulling away, Doubleday presumably below decks in handcuffs, with the local police. Mr. Darkly's remains had been put in a body bag and stowed aft. He'd be taken to town for a proper autopsy and examination before being returned to Dark Point for burial next to Nigel, together once more and forever.

The temperature had warmed into the sixties, and the sun was bright, the sky cloudless and blue.

"Quite a weekend, Heath," Alan said, exhaling loudly.

"Glad you were here," I replied, grinning at him.

"Yeah, me too, though it's not what I had in mind."

I laughed. "Me, either."

"I've been thinking, Heath."

"Oh?" I said, as the *Mercury*, smoke billowing from its stack, moved farther out onto the lake.

"Just wondering. Why do you suppose Mr. Darkly really invited you here?"

I looked at him. "Probably because I reminded him of his son, of the one person he truly ever loved."

"Strange."

I shrugged. "Love can be strange. I doubt when he was

planning all this he originally intended to have a police detective on the scene. But when he saw my picture in the paper, he couldn't resist wanting to meet me. And after all, Mr. Darkly knew the police would have to be involved when his body was discovered. Maybe he thought having a hotshot detective on the scene would actually work to his advantage. He'd get to meet me, relive some old times with the memories of his son, and influence me to thinking Acres so hated him that he'd murdered him."

Keyes shook his head. "How could anyone be so calculating?"

"Just his nature, I think. It's what he knew. And despite what he may have said, he did feel responsible in some way for Nigel's death. Perhaps more so as grief overcame anger. In his grief, he blamed everyone else, shoving them away until he was all alone in the world, and the world can be a lonely place. Then in his anger, he blamed himself, but he couldn't accept that. His shoulders were sloped, as Woody said. So he turned his anger to Woody, and he let that anger consume him, much as the cancer did."

From behind us a gust of wind blew up, and I pulled my fedora down low to keep it in place.

"The feather!" Keyes said. "It blew out of your hatband."

I looked up to see the white feather being blown aloft on a breeze. Together, Keyes and I watched it until it vanished from view over the lake.

"Bonsoir, Nigel," I said softly.

"Heath?"

I looked at him, his handsome face rather puzzled.

"Perhaps Nigel can finally rest in peace," I replied quietly.

"I hope so," Keyes said, nodding. "What about Woody?"

"I don't know. He'll be all right, I think. He's said his good-byes, now maybe he can say some hellos. He'll stay around until after the trial, and maybe he'll keep in touch afterward."

"And Mrs. Darkly and Dr. and Mrs. Atwater?"

"Well, unfortunately there won't be any insurance money coming their way, even if the official cause of death is listed as murder."

"Why's that?"

"Mr. Darkly falsified his insurance application, which makes it null and void."

Alan whistled. "So it was all for naught anyway."

"Afraid so. But Mrs. Darkly's a survivor. She'll go on as she has the past few years, and Dr. and Mrs. Atwater didn't really need the money anyway. I think for Mrs. Atwater, just knowing her father in his own sick way was trying to make amends with her will be enough."

"What's going to happen to Dark Point?" Alan asked, looking back and up the hill toward the tower.

I turned and looked back at the house, too. "All depends on if and how much Mr. Darkly borrowed on it, and what Mrs. Atwater wants to do with it. I suspect it will be sold."

"I wonder if they'll find Doubleday guilty."

"They'll find him guilty of something, I'm sure. Strange how things turn out. If Doubleday hadn't turned up and tried to kill Darkly on his own, Woody probably would have been accused."

"Surely you would have seen through it all, just like you did anyway."

"Thanks, but I'm not so sure. Doubleday's mistakes made the whole thing easier to see."

Keyes whistled softly. "It is funny. Woody actually has Doubleday to thank, then!"

I nodded. "Yup, from the way I see it."

"When did you first know it was Doubleday for sure, Heath?"

"I suspected him when he mentioned that the book was Woody's. He couldn't have known that unless he'd been in the room when Woody went back in after it. Remember Woody said that just before he knocked on the study door he thought he heard noises inside. That would have been Doubleday fumbling about. But even when we were all gathered together, I still didn't know for certain until he mentioned the strychnine. That sealed it for me."

"Gosh, what if he hadn't said that?"

I shrugged. "I'm not sure. Probably wouldn't have mattered. He'd still be arrested and taken in for a trial. But the fact that he did say it makes for a stronger case."

"So I guess that's that."

"Yup." The wind dropped off again, and I smiled once more at Keyes, squinting in the sun, still staring up at the house through the trees. "Say, Alan, it will be a while before the steamer returns. How about another walk in the woods?"

"But we still have to pack," he replied, ever practical.

"Packing can wait. We still haven't found that cave," I answered mischievously.

He grinned at me then. "Now you're talking! Last one up the stairs carries the bags back down to the dock. After we get back from the woods, that is!"

And as we raced up the stairs, I knew that though death may come darkly, life must come lightly.

ABOUT THE AUTHOR

David S. Pederson was born in Leadville, Colorado, where his father was a miner. Soon after, the family relocated to Wisconsin, where David grew up, attending high school and university, majoring in business and creative writing. Landing a job in retail, he found himself relocating to New York, Massachusetts, and eventually back to Wisconsin, where he currently lives with his longtime partner and works in the furniture and decorating business.

He has written many short stories and poetry and is passionate about mysteries, old movies, and crime novels. When not reading, writing, or working in the furniture business, David also enjoys working out and studying classic ocean liners, floor plans, and historic homes.

David can be contacted at dspederson@sbcglobal.net.

Books Available From Bold Strokes Books

Death Comes Darkly by David S. Pederson. Can dashing detective Heath Barrington solve the murder of an eccentric millionaire and find love with policeman Alan Keyes, who, despite his lust, harbors feelings of guilt and shame? (978-1-62639-625-8)

Men in Love: M/M Romance, edited by Jerry L. Wheeler. Love stories between men, from first blush to wedding bells and beyond. (978-1-62639-7361)

Slaves of Greenworld by David Holly. On the planet Greenworld, the amnesiac Dove must cope with intrigues, alien monsters, and a growing slave revolt, while reveling in homoerotic sexual intimacy with his own slave Raret. (978-1-62639-623-4)

Final Departure by Steve Pickens. What do you do when an unexpected body interrupts the worst day of your life? (978-1-62639-536-7)

Love on the Jersey Shore by Richard Natale. Two working-class cousins help one another navigate the choppy waters of sexual chemistry and true love. (978-1-62639-550-3)

Night Sweats by Tom Cardamone. These stories are as gripping as the hand on your throat. (978-1-62639-572-5)

Soul's Blood by Stephen Graham King. After receiving a summons from a love long past, Keene and his associates, Lexa-Blue and the sentient ship Maverick Heart, are plunged into turmoil on a planet poised for war. (978-1-62639-508-4)

Corpus Calvin by David Swatling. Cloverkist Inn may be haunted, but a ghost materializes from Jason Dekker's past and Calvin's canine instinct kicks in to protect a young boy from mortal danger. (978-1-62639-428-5)

Brothers by Ralph Josiah Bardsley. Blood is thicker than water, but you can drown in either. Jamus Cork and Sean Malloy struggle against tradition to find love in the Irish enclave of South Boston. (978-1-62639-538-1)

Every Unworthy Thing by Jon Wilson. Gang wars, racial tensions, a kidnapped girl, and a lone PI! What could go wrong? (978-1-62639-514-5)

Puppet Boy by Christian Baines. Budding filmmaker Eric can't stop thinking about the handsome young actor that's transferred to his class. Could Julien be his muse? Even his first boyfriend? Or something far more sinister? (978-1-62639-510-7)

The Prophecy by Jerry Rabushka. Religion and revolution threaten to bring an ancient civilization to its knees…unless love does it first. (978-1-62639-440-7)

Heart of the Liliko'i by Dena Hankins. Secrets, sabotage, and grisly human remains stall construction on an ancient Hawaiian burial ground, but the sexual connection between Kerala and Ravi keeps building toward a volcanic explosion. (978-1-62639-556-5)

Lethal Elements by Joel Gomez-Dossi. When geologist Tom Burrell is hired to perform mineral studies in the Adirondack Mountains, he finds himself lost in the wilderness and being chased by a hired gun. (978-1-62639-368-4)

The Heart's Eternal Desire by David Holly. Sinister conspiracies threaten Seaton French and his lover, Dusty Marley, and only by tracking the source of the conspiracy can Seaton and Dusty hold true to the heart's eternal desire. (978-1-62639-412-4)

The Orion Mask by Greg Herren. After his father's death, Heath comes to Louisiana to meet his mother's family and learn the truth about her death—but some secrets can prove deadly. (978-1-62639-355-4)

The Strange Case of the Big Sur Benefactor by Jess Faraday. Billiwack, CA, 1884. All Rosetta Stein wanted to do was test her new invention. Now she has a mystery, a stalker, and worst of all, a partner. (978-1-62639-516-9)